Reyna rested her  **head and stared think it happene**

"What?" Sean asked as he held out his hand to the dog. Dottie sniffed delicately and inched closer to him.

"Falling in love." Her eyes were steady on his. There was no way Sean could look away. "I've known her less than a day and I think I might die if something happens to her."

That was something he understood. Dogs brought it out in him, too.

What was less clear was what was happening the closer he got to Reyna.

Her hair was a mess, rumpled and sticking up. She was dressed a lot like he was, shorts and a T-shirt.

And he liked her for it. All of it. But right now, there was worry in her eyes and the glimmer of tears… He had to do something.

Dear Reader,

What was your dream job when you were a kid? Did you dream of becoming a veterinarian or a firefighter? A football player or a princess? My answer: teacher. Becoming a writer seemed out of reach, but being a teacher was a goal I could plan for and make happen.

Until I was in college and realized I didn't have what it takes to teach. Writing as a profession got real very quickly at that point.

Reyna Montero has a touch of both dreamer and realist. She's leaving her air force career and going out on top, but making her "what do you want to be when you grow up?" dream come true will take some help. Sean Wakefield's military career is solid, steady, though he's nothing like the action hero he dreamed of being. But every day he makes a positive difference. Together Reyna and Sean will discover how dreams change and grow just as ours do.

Cheryl

HEARTWARMING

The Dalmatian Dilemma

——

Cheryl Harper

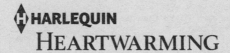

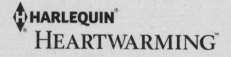

HARLEQUIN®
HEARTWARMING™

ISBN-13: 978-1-335-88982-9

The Dalmatian Dilemma

Recycling programs
for this product may
not exist in your area.

Harlequin Enterprises ULC
22 Adelaide St. West, 40th Floor
Toronto, Ontario M5H 4E3, Canada
www.Harlequin.com

Printed in U.S.A.

Cheryl Harper discovered her love for books and words as a little girl, thanks to a mother who made countless library trips, and an introduction to Laura Ingalls Wilder's Little House stories. Whether the stories she reads are set in the prairie, the American West, Regency England or Earth a hundred years in the future, Cheryl enjoys strong characters who make her laugh. Now Cheryl spends her days searching for the right words while she stares out the window and her dog, Jack, snoozes beside her. And she considers herself very lucky to do so.

For more information about Cheryl's books, visit her online at cherylharperbooks.com or follow her on Twitter, @cherylharperbks.

Books by Cheryl Harper

Harlequin Heartwarming

Veterans' Road

A Soldier Saved

Otter Lake Ranger Station

Her Unexpected Hero
Her Heart's Bargain
Saving the Single Dad
Smoky Mountain Sweethearts

Visit the Author Profile page
at Harlequin.com for more titles.

Writers depend on editors to make their dreams come true. Thank you, Kathryn, for making every book better.

CHAPTER ONE

SEAN WAKEFIELD WAVED away a puff of charcoal smoke as he checked the hot dogs on the grill. Some things belonged together. The Fourth of July, veterans and grilled meat were a match made in heaven. Concord Court, the community built to help veterans adjust to life stateside, was celebrating its first official Independence Day.

So far, the only fireworks at Concord Court had exploded between him and his boss, Reyna Montero, and they were now both on their best, most polite behavior.

Sean wished the celebration had come at the end of a better week at the complex. He handled the operations of Concord Court; most days, that covered the remaining construction, upkeep on the leased townhomes and grounds, and security. Reyna's last-minute celebration had caused some shuffling of priorities, but all of that he could take in stride. As the manager of the Court—and the daughter of the man bankrolling the entire experiment—Reyna set the priorities around here. She was the boss. His boss.

Their only problem so far was the result of a disagreement over those priorities.

The sun was setting. Some of the intense Miami heat had lightened. Almost everyone who had gathered was prepared to party.

He happened to be cornered with the one woman who never partied.

If he could come up with some required task far, far away, they both might enjoy themselves more.

"These are almost done. You can go ahead and start the show when you're ready." He turned to his boss, who was evaluating the small crowd gathered on the green grass in the center of the buildings that made up the townhome complex. A small wrinkle creased her forehead right between her eyebrows. Her posture was parade rest, her feet perfectly planted twelve inches apart. There was a muffled pop of fireworks in the distance, but here everyone was talking, ready for a movie to begin under the stars.

Everyone except her.

She was prepared for her next orders, whether she was giving them or taking them from a higher command.

"Everybody has a plate." Reyna nodded. Was that satisfaction on her face? Sean wasn't sure, but it would be nice to be able to read between the frowns, since she used as few words as she could during the day. Reyna held her cards close and treated every item on the to-do list as critical.

A good policy for an Air Force officer.

Exhausting at a cookout.

"But is everyone here?" Reyna bit her lip. That was easy enough to decipher. He knew the answer. She did, too. They weren't at full capacity yet. Some of the faces of the men and women who lived at the Court were missing.

"You can throw a party to celebrate the holiday, but you can't force people to show up," Sean drawled.

Not anymore. In her first career, she would have been able to demand participation. Here participation was usually voluntary. He studied the coolers lined up. Only lemonade and bottled water. She might benefit from something stronger.

He waved his oven-mitted hand again to chase the smoke away from her. The bacon-patterned mitt wasn't strictly Americana, but bacon was welcome at every party. She hadn't raised an eyebrow at the mitt. Or at the apron he'd chosen for the occasion—it said No Recipes or Opinions Needed. His grandmother had given it to him.

Sean said, "Independence and mandatory attendance. Mutually exclusive." Why was he still watching her? He couldn't look away. He might miss something.

Reyna didn't smile or agree, but her shoulders relaxed. "Logic. I can't argue with it."

They agreed on most things, and he'd been happier here at Concord Court since she'd taken over than he'd ever been on any job. As manager for the complex, Reyna set the budget and the goals, and she let him make plans for the physical facilities and operations. A good relationship, for the most part.

Until they'd butted heads over the first veteran who hadn't met the Court's main residency requirement. Fighting wasn't Sean's way, but when something mattered, he wouldn't back down. Sean had tried all the logic he could find to save the guy's spot in the complex. That conversation had turned tense, the explosive fireworks between them unavoidable. He was nearly certain his attempt had failed.

"Did you talk to Charlie? He's over by the pool gate." Sean turned the hot dogs. If he didn't face her, she wouldn't see his irritation at her insistence on following the rules this time.

Charlie loved it here, and Sean enjoyed his time with the old guy. His stories were wild.

"No. I've called around to five or six rehab facilities to find him a place. I'd like him to have a choice." She didn't look at Sean, either. Their first tense, loud discussion had only ended when someone came into the office to ask about local doctors. Now they were both on their best behavior.

Concord Court residents were required to go back to school or find a job, but Charlie couldn't meet those requirements. Right now his focus was on chemotherapy and recovery from surgery.

He might never go back to work, but Sean didn't see any need to kick him out of Concord Court until they absolutely had to have the space.

That had been his argument. Apparently he'd lost.

"When I know what his options are, I'll help him find the right spot." Reyna glanced at Sean quickly. "Charlie will understand. He spent a lot of time fulfilling the mission set before him. That's what I'm doing. Concord Court can't serve Charlie, but I won't leave him behind, either. And tonight, he's going to celebrate with the rest of us." Her posture was perfect again but stretched tight. She wouldn't bend but she might break.

Reyna had her orders. She'd execute them perfectly.

One of the first things he'd noticed about Luis Montero's oldest daughter was that while she might be petite and beautiful in the girl-next-door way, she would give Napoleon himself a run for his money as far as taking the lead. She was prepared to make hard decisions and stand by them in the face of opposition. Just like her father, the first Montero he'd encountered.

If he had to guess, Luis Montero was enforcing this "mission," which required evicting one of Sean's favorite tenants. Whatever Reyna might have wanted to do, she was in a tough spot.

She'd gone to bat for Sean against her father not long after she'd arrived home. That had earned his loyalty, even if evicting Charlie tested it.

And she'd made a good point. Tonight was not about leasing or dealing with Montero policies. It was about celebrating. And Charlie had come out to do exactly that.

"Might be time to…" Unbend? Relax? How could he end that sentence? "…make a plate. Are you hungry?"

She turned to face him then, her lips curved. "Why do I suspect that wasn't how you wanted to fill in the blank?" She crossed her arms over her chest. Maybe she was relieved to move away from the topic, because she added, "Next year, we'll make this bigger and do better publicity, increase interest and attendance. Brisa already has notes. There will be decorations, for one thing."

Sean watched Reyna's little sister work the crowd. There were few people Brisa knew, but that didn't bother her a bit. She was a social butterfly in her late twenties or early thirties, dressed in what had to be expensive, silky fashion. Her hair was done in an elaborate braid, and the red, white and blue fabric of her dress draped like fancy bunting.

"Are you paying her to sing tonight?" Sean asked. He wasn't certain where Brisa worked, but a fancy style like hers would demand a good paycheck. Or the support of the Montero bank account.

Luis Montero was an investment banker, and, if the charitable donations in the Montero name throughout southern Florida were any indication, he was very good at his job.

"She offered to help with the party as long as she got to perform one song." Reyna shook her head. Her voice was so dry that Sean did a double take. Then her lips curved again. He was sure he'd never seen her real smile. He would remember it.

"Public adoration is my little sister's favorite form of payment." She met his stare again for a quick second. "I love her, even if I don't understand it. I'll lead from the front, for sure, but do not put me up on a stage in front of strangers." Reyna shivered as if it was too much to consider.

He understood that aversion. Center stage was no place to be. Cracking jokes under his breath was more his style.

Sean was caught off guard at the connection that snapped into place in that heartbeat.

He cleared his throat. "How would you like your dog?" He pointed at the grill. "Last chance."

"Burn it, chef." Reyna straightened her shoulders and walked through the crowd, acknowledging each vet with a quick dip of her chin. In her Concord Court navy polo and shorts, she was the official welcome compared to Brisa's gushing celebrity appearance. Reyna joined her sister in front of the complex's well-lit flagpoles. Sean knew to the penny how much it cost to light and fly the United States flag, Florida's flag and one flag for each branch of the military. He also knew it mattered to every man and woman lucky enough to get a place at Concord Court. And it mattered to Reyna. She would happily pay the bill. Neither she nor her father had pinched pennies where it counted. It was the only decoration required tonight.

"Thank you all for coming." Reyna tangled her fingers together.

Most people would never guess she was uncomfortable in the spotlight. That made Sean wonder what else he might not know about Reyna Montero.

"We wanted to make sure we marked this day and made it clear to each of you how much we appreciate your service and how happy we are to have you here. My sister, Brisa Montero, is going to sing the national anthem. After that, we'll start the movie. Don't forget we've got cold watermelon and lemonade whenever you'd like refills. And if you have any suggestions on ways to improve your time here, please come by the office. I'd love to talk with you."

Awkward silence followed Reyna as she retreated through the crowd.

Brisa watched her go with a small frown. Had she expected a bigger intro?

Reyna stopped in front of the grill but didn't face him until Brisa started to sing. Then Reyna inhaled slowly and exhaled.

"Good job, boss." Sean offered Reyna a plate with a blackened hot dog in a bun. She raised her eyebrow but didn't argue.

She pointed at the plate. "This is perfect. Thank you." She ducked her head and darted around him to brace a shoulder against one of the wrought iron posts surrounding the courtyard. "You have a seat. I'll stay here and handle the rest." Then she took a bite big enough to stuff her mouth.

The weird uncertainty, which was completely out of place in her normal confident pose, made it harder to walk away from her. Everyone else at Concord Court was comfortable, content. He could help Reyna.

Sean studied the backdrop that would act as a screen for the projector. Troy was behind the projector, ready to hit Play. "Everything is under control," Sean said, pointing at the blanket he'd spread out before he started the grill. His service-dog-in-training, Bo, the hound dog, was relaxed, but both eyes were locked on Sean. He'd done so well. Bo would be leaving for his new home soon.

Then Sean would have to decide what came next for his program.

He'd watched Reyna defend his service dog training to her father the first week she'd been in charge. She hadn't backed down. He owed her.

"If you don't mind hanging out with hound dogs, you can share my blanket," he offered.

"So we declare a truce for the evening? No more fighting about Charlie?"

"You have your mind made up. I'm not foolish enough to hope I have a chance of changing it." Sean waved his plate. "And we have dinner and a movie to get to."

Reyna had always been careful to keep distance between them. They'd never been the "hey, you got big weekend plans?" kind of coworkers.

But tonight she hesitated to refuse.

Eventually she nodded. "I'll make sure Charlie is okay. Trust me, Wakefield." That was an order. Her tone had no "please" in it.

Reyna took one corner of his blanket while he settled on the other, Bo forming a comfortable wall between them. The screen lit up.

"One more condition," Sean said and watched her eyebrows rise. She didn't like an addition after she'd agreed. He could respect that. "I'm Sean. 'Wakefield' reminds me of my short and not-sweet career with the Marines. Now I like Sean."

Reyna pursed her lips. "Fine. As long as I'm Reyna. 'Boss' gives me the urge to fight." She arched one eyebrow as if to remind him that they'd already tried arguing once.

Sean cleared his throat. It might have a whiff of insubordination now and then to drawl "boss" at his actual boss. "Agreed."

"Good. Sean." Reyna picked up her plate.

"Why a movie?" Sean asked as he bent closer to Reyna. "No fireworks?" He'd thought *A League of Their Own* was an unusual choice, but he wouldn't be the only one who would appreciate some easy, fun entertainment. History, but no bullets or bombs.

Sean still wanted to understand her reasoning. It would be a hint to who Reyna was, the Reyna that didn't make it to the surface. *Reyna.* Not *boss.*

Reyna turned. In the same moment, they realized how close they were and shifted farther apart.

"So many vets have trouble with the booms and pops, and there are lots of places with fireworks already if someone wants to find them. But baseball? It's one of the top three." She held out her hand and ticked items off on her fingers. "Mom. Baseball. And apple pie." She rubbed one of Bo's ears between her fingers. "Besides, I'm a big fan of girl power, you know."

Bo turned molten brown eyes Sean's direction. He was working, so he shouldn't be distracted by anyone.

"Okay, Bo," Sean said, giving the dog permission to relax. Bo immediately inched forward and braced his chin on Reyna's knee. Sean waited for Reyna to protest, but the precisely straight line of her back bent a fraction as the movie started.

Reyna had flown jets.

She was a decorated military officer.

That much he knew from web searches and her father's boasting.

They'd butted heads exactly once. Over Charlie. And he was having trouble letting that go.

But he did trust her to do the right thing.

For one night, he wanted to forget that she was the hero he'd never be and that she was about to evict a friend because of her commitment to the rules.

He wanted to pretend he was just a guy sharing a blanket with a pretty woman, a perfect dog and a movie under the starry night sky. It wouldn't happen often.

He should enjoy every second.

CHAPTER TWO

A WEEK AFTER the Fourth of July cookout, Reyna Montero brushed sweaty hair off her forehead and tried to pretend she didn't mind losing.

She wasn't doing it well.

Losing was the worst and she'd never been good at faking. A lifetime of leading instead of following meant she had a lot more practice with being a gracious *winner*.

"You okay there, Montero?" Sid Fields, the instructor for the final required course at the South Florida First Responder Academy, yelled down from his perch on the second floor of the massive garage. The class had left the academy for real-world exposure at Sawgrass Station, one of the largest fire houses in the Miami area. They were gathered in a two-story building. The fire trucks and engines had been moved out, leaving concrete floors, cinder block walls and plenty of space. Open bay doors on opposite ends of the building provided the only breeze.

Sid and his younger brother, Mort Fields, the fire chief at Sawgrass, leaned against the railing and tested students' times in responding to an alarm. Mort held a stopwatch and a clipboard. The task was simple. Put on the full turnout gear of a firefighter and move as quickly as possible from the starting line to the opposite wall.

"Fine, sir, thank you," she answered and carefully placed the helmet and face mask in one of the cubbies above a long line of hooks on the wall. To buy time to catch her breath and shove her disappointment down, way down, Reyna studied the gear and straightened a few pieces. "Organization is key here."

Seventy pounds of gear had made the simple task—walking a distance she should be able to run without breathing hard—a challenge.

Slipping off the air canister lightened the load considerably, almost thirty pounds' difference in one simple change. Strapped to her back, that weight had made moving in heavy boots difficult.

"You can't do this, you'll never pass the physical aptitude test," Sid barked. He held up a clipboard. "Burns, Monrovia, McQueen, Jones, Pulaski and Montero, decent times. The rest of you need some practice and better conditioning before you try the PAT."

Reyna relaxed. Her name was on the good list. She was going to get her firefighting certificate, even if she didn't win the instructor's recommendation. Sid had announced he'd write one letter of recommendation and only one. Today's relays had been his tool to decide who would be the lucky one to get it.

And it wasn't going to be Reyna, because she hadn't had the fastest time today. That stung.

Ryan Pulaski had already shrugged out of his jacket. "Guess Air Force training is different than learning to fight fires."

Tall and blond, Pulaski would have made the perfect poster boy for an all-American firefighter. Reyna had beaten his test scores in every class they'd shared, so he was taking his turn to gloat.

Reyna was used to dealing with these men and their inflated egos when they had finally managed to push her to second place.

To show how unaffected she was by his dig, Reyna picked up his ax, flashlight and utility belt. After she'd stored them correctly in the cubbies along the wall, Reyna removed her own jacket and hung it on a hook. As she stepped back, she surveyed the line of turnout gear. She was leaving it better than she'd found it before the test started.

Cooler air immediately hit her soaked T-shirt. Reyna pinched the knit between her thumbs and fingers and pulled it away from her damp skin.

Summer in Miami. Sweaty clothes were her norm. She'd been relieved the fans she'd set up for the Fourth of July movie had made the last-minute inspiration to celebrate outside tolerable. Sawgrass Station could use those fans right now.

"The city's physical aptitude test is no joke," Mort drawled. "Passing it is tough, but I'm happy to see there are a few strong candidates here. You never know who will show up on the day. Bad news is I've only got room for one, maybe two of you here at my firehouse. If you're lucky enough to get on at Sawgrass, you stay here." His proud expression made it clear that he knew it was the best station in the city.

Reyna struggled out of the turnout pants and boots and turned to face the men on the second floor.

"Good job, Pulaski," Mort added. "Look me up when you have the certificate in your hand."

The tight burn in her jaw was Reyna's reminder that clamping her jaw shut was her best answer here.

So what that she'd been at the top of every class the academy required to get the firefighter certification?

Or that she'd outscored Pulaski on every written exam in Fields's final class?

Or even that she was a decorated Air Force veteran who'd served her country overseas?

Flying jets required precision, skill, command of all her reflexes and the ability to think under pressure.

Being slower physically than Pulaski to put on her turnout gear negated none of that.

Sawgrass Station was where she wanted

to work. It was a big operation with multiple crews. When any news reporter wanted the fire department's contribution to a story, they chased down Mort Fields. He had served the metropolitan Miami area for thirty years. She could remember the first time she'd met Mort and his firehouse dog, Smokey, at a summer event in Bayfront Park. She'd been ten years old and starstruck. The now-bald chief had had a full head of blond hair then.

Mort had been in her favorite snapshot of her family, the one she'd carried with her when she left Miami. That photo of Reyna, her father, her little sister, the fire chief and his Dalmatian had been a piece of home no matter where she was stationed.

Now he and his brother were watching her closely. They thought she was going to be a sore loser.

Reyna held her hand out and waited for Pulaski to shake it. "Don't suppose I could talk you into going for the best two out of three?" she asked.

"Got nothing to gain from that, Montero," Pulaski answered. "I'm either going to win again or I lose and throw away my only advantage here." He motioned between them. "Of course we're the fastest. That's why they put us up against each other. Army basic training versus that Air Force easy life. Here I came out on top." He motioned over his shoulder. "A job interview like this can't be beat."

Both Fields brothers were still watching them, even though they couldn't hear the conversation. This was not the time to wade into which branch of service was the best, strongest or hardest.

Reyna nodded and dug in her bag to pull out her phone. "Then can you do me a favor?" She pulled up the camera. "Film me as I run this again. I can work on conditioning, for sure, but I'd like to know where I'm getting hung up with the gear."

She held out her phone and waited.

Pulaski tipped his head back and then took the phone. "You're going to go through that again? With an audience watching. Why? It won't help." He glanced over his shoulder as if he weren't entirely convinced that what he was saying was correct.

"I want to be a firefighter. I need to improve this skill. Winning or losing only matters here, in this class, but when I'm on a shift, answering a call, I have to have this down." Reyna stared at the heavy gear and did her best to ignore the heat. She'd been through plenty of physical training over the years. She could do this one more time today.

Pulaski shook his head. "It's your funeral" was easy to read on his face. Then he turned around to make an announcement. "Montero's going to run it again, everybody, for her own personal development." He waved the camera. "And we're filming it."

He nodded at her. "Go when you're ready."

Reyna inhaled slowly to steady her nerves. The pounding of her heart was distracting and she needed to focus.

Sometimes visualizing the target helped, so she pictured the bunker gear, thinking about the order she would put it on in, and nodded in return.

Everyone was watching her, waiting, but her only competition was herself.

That had been true often enough in her life.

Under her breath, Reyna counted, "Three, two, one…go." Fast but not clumsy.

That was her last thought before she reached for the pants and boots.

Jacket. Utility belt. Flashlight. Air canister on her back. Face mask. Helmet. Gloves.

Then she was walking and she poured every bit of energy she had remaining for speed. When she touched the wall, she felt good. Right.

As she yanked the face mask and helmet off, she turned to Pulaski.

"I think you were faster this time," he said, both eyebrows raised.

"Because she was," Mort Fields yelled down, waving the stopwatch in his hand.

This time it was easier to catch her breath. Pulaski waited patiently for her to rehang her jacket and offered her the phone.

"Easier the second time," Reyna said. "Maybe one more time…"

His groan almost made her smile. "Don't be a martyr, Montero. We get it. You're strong." He walked over and snatched a backpack off the floor. "Tales will be told all over southern Florida of Reyna Montero's dedication. I'll take care of spreading the word here at Sawgrass." Pulaski held out his arms. "Because I'll be taking this job. See you at the physical aptitude test. Hope you're ready to finish second there, too." He was halfway across the wide-open room before Reyna gave up on finding a clever answer. If it didn't happen immediately, she'd only look silly yelling her "Oh yeah?" response.

Silly was no way for a Montero to look.

Reyna fell into line behind the rest of the class and listened to subdued chatter as everyone headed for the parking lot. None of it was directed to her, so there was no need to come up with anything brilliant to say.

Listening was easier than making conversation. Standing on the outside instead of serving as the glue for her team was something she was still coming to terms with. Her family came with some challenges, which had made joining the Air Force a simpler decision. It had been easy enough to make a new family with the men and women she'd served with. In South Korea, every holiday presented another chance to build that family's bonds. Thanksgiving dinner might not include turkey, but they'd done their best to observe traditions together.

Even so, loneliness had sometimes been overwhelming while she was in the service.

Reyna hadn't expected it to get worse after retirement.

She stopped at the SUV her father provided as a part of her role as manager of Concord Court, a cushy job he'd created to entice her home.

"Montero," Sid Fields yelled from the station's doorway. "Hold up."

Reyna dropped her bag inside and leaned against the hot metal car door. Maybe her clothes would miraculously dry while they talked.

"Second place. There's no shame there." Sid motioned back toward the firehouse with his chin. "My brother? Of the two of us, most people would say he's number one. Finished first. Fire department's spokesman when it counts." He tapped his chest. "But when it comes to training firefighters, I'm the guy chiefs call on. You understand?"

Reyna brushed her hair back. She really didn't get what he was telling her, but admitting that wasn't a smart move.

His sigh of disgust confirmed her suspicion. "Different jobs, Montero. Different skills. Think on that." He turned on his heel.

"A fine last impression to leave," she muttered as she spotted Mort Fields standing in the shade near the building, his arms crossed over his chest and a frown wrinkling his forehead.

Should she wave?

No waving.

The size of the station had been what first caught her attention when she was making plans for her second career as a firefighter. If she wanted to further specialize her training, Sawgrass would offer more opportunities.

Hazmat cleanup was interesting. They'd covered the basics at the academy, but on-the-job training would make any specialty training she might want to pursue clearer.

Reyna slid behind the wheel and carefully drove out of the parking lot. It was a beautiful sunny day and the roads were filled with people riding bicycles. Late afternoon could be that way. The heat eased marginally, so runners and riders came out.

The distance from Sawgrass Station to her town house was short. That was the second reason she wanted to work at Sawgrass. If she got the job, it would be easy to keep an eye on Concord Court, the bridge community of townhomes that offered veterans a place to stay for two years while they adjusted to coming home.

Veterans got a chance to pursue education or to find the right jobs, and space to get their feet under them.

Warm brown stucco and red-tiled roofs, along with the sparkling pool in the center of the complex, wrought iron fencing and lush vegetation gave the whole place an inviting atmosphere.

Luis Montero wouldn't have had it any other way.

He'd conceived the project as a way to encourage Reyna's retirement.

He'd always been protective of his daughters, and he'd felt the need to persuade Reyna to leave the Air Force, to come home where it was safe.

Without his pressure, she'd still be in South Korea. She'd be meeting her "family" at their favorite bar in Pyeongtaek, the place with the bartender who spoke English and blasted country music on the jukebox.

The restlessness and dissatisfaction she felt behind the desk at Concord Court would be a long way away. This plan to become a firefighter would still be hazy and in the future. The pressure to either join a fire crew or settle down in her position at Concord Court would not be a problem.

She'd tried things her father's way for a few months. Focusing on getting Concord Court up and running had taken some energy when she'd first gotten home, but the smaller that challenge grew, the harder it was to face spending the rest of her life behind the desk in the Court's office.

Coming home had been like racing at the speed of sound into a brick wall. From Mach 1 to done.

The first time she'd mentioned her interest in a second career to her father had not gone well. Luis Montero had never taken disappointment gracefully, and his plan had been for her to return and take the nice, safe job running Concord Court.

She hadn't attempted the conversation this time.

One father. One stepmother. One sister. With her no longer being in the service, that was all the family she had now.

It made no sense to upset the peace until she got a job offer. When that happened, she'd deal with her father.

As Reyna drove past the office, she noticed the lights were out. Sean had manned the desk for her, and he'd closed up for the day.

She continued on to her unit and saw that he'd made it as far as his own front steps. He was clearly waiting for her. They were neighbors, something she'd spent a lot of time thinking about when she'd moved in. Their setup was logical. For now, it was the two of them managing the complex and small staff and that was a job twenty-four hours a day, seven days a week.

Unfortunately, there was something about Wakefield that made their conversations tense, like there was an undercurrent of something she couldn't name. He was good at his job. Very good. She didn't have to worry because he took care of security, maintenance and construction, leaving her the people part of the equation.

Why did finding him now, when she wasn't expecting it, provoke this restlessness? It made her alert and unsettled and ready to move all at the same time.

It had to be because he was so handsome. Messy brown hair and hazel eyes that reflected his mood, good or bad. And tonight, he had the beginnings of a beard. Later she'd try to decide if that scruff was better or worse than his usual clean jaw.

Good-looking men should come with some advance warning system.

"Everything okay?" she asked.

He nodded. "Yes, ma'am. I expected you'd require a sit report. All quiet. Received two referrals from the hospital and left notes on your desk as requested." He frowned down at the grass. "And not that you asked, but I got Charlie moved to Punto Verde yesterday morning."

The fatigue that had been fading buried her in a landslide. It was hard to lock her knees. All she wanted to do was sit down. Had to be the heat. "Good."

"He wasn't happy." Sean met her stare then. "Again. Not that you asked."

Reyna pressed one hand to her forehead. His anger was understandable, but this was part of the job. "I'm sorry."

"That he wasn't happy or that you didn't ask?"

Valid point. Reyna huffed out a breath. "Both. Too wrapped up in something else, so I'm sorry he's struggling and that I didn't think to ask." Failing on both fronts of her career wasn't something she'd considered. She hadn't won Sid Fields's recommendation, and she was letting down a fellow vet.

She needed to get inside before the day got any worse.

One corner of Sean's mouth quirked up. "Enjoy your day off? Looks like it gave you a run for your money, boss."

Boss. The way he drawled the word... She'd never been able to decide if it was irritation or something else that turned her stomach all...loopy.

"Joined a new gym. I think it's working." Reyna climbed the three steps up to her door. "Thanks for taking care of the office today. I'll get an assistant manager in here soon. Can you handle next Saturday, too?" Casual. She'd been asking him to change his normal schedule to cover her Saturdays pretty regularly for the past two months. Trusting him not to catch on made no sense, but she needed his help one last time.

He slowly shook his head. "Can't do it, boss. My grandmother is turning eighty this year, so my aunts have got this big blowout planned. I'm on duty Saturday to put up the decorations and build whatever is required. There will be building." He braced his elbows on his knees, calling her attention to those legs. Surely that hadn't been his purpose.

"You wouldn't want me to disappoint Mimi, would you?" He tilted his head to the side.

"No." Reyna unlocked her front door. "I'll find someone else to cover for me." She'd almost stepped inside when she stopped. "Is Mimi her name? Or is it a cooler version of *Granny*?"

His eyebrows shot up before Sean chuckled. "Cooler? I'll have to tell her you said so. Her full name is Mary Elizabeth O'Malley, so it started as one and became the other."

Since she'd never had a grandparent to call by any name, Reyna thought that was pretty sweet. Her father's parents had lived in Cuba until they died, so she'd never met them. And her mother had taken her father's generous divorce settlement and headed for Europe when Reyna was still young. They mainly communicated through an occasional email and yearly birthday cards.

The temptation to linger was too strong. "Should I call you Wakefield? I thought we had an agreement, but that 'boss' is back."

He grimaced. "Sean and Reyna, please. The urge to salute is too strong otherwise."

She nodded. "Good night."

Reyna closed the door and locked it before heading for her shower. The problem with living next door to Sean Wakefield was how easy it would be to check to see if he'd gone inside, too, especially now that he was "Sean." Last names meant distance. Would she regret eliminating that?

If he was still sitting outside, Reyna wasn't sure she'd be able to control the urge to go ask more about Mimi or spill some of the anxiety about what would come next for her career. He had broad shoulders and a calm certainty that things would work out.

The temptation to rely on both was new. And dangerous.

CHAPTER THREE

ON SUNDAY MORNING, Sean completed the necessary run with his informal support group only because Mira Peters would make him miserable otherwise. Living on-site gave him access to a good group of vets-turned-friends to discuss his problems with and a dedicated physical trainer who did not understand sleeping in. Mira accepted no excuses.

"Good run, everyone," Mira said from the sidewalk leading to her building. "Same time next weekend?"

Sean knew better than to groan out loud, so he waved a hand in surrender. He made the short walk to his townhome and managed to let himself in without staring for too long at Reyna Montero's front door.

He'd had a few more things to say to her last night, but it was for the best she'd slipped inside before he had the chance. Her question about his grandmother had thrown him. Over the months they'd worked together, Reyna hadn't done much to make a personal connection. Sometimes it seemed like she was surprised to see him when he walked into the Court's lobby.

Since he did that pretty often to get to his small office set off the lobby, it confused him. He'd thought when he was introduced to her that it would take them some time to settle into a comfortable routine. Reyna was reserved. The urge to ruffle her serious demeanor bubbled up, but he did his best to control it because she signed the paychecks at Concord Court. The routine had arrived, but he would guess neither of them would call it comfortable. Now, with this disagreement over Charlie planted right between them, they might never have that easy working relationship.

Sean had expected her to demand an update on Charlie's situation. Instead, she'd given her order with the firm expectation it would be executed properly and never thought of it again.

Like the boss she was.

After a shower and change of clothes,

Sean asked, "Bo, you ready to go see the gents?" and patted the hound dog stretched out on the cool tile in the kitchen. Identifying Bo's lineage would be difficult. Anytime Sean was asked, he answered, "Forty pounds of hound," but Bo was smart. He knew exactly what going to "see the gents" meant. The three old guys holding court at Punto Verde always gave his dogs lots of attention. Sean had argued hard in favor of the facility he visited with his service dogs, so that he'd have plenty of reason and opportunity to check on Charlie Fox.

Charlie had gone with his recommendation, but it had been about choosing the convenient option instead of one he'd put any time into. When Sean helped him move in, Charlie had shown zero interest in the list of amenities available at Punto Verde.

Checking in on him today seemed important.

After a hard thump of his tail, Bo rolled up slowly to stand and stretch. He had learned new commands in the weeks Sean had been training him, and he'd passed the test to gain service animal certification, but that laid-back personality was genetic. It was also the most valuable trait Sean looked for in rescues to train as service animals for veterans, his *pet* pet project.

"Bad puns and no one around to enjoy them," Sean muttered. "I should definitely spend some time searching for human companionship, shouldn't I?"

The dog's soulful eyes were locked on his face. Bo didn't nod in agreement, but the slow wag of his tail could be interpreted as support.

"All right, let's get out of this apartment." Sean draped the vest that read Service Animal in Training over Bo's head and snapped on his leash before opening the front door. They'd take a mini stroll over the grass in front of his townhome to be sure there were no accidents on the way to the rehab facility.

He'd stepped outside when Reyna's door swung open. She slammed to a stop on the first step, the loose skirt of her floral sundress swirling around her knees. He realized he'd been mesmerized by the sight of her legs for too long when she finally spoke.

"Good morning." Reyna brushed a hand through her hair. "To both of you."

Sean nodded. "Good morning." Why wouldn't anything else come to mind?

The tense silence stretched until Sean snapped back to himself. "Where ya headed on this beautiful Sunday?" Something about Reyna made him turn up every bit of Georgia drawl he possessed.

"Brunch." She heaved a sigh. "With my father."

"That explains the fancy dress. I'm used to polos and khakis." And why was he commenting on what she was wearing? He wasn't a fashion reporter. "We're headed out to Punto Verde." He pointed at the dog. "Bo'll get to practice his manners and I can check in on Charlie. Make sure he's okay in his new home."

Reyna clutched her tiny purse in both hands. He made sure to study her face when he mentioned Charlie. Of the two of them, it wasn't him who should experience guilt over Charlie's new home. "Want to come with me to see him?"

Before she could answer, he said, "Oh yeah. Gotta do brunch." Then he mimicked her heavy sigh.

"A command performance. I hate those."

Her lips tightened. "But complaining is a waste of time and words. Nothing moves my father." She brushed a hand over her skirt uncertainly before touching the pale pink rose dangling on a thin gold chain around her neck. Sean wondered if she was uncomfortable in the dress or if the meal with her father made her anxious. If Reyna was intimidating, her father was imposing. Sean had been hired by him before Reyna made it home, and he was glad Luis spent less time inspecting his work now.

"Did you need something?" Reyna asked before going down the steps. Bo moved closer to sniff her toes, and Sean was distracted by the soft pink polish peeking from her sandals. She bent down to scratch Bo's ears. When the dog blinked up at her, Sean understood how he felt. Caught and happy about it.

"I meant to let you know last night that we've rekeyed Charlie's unit. It's ready to go again." Charlie Fox wouldn't be coming back to Concord Court even if he managed to get strong enough to leave the rehab facility.

"Good. It's fully outfitted with the assistive devices the kid coming in from Walter Reed will need. I hope his parents are right and that he can handle living alone here. I can't cope with another failure right now." She cleared her throat. "Not that Charlie was a failure. I mean…" She licked her lips. "I want to give everyone a chance who asks for it. If we have too many who can't meet the requirements, I'll have to revise my policy."

When he didn't answer, she straightened. Whatever her personal beliefs were, she'd go to battle to uphold the importance of proper policy.

Reyna could make a killing in a competitive poker game. Her face gave nothing away.

Reyna lifted a shoulder. "Charlie needed a different kind of facility."

Sean nodded his head slowly. Neither one of them liked her answer, and it hadn't changed. "Hope you're right."

Her eyes snapped up to meet his. "My father built Concord Court to fill a need, Sean. There are places for men like Charlie, the guys who need daily medical support. This is not that. We are not doing that."

Sean didn't argue. Whatever she had to

tell herself to live with the consequences didn't mean much to him or Charlie.

"I'm glad he's still here nearby where we can check on him. When I get a minute, I'll drop by to make sure he has what he needs. We won't forget about him." She straightened her shoulders. With that tone and the conviction on her face, she was a leader. She'd made a hard decision, but somewhere inside, there was enough good that it hadn't been easy and it wouldn't be forgotten, either.

That was why he still came to work for Reyna Montero. There was a heart under the policy.

It had to be enough. She wasn't going to change.

"Do you have further suggestions, Wakefield? I'm happy to listen to them." Her arms made a tight knot in front of her chest.

Wakefield. They'd taken one step forward at the cookout, and now they were two steps back.

"You *seem* happy," he drawled, the sarcasm he normally tried to control around his boss leaking out. He pointed to her arms with his chin. Her body language was defensive, not happy. "No, ma'am. Place runs like a precision instrument. Anything you need, boss?"

Reyna shook her head. "You and Bo have a good day." She marched down the steps to her SUV and slid inside. He waited to see if she would meet his stare as she left, but she backed out slowly and drove away.

Bo plopped down on his foot.

Almost as if he was affronted by how easily she'd left them behind.

"Don't take it personally, buddy," Sean said as he ruffled the dog's ears. "We'll go find someone else to scratch your chin."

After he got Bo loaded into his car, Sean pulled out of Concord Court and headed for the interstate. Homestead was a quick hop on and off, and he'd barely gotten the air conditioner to cool down the truck before he was parking in front of the nursing home and rehab facility.

Instead of howling with excitement, as he had every time he'd gone for a ride in the early days, Bo sat up straight, his eyes and ears alert. He was still excited, but this dog was under control.

"Good boy," Sean murmured and let him

out. He held the leash loosely to make sure Bo followed his pace, and he couldn't contain his proud grin when the dog stopped perfectly to wait for the door. "You got this." He was ready to go to his new home.

The mix of pride and happiness and sadness that always hit when it was time to send a dog on to a veteran's home washed over Sean. He did his best to shake it off. This was the goal, his whole reason for taking this project on.

The nurse working the front desk and registering visitors flashed a wide grin. "My favorite hound dog! And Bo is here, too!"

Sean nodded, even though her joke was a part of the routine. Working in a facility like this had to include some hard days. He'd never seen Monique with anything less than a smile. "Before we leave, you'll have to give Bo a good-luck kiss. He's headed home this week."

Monique clapped her hands. "Way to go, big guy." She came around the desk and ruffled Bo's ears. The dog peeked up at Sean. Since he was working, people were supposed to wait for permission to approach him and he had been trained to wait for the okay.

"Okay, Bo," Sean said and shook his head as the dog immediately swiped his tongue over Monique's cheek in a hello kiss. That might need refining before he sent the dog off.

Her grimace and giggles were cute, though.

"The gents are in the common room, 'watching'—" she made air quotes "—the news. Your friend Charlie won't leave his room. Fix that." The phone rang and she stepped back behind the counter to answer it, but tapped the sign-in sheet and raised an eyebrow at him.

Sean dutifully signed his name and saw that Dan Martin's daughter had been in, too. She came to see her father almost every day, and her visits put him in a sunny mood. Sean hoped he was having one of his good days.

"Let's go, Bo. Time to work." Sean walked down the tiled hallway. As usual, there were residents sitting here and there. Some were practicing their exercises in their wheelchairs. Some sat in doorways, content to watch people come and go. Bo calmly navigated the course. He didn't react to the wheelchairs or walkers. "Good boy."

When they reached the common room,

the blare of the news was impossible to ignore, but tucked into a sunny corner was a sofa and four chairs. The three old guys whom everyone called "the gents" were arranged as they always were, with Dan seated front and center. It was his group. And as always, when he spotted Sean and Bo, he held out one hand and waved gaily. "I knew it was going to be a good day." He tapped the carnation boutonniere his daughter brought daily to pin to her father's seersucker jacket. "I dressed for the occasion."

Fashion at Punto Verde varied. Some people wore hospital gowns. They were undergoing the early stages of rehab. Others preferred comfortable sweats or cotton shirts. Dan wore a suit and tie. Every day. Because that was what he preferred.

It was hard to argue with style like that.

"Good to see you. Okay, Bo." He dropped the leash. The dog walked over and sat, bracing his chin on Dan's knee. This always delighted the gents and they made a big deal out of it. Bo's tail wagged. As usual, it was a happy reunion.

"I thought you were getting out of here,

Dan. I'm surprised to see you still here."
This was Sean's part of their routine.

"Doctor thought one more week would be better. Build my strength up." Dan waved a hand around the group. "And I'm still needed here, Sean."

On his first visit to Punto Verde, Monique had explained that all three of the gents were fighting Alzheimer's. On a good day, they were the life of the party. And on bad days, they were still charming, even if you weren't sure what year they were in. Most often, Dan slipped back to his childhood. Seeing Bo led to at least one story about his favorite hunting dog, who could tree squirrels with the best of them.

No matter which Dan was sitting on the couch when he walked in, Sean enjoyed their visits.

"I'm going to take Bo on his rounds." Sean shoved his hands in his pockets. "Have you guys met my friend Charlie?" If he could get Charlie in with this group, the guy would be okay. They loved good stories and he had thousands of them.

Dan frowned and studied his gleaming wing tips. "I might remember a new face around the dinner tables last night. Handsome guy with a wheelchair?"

Sean paused to evaluate Charlie's "handsome" factor, then nodded.

Dan sighed. "Hasn't been social at all." He shook his head sadly, as if that was the worst comment there was to make.

"I'll talk to him," Sean muttered and took Bo's leash. "Let's work, Bo." And the two of them started their route down the next hallway. Bo had learned where all his fans lived and he gently and insistently collected every bit of love and affection he could from Punto Verde. Days like this made Sean reconsider giving dogs up once they'd finished their training. Bo was doing so much good at this facility.

But he could be some vet's entire world. And another dog would have the chance to soak up this love. Sean just had to find the dog. And if he could get Reyna on board with his plan, he'd have more people and more dogs out there, changing days from okay to great.

When they arrived at Charlie's room, Sean knocked on the closed door and opened it without waiting for an answer. Charlie was stretched out on the bed with the television on but the sound muted. "Special delivery," Sean said before he added, "Okay, Bo."

The dog crossed the room, sniffed the edge of the bed and jumped up beside Charlie.

That was not the correct protocol, but it was right for Charlie, whose rusty chuckle reassured Sean. "Dog, you don't belong here." Charlie grunted. "Guess that makes two of us." He ruffled Bo's ears. "You come to break me out?"

Sean dragged one of the cushy armchairs in the corner closer to the bed. "No breaking out required. You don't want to stay, you tell me where to take you and we'll go."

Charlie didn't answer. He didn't have another option.

"Bo and I are here for his last visit. Next time, I'll have a new dog. Bo's going to his new home this week." Sean stretched his legs out. He had time. He could wait for Charlie to settle in. If it didn't happen today, he'd be back. "Since I'm so popular here, I could introduce you around. I have connections."

Charlie snorted. "All the pretty nurses?"

Monique was the only nurse Sean could recall, so he said, "You realize there's a whole new audience here who has never heard any of your stories?"

Charlie sighed. "Yeah. It's a lot of trouble to go out there and meet people."

And he wanted to be alone. Depression was a threat to Charlie and vets like him. Sean's support group that met nightly at the Concord pool was his lifeline. The gents could be Charlie's.

"I can help you," Sean said as he stood. "Let me. You're going to like these guys."

Charlie finally turned his head to meet Sean's stare. "Make the best of a bad situation, huh?"

Sean tipped his head to the side. "Make the most of every day. As long as you're staring at these four walls, life is passing you by. Doesn't have to be that way."

"Jump down, Bo," Charlie said, his tone aggrieved and annoyed. "I have to make an effort." The dog jumped down and Charlie sat up. Sean shifted the man's wheelchair closer and waited for Charlie to wheel himself out to the hallway. He and Bo followed.

Charlie seemed to know exactly where he was headed.

Because he was smart.

Depression was hovering there on the edges, but the guy was a fighter.

When they made it to the common area, Bo immediately headed for Dan, and Charlie followed the dog's lead. "Dan, Tommy, Darius, this is my friend Charlie Fox. He was career Air Force and he has some stories you would not believe. Tell them about the London pub where you met Princess Diana."

Dan's eyes immediately widened. He gasped. "No, you didn't!"

The twinkle that lit up Charlie's eyes when he was about to tell a wild story—one that might even be true—appeared. "Let me see my friends out and I'll tell you all about it."

They'd reached Monique's desk before Charlie cleared his throat. Bo ignored the awkward silence between them as he chomped the biscuit Monique kept on hand for the dog's visits, and Sean and Charlie watched as if they had to memorize Bo's movements.

Then he couldn't delay any longer. "Guess it's time for us to go."

Charlie nodded. "Yeah. I've got a story to tell. Hope I can remember it." Then he coughed. "We okay?"

Sean glanced at him before busying himself with Bo's vest. "Yeah."

"Good." Charlie nodded. "Queenie evicted me, not you. I understand that, and I know why she had to do it." When he'd arrived at Concord Court, Charlie had asked Reyna about a million questions. One of them had been her call sign, something Sean had never heard until Charlie mentioned it. In the Air Force, they'd called her Queen, a play on her name. Charlie had changed it up to Queenie, to make sure everyone understood Reyna was a regular person, no better or worse than Charlie Fox. And Reyna had allowed it.

That was the part that still blew Sean's mind. "Boss" was the extent of his daring.

Charlie scrubbed his hand across his jaw. "You didn't have to check on me, but I thank you. I'll make an effort."

Sean crossed his arms over his chest. "Good. I'm glad. You deserve to be happy."

Then he added, "I should warn you about the gents and Dan. Some days he forgets."

"Some days, I'd like to forget. Maybe he won't remember that the Princess Diana story changes every time I tell it."

Sean said, "Ask him about his hunting dog. He has about a hundred stories about him and growing up in the country."

Charlie's jaw dropped. "The country? The suit and tie threw me off. We do have things to talk about." Before Sean could promise he'd be back soon, Charlie had backed his chair away from the front desk and wheeled toward the common room. He obviously wanted to enjoy Dan's stories.

Monique's grin was contagious. "Good work, hero. Take the rest of the day off."

Sean didn't have much to say to that. He'd washed out of the Marines at his first chance and now he delivered old men to nursing homes. How was that heroic?

"Ready to go home, Bo? We've got some arrangements to make. You're going to meet your new best friend this week." He followed Bo out, opened the truck door, and the dog jumped in.

Reyna had missed an excellent visit. Sean

hoped for Queenie's sake that the Montero family brunch was going well. She'd be in a good mood when he made his proposal. It was time to expand his project. If he had any chance of earning that "hero" title, this was it.

CHAPTER FOUR

REYNA TIGHTENED HER grip on the steering wheel as she stopped at the guardhouse to her father's exclusive club. There was no need to experience these nerves. She'd been to the Cutler Bay Club many times—her father had been a member for as long as she could remember. This was where he negotiated deals, showed off his family and occasionally played golf.

"Your name, ma'am?" the young guy in a spotless white uniform asked.

"Reyna Montero."

"May I have your driver's license?"

Reyna pulled it from her purse and slid it through the window.

While he clicked on his computer, Reyna had a flashback to so many times in her life of clearing such guardhouses to return to base. He had the same official manner she'd been trained in, as if this country club required safety measures equal to United States military installations. Whoever trained this young man had done a thorough job. When she looked back up, he was studying her with a squint, as if he was evaluating whether she could be an impostor.

When he was satisfied, he handed her back the license and raised the gate. "Thank you, ma'am. Please proceed to the main club building. You'll find parking straight ahead."

Reyna ignored her weird urge to salute his formal manner and followed his directions. "Straight ahead" took a minute because the road wound through parts of the golf course, complete with golf cart crossings. Brilliant green grass lined the road, along with palm trees and occasional plantings of lush foliage and bright flowers.

"How many gardeners does it take to maintain a golf course in southern Florida?" Reyna murmured. It was a good setup for a joke, but she couldn't find a punch line. So much money. She reached a fork with a discreet sign that pointed toward the marina. As far as she knew, her father had never fully committed to owning a yacht. The club had at least one that could be rented as needed. Members only, of course.

Her father had insisted on throwing a Sweet Sixteen birthday party for her on the Gold Standard, which had been his second wife's brother's yacht. Inviting every student in her class at the exclusive Ross Collegiate School had been embarrassing; being forced to waltz the first dance with her father had been worse.

But living with the snide comments about Daddy's money being able to buy her everything but a boyfriend had been the worst. She'd never fit in at Ross, and Reyna would have done almost anything to escape Miami, her father and his society friends. The Ivy League colleges her father had planned to send her to would never have worked. Montero money and its problems would have followed her.

Instead of using the valet, Reyna pulled into the first spot she could find. "Fine day for a walk." The number of cars in the lot didn't surprise her—the club's brunch was excellent.

Or it had been the last time she was here. Reyna walked toward the building and tried to guess how long it had been since she'd had brunch at the club. Ten years? Fifteen?

When she reached the front door, a young woman held it open for her. "Ms. Montero, we are happy to have you today. Your family is out on the terrace. The view of the water is lovely this morning." She motioned Reyna forward.

Apparently the guardhouse called ahead to notify them of visitors.

How efficient.

Reyna followed the young woman through a dining room filled with enough booths and alcoves to allow for plenty of private business dealings. When she stepped out on the terrace, she had to stop to take it all in. *Lovely* didn't do this view justice. She'd stepped into a shady garden. Vines made living walls and created thick coverings. Leaves stirred in a breeze no doubt created by hidden fans. And it all framed a view of the sparkling ocean. A sailboat was frozen on the horizon as if this was a landscape, an oil painting, instead of real life.

And at the table front and center, the one with the best view of all, sat her father. He was dressed in an expensive suit and silk tie, prepared to do business wherever it might pop up. He stood as she approached the table and accepted her hug before pulling her chair out. Reyna bent to kiss her stepmother Marisol's cheek. The third Mrs. Montero was by far Reyna's favorite, mainly because she was a genuinely kind person. Marisol had dressed for the occasion as well, but on her, silk was effortless. Small lines radiated from her eyes and gray hairs dotted her temple, but she was still the second-most beautiful woman Reyna had seen yet.

The first was her sister, Brisa, who was sitting beside their father. She didn't stand but it was easy to see relief settle over her. Her shoulders relaxed. "Hey, sis, wasn't sure you'd make it."

Since Reyna had used every excuse under the sun to cancel on her father's command performances, she understood what her sister meant. "Things are finally settling down. As soon as I have the assistant manager on board, Concord Court will be fully operational and we can ramp up admissions."

"Finally," her father sighed. "Then I can return to focusing on what I'm good at. The money to pay for all that won't make itself."

"It's a good thing Brisa's been such a help with your party," Marisol said mildly. "Isn't it, Luis?"

Reyna watched her sister's face closely. She was surprised Marisol had spoken up. And pleased. Brisa's eyes met Reyna's before returning to the view.

Their father grunted. Brisa raised her chin, and Reyna was sure no one else would ever guess he'd hurt her.

Some things never changed. Reyna had witnessed the same scenario a hundred different ways growing up.

"Brisa has been organizing this cocktail party for next month." Marisol shook out her napkin and spread it over her lap. "We've lined up the caterers, and I think the roof of the Sandpiper Hotel is going to make a memorable backdrop. Brisa worked on the guest list and the invitations. She's done a lot to make this big event a success." Marisol's lips were a firm line, and she'd wrapped her hand around Brisa's.

Reyna was glad to see that her sister had Marisol's support. Getting some distance had made it easier for Reyna to get along with her father, but Brisa had been here, enduring the brunt of his focus. It couldn't have been easy, since Brisa had eloped at eighteen with her high school boyfriend, a clueless kid from a similarly rich family. In one move, Brisa had scrapped her father's plans for her and college and an appropriate society alliance via marriage. It had taken two years for the marriage to fall apart, due mainly to lack of parental support through funding. Brisa had returned home, and she'd been dealing with the consequences ever since. Clearly, she and Marisol had made an unofficial pact to stick together.

"Glad to have the main attraction on hand. I've already told all my friends about my daughter, the Air Force pilot. Brisa, they know very well. Reyna will stir up more interest in our project." Luis raised his eyebrows at Reyna. "Next goal you need to tackle is to turn this opportunity into real dollars for Concord Court. I built it. I expect you to run it. That means paying the bills on your own someday, too."

"Actually, it's funny you should bring that up," Reyna said slowly as she formulated a weak plan in her head. Listening to Marisol outline Brisa's involvement in their father's plans had sparked an idea. "I'd planned to run something by you before I moved forward, but it's not necessary. Before I open the job listing for the assistant manager…" Reyna sipped her water before continuing. "Concord Court could use Brisa's skills and connections day-to-day, too."

Could it? Reyna wasn't sure, but she'd taken her usual position in their family: standing with her sister against her father's judgment. "She improved my shaky Fourth of July celebration, and there's plenty else to do."

Reyna had come home to get closer to her sister.

This would work.

Her father frowned. "She's a…model. That's right, isn't it, Brisa? You're still modeling." His tone made it clear that it was too hard to follow her sister's wild career path. Brisa had never been great at sticking with things past the fun stage. "What skills could she bring?"

The only one Reyna required was being able to cover the office on Saturdays until she finished her class and passed the physical aptitude test. That answer would do nothing to change the tension at the table.

"Connections, Dad. She moves in Miami society. You know I'll never be comfortable schmoozing those money people for funding, and it can't be a once-a-year thing, either. There are local businesses to contact, and we're at a growth stage. That's exciting." Reyna glanced at her sister. It was impossible to tell if she was hurting or helping Brisa at this point. "Besides, I've missed my baby sister."

That was easy to say; Reyna meant it from the heart. Ever since she'd returned to Miami, she'd expected some revelation that would make it easy to bridge the gap that had grown between them while she'd been in the Air Force, but nothing came.

"You've got no one to blame but yourself for the fact that you aren't comfortable in Miami society now. You never should have joined the military in the first place. The Monteros serve in a different way. If you'd done what I told you to do—gotten some kind of degree and married someone here— how different would your life be now?" Her father's dark eyes were serious as he waited for her to acknowledge his verdict.

Well, from a purely logical standpoint, there'd be no Concord Court if she'd followed her father's orders. Of course life would be different.

Saying any part of that out loud would lead to an argument, and she might be arrested by the military-like security guard at the front gate, so Reyna bit her tongue.

"I'd like to help at Concord Court," Brisa said with a sunny smile. "I already know the place pretty well, since Daddy used me as unpaid labor until Sean showed up. I worked with the architects. I supervised the design of the place." Brisa picked up her water glass to take a dainty sip, and Reyna realized that one or two things might have changed since she'd been gone.

Her little sister had learned to do some fighting for herself.

Reyna met her stare across the table and they shared a small smile.

"Unpaid." Her father grunted. "Right. Let me tell my accountant that so he'll stop the rent payments, car payments and credit card payments. Wouldn't want to insult your integrity with my money."

"If she moved into Concord Court to take over this assistant management position, imagine how much you'd be saving." Marisol smiled vaguely around the table and picked up her mimosa. "This is an excellent plan, girls. Let's toast to new jobs."

As Reyna picked up her own mimosa, she noticed the small tick in her father's jaw. Was he clamping his mouth closed to keep from saying what he wanted to? Another trait that ran in the family.

"To new jobs." Reyna happily clinked her sister's glass. "Let's meet this week. We can make plans."

Brisa nodded.

"Better wait three months or so to make sure this job sticks before you move her into the Court," Luis said. "Moving her out again will be a hassle."

Brisa's smile didn't slip, so Reyna pasted on her own smile. "I've got a good feeling about this."

Marisol patted her hand. "Me, too. Now tell us what's been keeping you so busy." Waiters approached their table silently.

Reyna raised an eyebrow at her sister when plates of food were placed in front of them. They hadn't ordered yet. Her father raised his phone and pointed at it to give someone across the room a directive to call him. Reyna wasn't certain but she thought the balding man in the corner was a former governor.

"Since you were late, Daddy went ahead and ordered for you," Brisa said. "Time is money, et cetera, and so on." She picked up her fork. "Early is on time, and on time means you take what you get."

Silence except for the faintest clinks of silverware on plates fell over the table while they all sampled the brunch offerings. Reyna scooted the chunks of avocado over to one side. In a world of diverse cuisines, there were only a few things Reyna didn't like. But avocado made the list. Either her father had forgotten that or he'd never paid attention. She wouldn't have chosen that for herself, but everything else was delicious.

"You took care of the problem we discussed the last time I dropped in?" her father asked.

Charlie had been that problem. She would

have let the old guy live in his town house as long as it took to fill up the complex, but her father was still in his hands-on phase of this project. Over the months, thankfully his standing Wednesday meetings had become more sporadic. Eventually he'd move on.

Once he was certain she'd instituted all of his policies correctly.

"I did. He's been moved to a rehab facility in Homestead. I'm going to stop in and check on him as soon as I have a chance." She would. It would help with the guilt.

"That's not what I was asking. You mean you haven't contacted that family Senator Nixon called me about?" Her father's dark eyebrows smashed together.

With that one comment, Reyna came closer to understanding her father's willingness to pay for a project like this—for him, politics could mean profit.

"Yes. I have. Last week. I meant the veteran who has been evicted from his home." Reyna met his stare for a hard second and then turned away. Her father hadn't cared enough to ask about Charlie Fox. If Sean hadn't made a point to show her how cold that lack of concern seemed, would it ever have occurred to her?

Reyna was afraid the answer was no.

She swallowed to clear the hard lump in her throat.

For the remainder of the meal, conversation was easy but careful. They talked about Brisa's volunteer project funding new libraries for three local high schools, and her modeling career, stalled after a disagreement with the photographer for a high-end boutique in Miami's Design District. Marisol asked for opinions about whether the fall vacation she was planning would be better spent shopping in Paris or tanning on Fiji's beaches.

Since Reyna had spent a lot of time in faraway places but hadn't done much shopping or tanning, she didn't have a lot to contribute. She did wonder why someone would travel halfway across the world for a beach when they were already surrounded by them in Miami, but she swallowed that thought.

"Or a family vacation!" Marisol clapped her hands. "We could go somewhere together, a place we'll all enjoy. I like this. Lots of time to spend together."

When no one jumped on her suggestion, she folded her napkin. "Everyone check your calendars. We'll talk more about where when we know when we're going."

That would never happen. Reyna understood Marisol's impulse, but they barely managed a meal without arguments. A week of togetherness would require intervention by either law enforcement or perhaps foreign governments. The Monteros needed space and lots of time apart to stick together.

When the meal was finally over, Reyna said, "We're on for a three-month trial, then, right, BB?" She wrinkled her nose as her sister rolled her eyes at the old nickname.

"Yes. I'll call you and we'll set up a time to start my training." Brisa stood and Reyna gratefully followed suit. They'd both hugged Marisol when their father said, "I see someone I need to talk to. Marisol." He held out his arm. She'd be the right accessory for whatever kind of meeting came next. "Reyna, you'll need an escort for this party. I've got someone in mind." Her father pinned Reyna down with a stare. "Brisa will bring whoever she's dating at the moment. They're always good for publicity, but for you, I'll find someone with the right connections. I'll have someone text you with the details."

Arguing here would be too public, too much.

That was why her father had chosen his manner of delivery. He'd known she'd object to being set up with whatever associate he deemed advantageous.

That didn't mean she would go along with his plan, though. Now that he'd warned her, she could make her own plan.

"Thanks for brunch, Dad," Reyna said and wrapped her hand around her sister's wrist. "We're going to take a walk down by the water before we go."

He held up a hand, but he'd already moved on to the next conversation. She and Brisa followed the stairs down to the boardwalk leading to the marina.

Before Reyna could say anything, Brisa had wrapped her arms around her neck for a hug. "I'm glad you're back, Reyna."

Frozen, Reyna stood there, overwhelmed by the emotion, until she remembered to return the hug. "Me, too." This was what she'd hoped for and had been missing. Her sister.

"And you won't regret bringing me in to Concord Court. I have ideas." Brisa eased back and framed her face with jazz hands. The ideas were big and exciting. For now.

"Great." She wouldn't mention Brisa's terrible track record at sticking with anything for more time than it took for the next exciting idea to show up.

Not today. They were happy.

Brisa touched the rose pendant dangling on the gold chain around Reyna's neck. "I can't believe you still have this."

"What do you mean? You don't have the stuffed purple unicorn I gave you when you were ten?" Reyna had been so proud of that Christmas gift. The unicorn had been life-size, if you could say that about an imaginary creature. Brisa could sit on it and yell commands as if it was a trained show pony.

Brisa wrinkled her nose. "Not on me."

"This rose pendant has been around the world." Reyna fiddled with the delicate pink rose. "I'm not sure how many times I've replaced the chain, but I've kept this with me. It reminded me of you."

The weird tension between them thrummed while they tried to come up with a change of subject. Until Reyna left, it had been the two sisters against the world. They could get back to that, couldn't they?

"Do you want to walk to the end of the marina and back?" Reyna asked. "You can tell me about whoever you're dating. Dad is not a fan."

"That is usually the first quality I look for in a man—the ability to disappoint Luis Montero but not enough to get me kicked out of the family. Unless you want to be married off to fulfill dynastic dreams, I suggest you learn from my example," Brisa said with a sigh. "I can help you with that, too."

They shared a grin, like the other times they'd teamed up to outmaneuver their father.

Reyna threaded her arm through her sister's. This was how they'd ended every visit to the club when they were growing up. A trip to the water could wash all the family tension away. Bringing her sister on at Concord Court would ease the workload while she was pursuing her next career as a firefighter.

It might also eliminate some of the time and distance between them. This brunch had made it crystal clear what Reyna had escaped by joining the Air Force and how much Brisa had dealt with while she'd been gone. Brisa needed some room. Reyna could give her that at Concord Court.

What came after, she'd worry about later.

CHAPTER FIVE

As SEAN JOINED the unofficial therapy session that took place most nights around the pool in the center of Concord Court, he tried to shake off his weird mood that had settled over him while Bo was out for his nightly constitutional. Reyna's SUV was parked in front of her unit. That had been enough to make him wonder how brunch had gone. Knowing Luis Montero as well as he did, he'd understood her moody sigh that morning. What he was less clear on was why he was curious about how it had worked out. Reyna was his boss. Nothing more.

The memory of that delicate rose pendant against her skin flashed in his mind before he shook it off. Why that kept happening was something to evaluate the next time he was looking to get in touch with his emotions.

So, not tonight.

During the day, the pool showcased the

amenities to be found at the town house complex, the lush Florida landscaping and the cold, clear-blue water. At night, the shadows provided the perfect cover for whoever needed to show up to talk.

Even when he had nothing to say, staring up at the night sky was better than trying to sleep through nightmares.

Nightmares that were always worse with no dog at his side.

As he opened the gate, Sean reached down to scratch behind Bo's ears. He'd miss the hound dog on the nights when bad memories jolted him awake.

His nightmares shouldn't have so much power, not when so many men and women had been through so much worse than he ever had in his short military career. But the length of his time in the Marines meant nothing in the middle of the night.

The nightmares still came. Fire still blazed against a starless sky.

Cracking jokes to lighten the load of his friends was a much better use of his time than fighting tangled, sweaty sheets and wishing things were different.

When he closed the heavy wrought iron

gate behind him, Sean could see that only Mira Peters and Peter Kim had shown up. The group had grown to a steady five after fellow Georgian Jason Ward had moved in, but tonight he and Marcus Bryant were missing.

Since Sean hadn't mentioned his grand plan to Ward, the low attendance might be the best situation.

"Did you tell her?" Mira asked before he'd even stretched out properly in his seat. "You promised you were going to do it yesterday." Mira and Marcus had been a part of the first wave that moved into Concord Court, even while construction was still being finished. The three of them had gotten pretty tight, and Mira had never been one to let something go when she knew she had the right answer. She was the heart of the group. "If you want to make something of your program, Reyna could be a big asset."

"Sure. If a person can get her to slow down long enough to listen and sign on. I don't know who that person is." Sean tipped his head back to stare at the stars. Military life had never been a good fit, but he'd stayed as long as he could. Being a marine had fitted him like a silk suit. Constricting. Uncomfortable. This here was his home.

He'd wanted to be a hero, but watching the building he'd been sent to help clear explode in the middle of the night had been too much—there had to be another way. That ringing in his ears, the fire... That was the part that always woke him up.

Sean inhaled slowly, his heart racing in an instant. That image, bright orange on a dark backdrop, triggered the panic if he let it go too long.

When he'd gone back home to Georgia, he'd started working construction, but the urge to help, to be a part of the mission, had stayed with him. Training service animals had been the easiest answer to the hardest question, but to expand, he needed help.

"I tried, Mira. Twice," Sean said, even as his conscience pointed out he hadn't tried hard. "She was in a hurry. Neither of us is going anywhere. There'll be another time." Relaxing around the pool at night was usually easy. During the day, Reyna might keep him on edge, but he was good at his job; he knew everything there was to know about Concord Court.

After his mother died, leaving him with a whole lot of nothing in Georgia, Sean had been lost. He'd left the Marines to come home, but without her, he'd had no home.

The job posting for a construction manager for Montero Financial had coincided with his grandmother's request that he come for a visit. His mother had been one of seven sisters. Five of them had stayed close to home in South Florida, and having that connection had made it easy to move south. There were enough aunts and cousins in the area to keep him busy—he visited when he could.

Or when he was required to. At least Mimi's birthday party would save him another long day in the office. Sean hated being stuck behind his desk. That was something he'd have to remind himself of when he was being overrun by female cousins next weekend. Seven sisters had produced fifteen daughters and two sons. Now? The crowd of cousins was overwhelming.

Fingers crossed his uncle Manny showed up for the party.

Peter's drawl interrupted his thoughts. "Reyna never strolls when she can march, for sure. I'd say a man who wants her help would be motivated to catch her unless that guy only talks a big game." He softened the pointed words with a dripping cold beer, so Sean didn't do anything but twist off the top to release some aggression.

Everyone wanted to give him advice. But none of them understood how hard it could be to talk to Reyna Montero. She was intimidating. Asking for her help was the same as asking Michael Jordan to join his basketball team for a game of pickup. If she said yes, he'd have all the help he needed, but at the end, she'd outscore him and he'd be left wheezing on the sidelines. And if she said no…

"She signs the checks around here. Gotta navigate carefully." Sean thumped his feet up on the table to prove to them he was sure of his words. "Besides that, I push her too hard and she could tell me no more dogs around this place. That would shoot my whole plan to pieces." Sean draped an arm over his chair to run his hand down Bo's side. The dog had stretched out in his usual place near Sean's chair.

Neither Peter nor Mira responded. Weak

moonlight gleamed on their bottles as they drank.

"Where's the poet tonight?" Sean asked, ready for a diversion. Jason Ward had been opening up to them while he was taking classes at Sawgrass University. Missing a night could slow that down.

"He might be putting distance between us, now that we know about his leg." Mira huffed out a sigh. "Even though we're the ones he should be talking to."

Ward's amputated lower leg had never been a secret to Sean, but he'd also never been the guy to shoot his mouth off about other people's business. His position as Reyna's temporary right hand meant he saw the recommendations and applications that came through. Making sure the facilities at Concord Court operated and supported the vets it was meant to serve was his job.

Ward didn't want to talk about the leg. Sean understood that to a point. Pushing him to confide about it before he was ready would do more harm than good. "How much longer is his summer class?"

"Couldn't be more than a week," Peter

said. "If he's going to make a move on his writing professor, the clock is ticking."

Mira said, "I hope he doesn't try one of Sean's poems. They're bad, dude."

"Roses are red, leaves are green…" He ignored their groans as he tried to come up with an ending that would make them laugh. That was another part of his job. Comic relief. If that made it difficult for other people to take him seriously, fine. He could live with that. "Roses are red, leaves are green, the best beer is cold, and so is the queen."

Nobody laughed.

"What? That one rhymed. Give me some credit." Sean tried to read their expressions but the darkness hid them.

"You weren't referring to Reyna, were you?" Mira said, her words tight like she was pushing them through a clenched jaw, "because I will pick you up and throw you in the pool myself."

Mira was petite, but the former Air Force medic didn't make promises she couldn't keep.

Sean straightened in his chair. "Of course not. No!" Had that even been in the back of his mind? No way. Reyna wasn't icy. She wasn't. She was more like pure fire, banked but glowing, ready to burn with a grim stare. He'd watched her put pushy would-be suitors in line. Everyone knew she could turn a man to ash but she didn't, thanks to control. She'd been in command of airmen and airwomen and it showed. "I wouldn't. I didn't. I don't doubt her commitment to this place. She cares about every vet here."

Mira's dark form unbent and relaxed against the seat. "Weird combination of words to pull up, Wakefield. Consider giving up on poetry completely."

Sean rolled his head on his shoulders. That was solid advice.

"You're still mad about Charlie. I get that." Mira twisted her glass bottle on the table. He thought about stopping her there. If Reyna was around, none of them would escape a lecture. Glass in the pool area? It was a security risk.

Reyna Montero didn't take risks, but security? It was at the top of her priorities, something he appreciated.

"Not mad, just…disappointed, I guess." Sean had done his best to make a case to let Charlie stay. Reyna had listened carefully, asked for a couple of days to evaluate, and then she'd followed the written policy of Concord Court. Fairly. Evenly.

But not coldly.

"Yeah." Peter's voice was quiet. "I get that. How was he hurting anyone?"

"The mission. You guys understand that. We've all served. We all understand how our missions guided our work. Reyna's only following that example." Mira didn't appear any happier than Sean, but it was the only argument he could make. "There's one battle, but every branch, every team deployed, every man and woman has a piece of the mission. Medics don't fly planes or clear bombs. They still win wars."

Mira exhaled loudly. She didn't talk much about her own time in the service, but it had to have been intense. She'd also made her point. Concord Court served a narrow section of vets. Trying to do more than that would lessen its impact.

"Reyna said she'd check on Charlie. She's not cold." Sean hadn't spent much time absorbing the military way of life, but he'd had a few bosses. His loyalty to a boss was earned, not a matter of titles or paychecks.

Reyna was smart, organized and tough. She would run Concord Court well, serve the veterans who came here with experience and dedication. She had his loyalty.

That didn't mean anyone would ever get to know her.

"I caught her on the way out to brunch this morning when I was loading up Bo to visit Punto Verde and Charlie." Dressed like the perfect mix of the girl next door and old money. Beautiful. No-nonsense. Intimidating. The memory of that fragile pink rose flashed through his mind again.

In another lifetime, a construction manager from Georgia would never meet a rich, decorated Air Force pilot from Miami, but this was Concord Court. All types of people came through here. "She had the time to talk about Charlie. Nothing else."

Mira sighed long and loud. "She would have waited for you to make your case for your training program. She would have. I know it."

Peter added, "How many times do I have to say this? Set a meeting. Treat it like business. She's bound to listen then."

"Sure. I'll make charts and graphs showing zero money coming in while money actively leaves Concord Court for adoption fees and trainers to work with my volunteers, and then I'll mention I have a couple friends on board to help." Sean pointed at the two of them. "You're it. Marcus will be leaving soon, but I'm counting him, too. I will rope in Ward eventually, but is that even three slides in a presentation? Fifteen minutes for my huge sales pitch. Can I fill that?"

He ran his hand over his head, seriously regretting he hadn't gone back to school and gotten a degree in something that would help. Business. Accounting. Talking to important people. Did they offer degrees in talking good?

All things that required suits instead of work boots. No, thank you.

Construction suited him. Running the operations at Concord Court suited him. Reading and papers and homework never had.

"If you don't believe it, she never will," Peter said. "Hate to say it, man, but maybe you *don't* want it bad enough."

When Mira didn't jump to his defense and he couldn't even begin to form one, Sean had to wonder whether Peter was right.

"Fine. I'll set up a meeting this week. I do want this. There are three dogs at Hometown Rescue that would be perfect for this program. I'll go in, request approval to set the two of you up as volunteers. And when those three are successfully trained and sent to new homes, I'll talk to Reyna about presenting a formal program to her father to request start-up funds. I'll estimate expenses. And timelines. And each one of us will try to find another volunteer."

Mira gave a slow nod. "Finally, a plan. It's like, how many times can I poke a worm until it rolls up in a ball? One more time." She punched his work boot. "Poke. Poke."

Sean closed his eyes. His whole life, he'd wondered if he'd ever figure out his purpose. He'd drifted along until he'd landed here at Concord Court.

Then he'd understood how he could help.

Dogs for vets. He loved them both. He could help. And the lack of services here in southern Florida meant the door was open wide.

Did he want to be the organizer? No. He wanted to be hands-on, doing the work. That was his spot, but getting this up off the ground would take some leadership, a solid plan.

That was where Reyna could come in and make some magic.

His military service was over. Sean had grown up knowing his father only through a framed photograph on the mantel and his mother's and grandmother's stories of his service. He'd died way too young from a heart attack, but he'd live forever in that photo.

Sean would never fill the role of American hero, but he could do this small thing that mattered.

All he had to do was convince Reyna.

She owed him a favor for taking on her weekend hours. Surely that would be enough to get her to agree to a meeting.

CHAPTER SIX

REYNA WAS GLAD she had a couple of days to come up with a strategy to involve her sister in the running of Concord Court while limiting the amount of damage Brisa might do if she decided to drop everything for some other exciting opportunity.

Models got great offers all the time, even part-time dabblers like Brisa. Concord Court would have to continue to run smoothly if that happened.

As Reyna unlocked the door to the office on Tuesday morning, she watched Sean, high on a ladder, examining one of the cameras she'd had installed at the four corners of the property. Instead of his usual jeans and T-shirt, he was wearing khakis with a polo that did not have Concord Court embroidered on the chest.

"Does he have a job interview somewhere?" Reyna muttered to herself as she walked behind the large, expensive desk her father had insisted on for the center of Concord Court's office. The whole aesthetic of the buildings and grounds was suited to her father's notion of what was expensive and, therefore, acceptable. The warm Spanish Mission style her father preferred suggested both high end and history. Her father had always believed old was better than new.

A flash of sunlight caught her attention as her sister opened the door.

"Morning, Reyna," Brisa sang as she held up two cups of coffee. "I brought us some energy." She slid one across the desk and plopped the other down in front of one of the chairs opposite. "Am I meeting the Concord Court dress code?" She indicated her ensemble. "A friend designed it." She shifted backward and forward as if she perched at the end of a runway in her perfect sundress and huarache sandals.

"Yes, of course." Reyna gestured at the seat across from her and tried to ignore the pinch of dissatisfaction at her own khakis and monogrammed polo shirt. Her outfit suited the atmosphere of Concord Court, it was father-approved and it was practical. It wasn't mandatory, but Reyna was comfortable in uniforms and they served an important purpose.

But maybe she didn't have to wear it every day? She could buy a few dresses that might be more...

"You'll have to give me the address of her store. I could use a few more options, now that I'm out of uniform," Reyna said. Her sister had good taste. It would be easy to follow her recommendations as far as clothing went. The freedom to wear whatever she wanted whenever she wanted was something Reyna was still adjusting to. Maybe she'd leaned too hard on the Concord Court polos.

"Well," Brisa said with a sigh, "no shop yet. No money yet. Like a bunch of my friends, she pays her models with clothes, so..." She shrugged. "But I could introduce you sometime."

That explained a few things. Modeling. For friends. Who paid with clothing.

While their father covered the expenses. It was no wonder the tension between them was so thick.

There might be less chance of Brisa jetting off to Fashion Week than Reyna had originally feared.

And things were going well, so pointing out that being paid in clothes wouldn't do much to gain any independence from Luis Montero might be a mistake. Brisa had managed to stick it out at home. What if she was completely content with her situation? Was listening to her father complain about credit card payments all that different from taking the job he'd custom-built for her anyway? Reyna's superior position was shaky.

"We'll have to go shopping sometime. I'd love to have some professional guidance. Without uniforms to fall back on, I need to expand my wardrobe." Reyna cleared her throat. "I have a few thoughts on how this arrangement might work, but you should give me a description of what you want to do. How much time you can give."

Instead of taking a seat, Brisa paced. She went from Reyna's right to her left, made a graceful swing to turn and then returned to her starting point, the skirt of her dress twisting around her legs in a swirl that Reyna admired. Brisa even walked beautifully. Of course she did. While Reyna was… efficient.

"Assistant manager. What would you have an assistant manager do?" Brisa asked.

"Well. I had drawn up a proposal to hire part-time help in the role." With a view to taking it herself when she went to work for the Miami Fire Department. Facing off against Luis Montero required long-game strategy. "In the beginning, the assistant manager will cover the desk on the weekends, answering calls from prospective veterans and current tenants. Sean covers the weeknights and any emergency calls."

"Answering phones. You need a receptionist, not an assistant manager." Brisa shook her head. "I don't want to do that again. What else?"

Since Reyna had experienced her father asking a similar question in the same tone, she already knew how to expand on her goals.

"Day in and out, I'm reviewing applications, paying bills, updating accounts receivable and signing two-year contracts that require follow-up. Anybody could do that.

We're no different than any other well-run apartment complex there."

Reyna tapped her fingers on the desk. "What makes us different is the programs we offer. When I add an assistant manager, that person is going to help me brainstorm new ways to help the men and women who live here. They will also need to do a lot of research, finding the right people and programs to work with. I can do some, but having another dedicated person on hand to help will make all the difference." This was the part of her plan that bothered her the most. If she stepped down from managing Concord Court, what would happen to all the carefully established relationships she'd built with employers, staff at Sawgrass University, the therapist who was making a difference every day with these vets? Reyna didn't trust anyone to take that over and run it the way she would.

And her baby sister? Reyna wasn't sure she could be trusted with any of it.

But for now, she mainly needed someone to be here when she couldn't. Thursday night, Friday night and all day Saturday. After she'd gotten her certificate and passed the physical aptitude test, she'd need to complete her training with any crew that hired her. That would mean three days where she'd be away from Concord Court every week.

Reyna wavered back and forth on the proper time to tell her father, but she should be able to figure everything out within a couple of months.

Surely Brisa could stay in one place for that long.

"Fundraising to support those programs." Brisa tilted her head to the side. "You forgot that part?" She resumed pacing.

"Good point." Reyna didn't want to do any fundraising, but it was the key to Concord Court's true reach. Montero money had done a lot of the heavy lifting, but growth would depend on finding partners. "If we can iron out a plan together, I need to take more of that on." Dread would have settled into her bones, but Reyna shook it off. It was part of the job.

When Reyna looked up because Brisa hadn't responded, her sister was biting her lower lip as if she had something to say but definitely wondered if she should.

"Spit it out, BB." Reyna untangled her fingers to loosen up her body language. How many leadership training sessions had she attended over the years? Being open was important.

"Sure, you could help with fundraising. You're the veteran, not me," Brisa said slowly as she perched on the edge of the chair, "but I might have an inspiration for a program." She clenched both fists. "Or two."

Reyna blinked. "Two?"

"Or more." Brisa tipped her chin up. "Fashion. You think it's silly, but we could help people going for interviews to grow some confidence. One session. A loaner suit or two, and if they get the job, we can help with the first month of clothing. Going from an approved military uniform to dressing for today's workplace could be intimidating." Her pointed stare at the logo on Reyna's polo spoke more than a thousand words. "I have connections who can help."

Of course she had connections. Reyna had escaped Miami at her first opportunity, but Brisa had settled in. If Luis Montero valued social standing, Brisa had learned how to leverage it for good.

But clothing?

"These aren't homeless people, Brisa." Some of them might be, but for the most part, no. "And they haven't arrived from another planet. I'm not sure…"

Her sister's shoulders firmed. Instead of deflating, Brisa stood taller. "You just mentioned needing a professional's opinion for your own wardrobe, Reyna." Brisa was ready to fight for herself.

"Fine." Reyna offered her sister her hand. "Let's flesh this out. You work here with me for three months, learning the programs and the veterans we're already working with. If we still think it's the best plan at the end of that period, we go for it."

Brisa reached to take her hand but hesitated. "Why are we waiting?" Then she nodded. "Because you don't have any faith in me—you don't think I'll still be here in three months. I will."

Reyna pushed her hand farther forward. "Okay. Do we have an agreement?"

Reyna could tell that Brisa wanted to argue. She did. But she shook.

"Great. First thing I want you to do is help me convince one of our current tenants, Jason Ward, to act as a job counselor.

He'll work with the therapist we partner with, but he'll serve as hands on deck to help with internet searches, résumés, practice interviews, whatever. I'll set up a meeting. You just…" Reyna shook her head. She was never certain how Brisa got people to cooperate, but she did. Time and time again, she drew people into her web.

"Fine. Why him?" Brisa sipped her coffee. "I'm sure you have a solid list of reasons."

"Military experience. He was a crew leader. People followed him. He's facing his own confusion on how to enter civilian daily life. Right now, he's in school, but he's not sure why." Reyna pulled open her desk drawer and dug around until she pulled out a file she'd put together on the job program. "People will trust him because he understands where they're coming from."

Brisa pointed at the drawer. Reyna glanced down to guess what the problem might be. From her vantage point, her files were a pretty rainbow of order and organization. Color-coded according to function, labeled in a perfect stair-step that had taken some work.

"Your files." Brisa widened her eyes. "They're so…scary."

"Scary." They stared at each other while Reyna puzzled that out. "Organized. That's what you mean. I have a system."

Unfortunately, this was not the first time she'd listened to criticism of her system.

"Color-coded. Alphabetized. Cross-referenced by date. I also have digital files to track leases and spending and… We can get to all that as we go." Reyna handed Brisa a folder. "Here's an outline of the job counseling program. I'll put together a meeting with all the players. You just…help."

Brisa flipped open the file and scanned the first page. "The problem with being truly excellent at everything you do, Reyna, is that it's awfully difficult for the rest of us mere mortals to follow."

Reyna tipped her head to the side. "Mere mortal?" This wasn't the first time someone had made a dig like that, like she wasn't human. She hadn't appreciated it. Ever.

Coming from her beautiful baby sister, though, it burned.

Brisa shook her head as if she was waving off the argument. "Never mind. Organization is fine, but I can show you great things happen when you're open to them."

Reyna wanted to argue. This was her project, her place—she'd given up more time flying because her father had hammered over and over how much she was needed at home, how much good she could do here. Her system was more than up to the low-key demands of running a comfortable town house complex and a few programs.

What she needed was a bigger challenge. More excitement. Burning-building or chemical-spill levels of adrenaline, please.

She had two options: she could let her sister think whatever she wanted for as long as she could cover the front desk, or she could set her straight while risking that assistance. Before Reyna could make a decision, the door opened and Sean Wakefield entered, carrying a laptop.

It was unusual to see technology under his arm. He used the computer in his office for email and researching contractors, but he was mainly a hands-on fix-it guy.

But that surprise was nothing compared with the way her baby sister lit up when she saw him. Her shoes clattered across the tile floor as she hurried to throw her arms around his neck in a hug. Reyna blinked slowly when Sean lifted Brisa off her feet. Neither one of them hesitated. This was something they'd done before.

Why did that sit like a hard knot in her stomach?

"I take it you two have met?" Reyna drawled, determined not to let the weird emotion that tangled and shifted in her stomach show. Some people might call it jealousy. She would not.

"Yeah, Brisa was a huge help on getting this place up and running." Sean draped an arm over her sister's shoulders.

In a very familiar way.

"It's been a while, Breezy. What you been up to?" Sean asked as they approached Reyna's desk. "What happened to your plans?"

Breezy? A nickname? Reyna leaned back in her chair. Brisa had had plans that she'd discussed with Sean. Plans for Concord Court?

"Oh, you know." Brisa fidgeted with her dress. "Life happened, but I'm here to help run the place now. Got myself a trial period of three months to prove I'll stick around."

Reyna met Brisa's stare, and Sean cleared his throat.

He nodded once and tapped his laptop.

"Great. Somebody else to help cover the front desk and phone calls on the weekends would be nice. I've been able to do it for the past month or so, but my grandmother will murder me if I miss her birthday party this weekend." He studied them both and then pointed at the chairs in front of the desk. "While you're both here, I wanted to talk to you about something."

Reyna nodded, and Sean and Brisa sat down across from her.

"What is it?" she asked. She was glad for the change in topic—she didn't want to keep talking about Saturdays and risk their asking why she needed them covered.

Sean held up a finger and then opened his laptop. The silence stretched in the room for the eternity it took him to load his slideshow, but it finally opened on a picture of his dog, Bo, wearing the vest that marked him a service companion.

"Service animals for veterans. I want to formalize a training program where volunteers foster and train shelter dogs to receive certification." He straightened his shoulders. "I want to do it here, at Concord Court."

"We have a no-pet policy, Sean, which I stretch beyond the bounds of good business by letting you bring in the dogs you're training." Reyna shook her head. "No way can we allow more dogs."

"Yeah, Dad would never go for that." Brisa rolled her eyes. "The cost of repairs and upkeep. The liability of dogs on the grounds. I've already listened to it all."

"Not even adorable four-year-old Brisa was able to convince Luis Montero to allow a dog at the Montero home. Too much mess." Reyna was still unhappy about that. If they'd managed to win the argument over having a dog, it might have changed the whole family dynamic. She and Brisa both had fallen hard for Mort Fields's station dog, and Brisa had asked for a puppy for months after their family photo op.

Neither of them had forgotten the hard, firm rejection that had ended the conversation on Christmas Eve that year.

"But you'd allow service animals, support dogs, after they have the certification they need." Sean tapped his fingers on his knee, the one covered in khaki instead of denim. Was this meeting the reason he'd dressed up for the day? Reyna hoped so. She'd hate to lose him.

"I would." She'd have to. Her father would never argue over allowing service animals.

Sean didn't give up easily. Eventually he said, "Okay, but that's not exactly what I came in to discuss." He cleared his throat. "I had more of a service in mind, not a new policy."

He leaned forward. "What if the veterans here at Concord Court could help other vets by training the dogs? I have two volunteers already, and the shelter's identified three dogs that might work. The three of us will do what I've been doing, fostering and training, getting the service animal certification, and sending the dog on to the lucky veteran who needs the support. Until I have the certification needed to be a trainer and tester, we'll set up a dedicated class at the Dade Dog Training Club. It's not a lot of expense, and three veterans will benefit."

"Six veterans, actually," Brisa murmured. "The three who get the dogs, of course, but the three doing the training have a chance to give something back, and that is part of the mission here at Concord Court. Plus, you're saving the dogs. I mean, it's pretty genius."

Reyna watched Sean's face as he absorbed all of Brisa's words. It was the same as the sun burning through heavy cloud cover on the only Saturday you have to spend at the beach.

He immediately sat up straighter.

Because everything she'd said was correct.

"But." Reyna hated to do it. Both of them had such hopeful expressions. She, as the Luis Montero representative in the room, would have to be the hammer. As usual. "Concord Court is meant to first support the men and women who stay here. This would be a distraction from the main mission."

Brisa rolled her eyes. Sean obviously wanted to do the same.

"And spending money on something that isn't a part of the mission will be a problem." Reyna picked up her pen. "It's not that I don't like the suggestion, but…"

"Should we wait and take some time to think this through?" Brisa asked and flashed a fake grin. "Why do I have this hunch that the answer will still be no—to both good suggestions we've covered here today—because of some other perfectly valid reason?"

Reyna sighed. "Listen, we're getting fully up and running. I don't want to overextend what is limited staff right now. And you, Brisa…" She shook her head. "You understand why I hesitate. Sean has been here. He's been pulling more of the load lately than he should have, and it would be smart to give us more time to do things the right way than jump in because we're excited."

Not that Brisa would ever get that. She was a jump-in-with-both-feet kind of person and Reyna loved and hated that about her.

Brisa slowly crossed her legs. There was no pout on her face. Or anger or disappointment or any of the things Reyna expected. Instead, there was a shrewd expression, a serious consideration of the situation.

This was new.

Growing up, Brisa had followed Reyna's lead in everything.

Having her sister question her decisions could take some adjustment.

"Just exactly how many Saturdays have you covered, Sean?" Brisa didn't turn his way. Her gaze was locked on Reyna, so Reyna did her best to perfect her poker face in that instant.

Sean studied her before facing Reyna. "More than a month? I'm not sure. I could check a calendar and figure it out. I don't mind doing it, but sometimes…I can't."

Brisa nodded. "And have you been overwhelmed by the work and programs here at Concord Court while you've been waiting for an assistant manager to come on board?"

Reyna dragged her eyes away from her sister's to see that Sean had no clue how to answer that. If he said yes, he'd be saying he didn't have time to run his own program.

And if he said no, he'd look like a slacker.

"You expect something to be different at the end of three months, Reyna." Brisa pursed her lips. "What is it?"

Sneaking around had never been Reyna's strong suit. She'd learned that the hard way at ten years old, after she'd opted out of her first stepmother's thirtieth birthday party by claiming a bad case of the shingles. The news story that had inspired her lie had explained clearly that anyone who'd had chickenpox might be susceptible to the eruption of a painful rash due to the same virus. Since a shingles outbreak could also be contagious and a danger to others, it had been the perfect solution to a problem. Unfortunately, Reyna had missed the fact that a ten-year-old experiencing a shingles outbreak in 1990 might deserve her own news story.

The housekeeper who'd carried her message to her father hadn't seen the story. Fooling her had been easy enough, but her father had been certain shingles happened to older people. Much older. Even older than he was.

Now, Reyna would be able to support her claim with proof that shingles could occur at any age. Back then, she'd learned a few painful lessons.

Lying to her father had consequences. Both she and Brisa had been punished, even though the lie had been Reyna's alone. Her father understood then, and now, what mattered most to Reyna.

Sometimes she still felt guilty about the way Brisa had missed out on her favorite cartoons for months because her father had removed their television. Brisa had been confused and sad about it, and she'd never understood that she'd done nothing wrong.

If Reyna understood anything about sneaking around, it was that sometimes you had to double down. If you could do it with logic, so much the better. "I anticipate we'll have filled more of the units here, at least half of them, and we'll have a better grasp on what is required for day-to-day operations. Dad will have been satisfied I can run the place. That will open the door for expansion, and expansion the way I want to do it, not him." It made perfect sense.

"Fine." Brisa nodded. "I'll buy all that. But what you have to do is tell me what you've been doing every Saturday for a solid month or more. I won't complain about your lack of faith in me for at least three months. What's kept you away from Concord Court?"

Brisa's firm stance was new. In the past, whenever Reyna told her little sister to stay out of her business, she had. At some point, Brisa had grown up. This time, she didn't back down.

To buy time, Reyna answered, "Easy enough." Then she sipped her coffee.

The realization that she should have spent

more time learning to lie better burned all the way down to her toes.

In that moment, Reyna couldn't come up with a believable way to cover her plan.

What was she going to do?

CHAPTER SEVEN

Sean had never been more uncomfortable on the job in his life. Since he'd managed some large, unruly crews in his time, that was saying something, but watching two beautiful and completely different women face off was impossible to look away from. If he'd been a fly on the wall or separated from them by protective glass, he might have enjoyed finding out who would win. As it was, he shifted in his seat and considered stepping between them.

"If you keep this up, you're going to short out the electrical system," he drawled and then forced himself to stay perfectly still as both sets of blazing brown eyes turned his direction. "Whole lot of heat coming off the two of you." He held up both hands in surrender.

"If you knew her the way I do, you would understand that she can't lie to save her life.

Her only defense is silence." Brisa made a broad gesture to indicate that it was fully on display at that point. "The fact that she's admitting she needs help at all? Something big is going on. If we don't get the truth now, well…"

"We won't have it." He'd never dealt with a family showdown like this one. The Monteros butted heads; the Wakefields went along to get along because family was family forever. "Doesn't change the job or the fact that what the boss says goes. Reyna doesn't owe us any more." He waited for one of them to argue or agree with him. "And that's where we are, Brisa."

Watching Brisa's shoulders slump was hard. He had spent time with her over the course of getting the Court up and going. Facts were facts. She had a presence, and the world turned at her instruction. Few people told her no like her sister was attempting to do.

He'd stood his own against some of her crazier plans for decor, due in big part to having the Montero budget to swing like a sword. Brisa's father could shut her down with a stern frown, but Sean had never seen anyone else gainsay her.

Apparently there was one other person who could: her sister.

Since said sister was his boss, he owed it to her and his paycheck to come down on her side.

Brisa raised her eyebrows at him. He gave his head a slight shake. Reyna's priorities were solid. She was smart.

He *trusted* Reyna.

Then the muffled thump snapped them out of their silent argument.

Reyna had bent forward to press her forehead against her desk.

When she didn't immediately straighten back up, Sean reached toward her. "Reyna, are you okay?"

He could see that her eyes were closed. The uncharacteristic action shook him. Had they broken her? He stood and moved around the desk to bend down and wrap his arm around her shoulders. The extreme silence in the lobby meant his own breathing was too loud. "Come on. Use your words."

"This is new," Brisa whispered. "Just tell us. You can trust us."

Sean squeezed Reyna's shoulder, surprised at how delicate she was under his hand. The rose pendant was missing, but he was reminded of it as he inhaled slowly. Roses. He could smell roses. And she was strong. Capable. She'd flown a fighter jet and commanded a squad.

But at this moment, he might as well have been a banyan tree, big enough to hide her completely if she needed it.

Get a grip, Wakefield. As much grief as you gave Ward over his poetry assignment, you know you are no poet.

Eventually Reyna turned her head to stare up at him. "She's right. About the lies. I can't do it."

Sean's relief was immediate. "I was afraid you were dying. Good to know the threat of lying turns all your bones to rubber."

When one corner of her mouth curved up, he squeezed her shoulder again and then reminded himself that it might be more touching than was strictly required for first aid at this point. As she straightened in her seat, he eased back.

The sharp ache in his knee reminded him of where he was. If he didn't stand up now, he might not be able to. Old football injuries compounded by Uncle Sam's training and the bumps and bruises of construction had wrecked his right knee. Babying kept it working mostly like a knee should.

Squatting, while bent over, did not.

He tried hard to pretend he wasn't suffering any pain, but his grimace bled through.

Reyna offered him her hand for assistance, but he struggled through it to lean against her desk for a second. "Do you need my chair?" she asked.

Before he could explain he was fine, Brisa reminded them both she was there. "What he needs is the truth. Trust us, Reyna. Don't try to distract us by pretending to care about Sean."

Ouch. *Pretending* to care?

As he plopped back down in the chair, Sean sighed at the relief of taking the weight off his leg, but he could still feel the pain of Brisa's jab.

Which was silly.

He did a good job. It wasn't necessary for Reyna to care about him.

Was it?

"You said I'm no good at pretending.

I do care. About Sean. About all the vets here. And Charlie. And about you." Reyna scrubbed her hands over her cheeks and then shook out her arms, as if she was letting go of something. "I told myself if I came home, things would be different."

Brisa nodded. "Good. Trust me. Whatever it is, I'm ready."

Sean was prepared for almost anything.

Reyna's expression said, "I've killed an innocent person."

Brisa's was set on "Tell me the truth or you're next."

"I literally cannot stand the tension," Sean drawled and stood back up to pace.

Reyna cleared her throat. "But you stood up. You were sitting before, so…" She huffed out a breath as Brisa shook her head. "Fine. I've been attending school at night and on the weekends while Sean has covered the phones." Then she shrugged.

That was it? The big revelation that took all this buildup and the threat of sister-on-sister arguing?

He was ready to let that be enough. Brisa had asked; her older sister had finally answered.

And in a few months, they'd reevaluate all their programs. Nothing would change, and if the current "normal" wasn't everything he wanted, at least it was comfortable.

Except...

Now that he'd watched Reyna physically melt down in the face of a lie, something he'd never witnessed a grown human do, he recognized the symptoms on her face. She was still, like prey depending on camouflage to protect her from a predator.

Her weird, fake smile convinced him. They'd only gotten part of the story.

He knew a real smile from Reyna Montero would be memorable. And this broad curve of her lips was not authentic.

"What kind of school?" Sean asked as Brisa's head snapped his direction.

Reyna met his stare and he could see anxiety. He hated that. It was easier to believe Reyna was always confident and fearless.

Sean crossed his arms over his chest. He'd learned not to rush in with solutions when he'd told his grandmother about five minutes after he'd moved to Miami that she needed to be in an assisted-living facility, a place for active people that would keep her out of trouble, and she'd threatened to box his ears.

Old-school punishment.

And it had made an impression. Sometimes women needed space. Telling them what to do was hardly ever the right answer.

Reyna straightened her shoulders. "I'm getting my certificate to be a firefighter. I've completed the EMT training required in the state of Florida, so when I get this certificate and pass the fire department's physical aptitude test, I'll be ready to get a job as a firefighter. I don't want to run Concord Court."

Sean tipped his head to the side. He still didn't get it. What was the issue? Sounded like a good job. The quick flash of fire burning in the night sky irritated him. Fighting fires was nothing like the uncontained explosion of flames that woke him up in a sweat.

"But you haven't told Dad yet." Brisa's lips were flat. "Girl. I get it."

Sean sat back down. "You do?"

Brisa nodded slowly. "He's going to hate her decision. A lot. And when Luis Montero doesn't like something, he does not hesitate to throw all of his considerable resources at changing it." She wrinkled her nose. "We have Concord Court because he hated Reyna being in the Air Force."

Sean frowned. Luis Montero's stated reason for the development of the property had been the serious need for veterans' facilities in a metropolis the size of Miami—and not the same old solutions but something new to the city. Patriotism. Philanthropy. Those had been his speaking points at the groundbreaking ceremony and the ribbon cutting and every time Sean had seen Luis in any news story.

But Brisa believed Concord Court was only a string to tie his oldest daughter home.

"Is that true?" Sean asked. Luis Montero as a boss was easy enough to understand. He made all the decisions and expected them to be executed perfectly and with little input. Clear. Decisive.

Apparently Montero ran his family like he did his business.

Sean had no concept of what it must be like to live with a father who was determined to have his way. Luis Montero had gotten comfortable pulling the strings when he paid all the bills. Reyna and Brisa were still tangled in those strings.

The only tools the women in his family had at their disposal were noisy advice, which was really an order, and a lack of shame. He listened to their advice because he loved them, but every decision was his own. They could encourage, but there was nothing his grandmother or aunts could do to make him change his course.

"When I turned sixteen, Dad told me to pick out whatever car I wanted." Brisa raised her eyebrows. "Can you even imagine how wonderful that would be?"

Sean shook his head. He really couldn't.

"The car was parked in the driveway when he mentioned one little string. He was dating a new woman." Brisa straightened her skirt. "As long as I was friendly to her, the car was mine." She smiled. "Which was easy enough, since it was Marisol, and she's been the best thing to happen to the Monteros, but that's the sort of strategy our father employs. The strings don't seem so bad until you want something different. Because the strings stay until he decides to let them go."

The lobby was quiet for a minute. Sean

understood better, but they were adults now. Change was possible.

"You still don't get the whole picture, Sean. On one of our weekly phone calls while I was in the military, Dad reminded me it was time to retire." Reyna snorted. "Almost as if he had the first date I could do so circled in red on his calendar. I told him then I had no intention of leaving, and besides that, what would I do with myself if I got out?"

Brisa raised her eyebrows at her sister's explanation.

"Huge mistake," Reyna said. "We talked every week on Monday evening, like clockwork, unless I couldn't because of a mission. It was like brunch without the professional chef."

Brisa wrinkled her nose.

"Anyway, a month later, he texted me a link to his newest venture. At that point, the only thing on the website was an artist's rendering of Concord Court." Reyna gripped the edge of her desk. "He doesn't understand *no*. Refuses to."

Sean whistled. "He paid for that in a month?" And then he understood.

Brisa patted his hand. This time he understood it to be "you poor child" in tone.

"He'd been planning it for a while. Every time I turned down his advice to come home, he probably sank another few million in a rainy-day extortion fund to make me this grand offer." Reyna shook her head. "And it's almost the only thing that could have worked. What kind of terrible person turns her back on a chance to help vets like this?" She held out both hands to indicate the tasteful, comfortable lobby. "Lucky vets go home, where they may struggle to get back into life stateside. Some are wounded— they'll go to rehab facilities—but so many men and women need something else. Years spent going where the military sends you and then…what? Where do they go next? Where do they work? So build them a spot, but instead of government bare bones, you have a place like this, a home with built-in support, a place to acclimate. Only the worst kind of person would say 'no, thank you' to the man who is offering to build that."

She covered her face with her hands, and Sean understood some of the emotion burning in her eyes. Was it guilt? Maybe. In her heart, she was close to that terrible person, because she'd wanted to say no.

But she hadn't.

At least she hadn't said it yet.

"If I can't pass the class, if I can't meet the physical requirements, if I can't find a firehouse to take me on…then this is a worthy backup. It is." Reyna straightened her shoulders. "And until I know I can do all those things, I'm not going to rock the boat. There's no reason to dump us all into stormy Montero seas if I can't make this work."

It all made sense when she outlined her plan. Reyna was taking it step-by-step in a logical process, testing those waters.

For some reason, the deflation of being second best settled over Sean's shoulders. He'd chosen Concord Court and loved every bit of the job from the development to the day-to-day oversight.

Reyna only wanted this as a safety net, but she was used to soaring. For him, this was his first choice.

His best choice to do what he hoped.

"I'll help. However I can help, count me in." Sean swiped his laptop off the desk. He wasn't sure what Brisa would do, but he could see the wheels turning in her brain. She'd impressed him as one of those people who could be a criminal mastermind if she decided to go that way.

She offered Reyna her hand. "Fine. I'll help, too. I'll keep your secret."

As Reyna slipped her hand inside her sister's, Brisa added, "On one condition."

If he'd had the assistance of that protective glass, Sean might have laughed at the way the whole world froze in that instant.

These women? They were impressive. If they could get on the same side of the fight, they'd change history. As it was, he wasn't certain which one he'd back in a fight. They were evenly matched.

But only one of them was impossible to look away from. Reyna's face was set, the warrior in her close to the surface.

Why was that so…exciting?

At some point, he'd examine the reasons. Attraction to a woman who could eliminate him and hide the body without much help made no sense.

Since he could still feel the shape of her shoulder under his hand, he knew the attraction had already landed. He'd have to ignore it until it went away.

Even without a protective barrier, he was smiling. They were fun to watch.

"There's nothing amusing about this," Reyna snapped. This time, when he locked eyes with her, he didn't see fear, only an extremely irritated woman. Good.

"I'm not enjoying this." Sean crossed his arms over his chest. "I'm prepared to break up any fistfight, though. I'll have to make all the repairs to whatever it is you break, and I have big weekend plans."

"Tell me your one condition," Reyna said softly as she dragged her suspicious stare back to her sister. It was easier to think when she wasn't focused on him, but nothing was the same, either.

Brisa pinched her skirt as she considered. "I'll be your assistant manager and we will cover for you. I'm prepared to answer phone calls, arrange tours, do contracts—whatever it takes to keep this place going when you need time. In exchange, you'll give us what we want, your okay to explore Sean's Shelter to Service program and my...clothing idea." She waved her hands. "The title for his program came to me immediately. Mine will take a minute."

Would this work? Sean held his breath as he waited.

"Counteroffer. I'll give you a small budget and connections to a few of the veterans programs I work with. Let's give this professional attire program a try for a month or so." Reyna met Sean's stare. He couldn't read whatever it was in her eyes. An apology, maybe. "Then we'll reevaluate the service dogs. Thirty days. You build up your idea, Brisa. Show me what that looks like. Then we'll move to Sean's."

Brisa's slow-growing grin was easy to read. It looked like victory.

"Deal." They shook.

He tried to determine whether they were doing the he-man test of strength that men's handshakes sometimes resorted to, but it seemed friendly enough.

Brisa turned toward Sean. "My sister wants me to prove myself with something small before we move to your program. She thinks I'm going to get bored and move on and leave her with a mess to clean up. I'm not. I can do this." Brisa tilted her head to the side. "With her help, I can do this. I should argue for both programs now, but I'm going to stick with this until I prove to her and Luis Montero that I'm ready for more. I can wait one month, because she's going to owe me an apology and a favor then. Are you in?"

He'd been in since…forever, but he nodded. "You bet." He shook Brisa's hand and then looked back at Reyna.

Her hand was out, too, so he wrapped his around it, reminded again of how small she was in the face of an enormous personality. "Thanks for listening, Reyna."

Her lips curved. Her amusement was authentic. "I like the program, Sean. I hope you get that. I just…" She cleared her throat and did not glance at her sister. "Give us time to get everything in order and then we'll move forward."

He held her hand when she would have slipped away. "Okay. With both of you in my corner, this could be something important. That's what I want. A program that makes a difference."

She squeezed his hand. "You're the heart of this. Make sure you never let us forget it, either." She nodded at Brisa. "Whatever Brisa and I do, we're going to try to take over. Don't let us."

He returned the pressure before forcing himself to let her hand go. "I forgot to blink a couple of times during this meeting. You two are intense."

"We haven't spent much time on the same continent in years." Brisa sighed. "This could get interesting."

He liked his job, but this restless excitement he felt now had been gone for a while.

How much of that excitement was due to the go-ahead for his program? Most of it.

But there was another part that belonged to the slide of Reyna's skin against his.

It felt good.

CHAPTER EIGHT

WHEN THE DAY of the physical aptitude test arrived, Reyna knew that she had done everything she could to prepare. Memorizing the test elements and the scoring system had been easy enough. She'd watched the online video demonstrating the city's test for firefighters so often that, for at least two days, she'd barely stopped herself from ending every sentence with "Safety has no shortcuts," the reminder that ended every section. Nights staring up at the ceiling had given her plenty of time to dream up new ways to make sure she was ready.

She had nothing to worry about. Her sister had stepped up to cover for her at Concord Court. Once she made it past this hurdle, her next step would be clear. Probably.

Finding at least half of her academy class at the city's testing facility should not have surprised her. But when she'd imagined this, role-playing it to make sure she was comfortable with the plan, she'd been alone. No one had been there to make any cracks about Montero money or the academy's rankings.

The tests were given on a regular basis. Her whole life, she'd moved quickly. She'd imagined she'd be the only one rushing to take the first one offered after they all completed the academy training.

Being wrong was enough to shake her confidence.

Finding Ryan Pulaski front and center might have been a gift. She had to act confident when he was around—no way would she let him know she was nervous.

His only acknowledgment was one wary nod after she completed the registration process.

"Morning." Reyna flashed a quick smile at the group clustered in the entry of the training facility, which was situated in an expansive parking lot. Large windows on all four sides of the office gave views of the testing areas. The multistory tower where she'd take her test anchored one corner. At one edge of the lot, Reyna could see cones laid out in a course for some kind of driving test.

"Montero. I would have thought you'd already completed the test." Pulaski leaned against the wall as if he didn't have a single concern. "Haven't you been camped out here since the final grades were posted in Fields's class?"

Be nice. Make an effort.

"This is the first date that's been offered since we completed the academy classes. I'm here for the same reason you are." Reyna shrugged. "I was not expecting the group to be so large, though." She wasn't going to fight. She needed to focus.

"You two know each other?" one of the women asked. She had a long blond ponytail and a brilliant, friendly smile. "I brought my EMT certification with me from Orlando. I should have gone for the firefighter certificate, too—I could have done it here at South Florida First Responder Academy. The buddy system must be nice. It would be awesome if somebody I know ends up being hired in the same fire station as I am. We'd be the rookies together."

There were a few nods and some of the

tension in the group eased. EMT certification was the only requirement to joining the fire department. Reyna had gone for the firefighting certificate in addition, to better her odds of getting the job she wanted. The extra time it had taken away from Concord Court had made pursuing this career harder, but it might still pay off. She should be glad to have a connection, even if it was to Ryan Pulaski.

Reyna smiled even as her brain turned over and over the comment. A rookie. How long had it been since she'd been the lowest of the low on a team? She'd forgotten or tried to forget the pranks and all the extra duties she'd picked up as the new kid.

"Well, now we've all got the buddy system. Good luck, everybody." Reyna offered her hand to Pulaski. "I hope we'll get to work together." He saw through the big fat lie, but it made her feel like the better person to at least make the effort.

Reyna turned and shook every person's hand. She took a minute to commit names and faces to memory. That was a trick she'd learned early on in officer training. Yelling an airman's name was the quickest way to get the action she wanted.

"All right, huddle up," a large man said as he stepped out from behind the desk. He was tall and wide, and his muscles had muscles. "I'm Jenkins, one of the proctors here who will be completing testing today." He motioned with a thumb over his shoulder. "There are four of us. We'll get you in and out as quickly as we can. When I call your name, you will follow me to the tower. Your test will start there. It will end in fifteen minutes or less. If you hit fifteen minutes, you have failed. There will be no running. Ever. Move quickly, steadily, but do not take shortcuts. Shortcuts will get you disqualified. Safety has no shortcuts. One warning. That's it." He paused to study every face lining the wall. Reyna turned to see that everyone had wide eyes locked on him. They had to be as nervous as she was.

"If you fall, get up. Return to the beginning and try again. Do not stop until the proctor tells you to move to the next event." He tipped his chin down. "Finish in less than fifteen minutes. Those are the general rules. Any questions?"

Pulaski raised his hand.

Jenkins pointed at him. "Good. We have a volunteer to go first. Your name?"

Pulaski slowly lowered his hand. "Actually, sir, I wanted to ask..."

"Name?" Jenkins raised his eyebrows.

"Pulaski." Ryan stood. Everyone in the room knew that protesting would get him nowhere. Reyna had seen that trick pulled by more than one instructor while she'd served. She'd fallen for it more than once herself. "And I'm ready to go when you are."

Jenkins nodded. "Let's go, then."

After they left, Reyna considered trying to organize the rest of the group into a voluntary order. Some people would prefer to get the test out of the way and go next. Others would want to go last. If they organized themselves for the proctors, they increased their chances of getting the slot they wanted.

But stepping out like that was dangerous. She chewed her fingernail and tried to decide whether that initiative would be praised or derided. In a lifetime of classes and teams, she'd gotten both respect and a ton of grief for stepping up.

"I'm Alvarez," said the woman who

stepped out from behind the desk next. "Where is Montero? Jenkins says you're ready to go."

Reyna tried to be relieved that the decision had been taken out of her hands as she stood. "Here, ma'am. I'm ready."

"Aren't you a little old to be making this fresh start, Montero?" Alvarez didn't smile as she motioned Reyna to follow.

Reyna hesitated, caught off guard at the question.

"I decided to fly jets first. I got here as quickly as I could." Reyna fell into step behind her. They went outside and stopped in front of the five-story building behind the office.

"First, you will fully outfit yourself in the bunker gear. Do you need to examine the helmet or air tank before we begin? As soon as you touch the first piece of gear, your time starts." Alvarez studied her face.

Reyna shook her head. "I'm ready."

She studied the equipment and replayed the order as she'd done at the academy. This would be easy.

"Guess we'll find out how that Air Force training stacks up," Alvarez said as she pulled out her stopwatch. "Go when you're ready."

"You're military, too. Army?" Reyna stepped up to the starting line.

Alvarez nodded, the corner of her mouth turned up.

"Your posture. It's a dead giveaway." Reyna glanced at Alvarez. "Can I call you Alvarez?"

"To my face, yes, but call me whatever you have to in order to get through this test in under fifteen, Montero. Just do it under your breath."

Reyna nodded. She was ready as she would ever be, so she walked quickly to the equipment and methodically stepped in. Boots and pants. Jacket. Air canister. Face mask. Helmet. Gloves. This was where the academy training helped. She'd had a chance to get hands-on experience with the gear.

"Good. Pick up the bundle and carry it to the fourth floor. Set it down in the designated area. You'll find an X painted on the floor near the wall." Alvarez pointed at the bundled hose on the ground. Reyna knelt to pick up the weight and placed it on her shoulder before turning toward the stairs.

A small alarm rang in her head when she reached the second landing and had to gasp for breath. She was in good shape. The extra weight took some adjustment, that was all.

"Touch every step, Montero." Alvarez followed her and pointed at the window. Reyna set the hose down and forced herself to inhale and exhale steadily. "Pull up the equipment bundle. Hand over hand. Do not wrap that rope around any part of your body. Using any part of your body as an anchor is a safety violation." Alvarez watched closely as Reyna worked. Her biceps burned but she carefully brought up the bundle. "Lower it the same way, hand over hand, and complete one more lift and lower. Do not drop it."

Reyna nodded. She wouldn't waste a bit of air trying to speak. As soon as she'd completed that, Alvarez said, "Pick up the hose and go back down to the ground. Do not skip a step."

Reyna hurried and told herself this would be easier than climbing up. She had no concept of how the time was ticking, but she never stopped. On the second landing, she struggled to keep her balance in the turnout pants and boots and missed the first step.

"First warning, Montero. Every step," Alvarez shouted. Reyna considered arguing and asking to return to the fourth floor to try this descent again.

Then the weight of the hose bundle settled heavily on her shoulders, so she continued down to the ground level.

"Set the bundle on the X. We're going to raise the ladder next." Alvarez pointed at the designated spot for the hose and waited for her before moving around the side of the tower. "Hand over hand. You pull, the ladder rises. Then you release it and lower it. Go, Montero."

Reyna had to ignore the burn down the backs of her arms.

Her breath was loud in her ears, but she was doing it.

The ladder went up, then lowered.

"Now raise the ladder again. Climb up to the tenth rung and back down." Alvarez crossed her arms over her chest. "Do it the right way, Montero."

Reyna gritted her teeth and raised the ladder. Then she climbed steadily to the rung painted red and back down to the ground.

She immediately released the ladder and lowered it.

"Good job. Now we hook up the hose." Alvarez pointed her to the fire hydrant. "Hook it up. Open the hydrant fully. Then close it." Reyna fumbled with the hose and fought the urge to yank the gloves off. They'd practiced this at the academy, too. If she could use her fingers better, this would be easier. On the third try, Reyna got the hose hooked and started turning the wrench on top. And turning. And turning. Was she doing this wrong? Eventually she could see the hose changing, filling, so she kept pulling the wrench around. Her stomach hurt and her arms were going numb, but she was close.

"Now close it." Alvarez had stepped under the shade of the single tree in the parking lot, her focus on the stopwatch. "You're doing good on time."

That small encouragement was all it took for Reyna to pour speed into pulling the wrench the other direction. She could do this. It was hard, but it was never supposed to be easy. When the hydrant was closed, Alvarez said, "Watch closely, Montero." She stepped up on some kind of machine with a mallet in her hands. She braced her feet on either side of the heavy metal beam in the middle. "Swing carefully, methodically, to move this beam all the way down. When it crosses the line, you're done." Alvarez swung the mallet as if she were splitting logs of wood to hit the metal beam between her feet. When it moved, she scooted her feet back on the sides and repeated the swing. Two men hurried to reset the beam and Alvarez motioned Reyna forward with the mallet. "Do not try dragging that beam down by hooking the mallet on one end. Do not lose control of the mallet. Both are automatic disqualifications because of the danger. Proper form, Montero."

Reyna nodded and stepped up on the machine. The first swing of the mallet shocked her. The impact reverberated up her arms and she nearly lost her grip on the mallet, but she held on. The next two swings were disappointing, but then she understood the rhythm required and the beam started to move. Reyna would swing the mallet. The beam would move a couple of inches. She'd scoot back and repeat. It took forever, but eventually Alvarez said, "Good. Let's drag the dummy."

Reyna followed her across the lot. If she'd had any breath left, she'd have asked whether she was the dummy getting dragged, but no one had time or energy for that much fun. Her legs had started melting, the muscles sluggish as she walked. Whatever she had left was fading.

Her Air Force conditioning was good, but the Miami heat was something else.

Reyna shook her arms and followed. Alvarez pointed at the dummy stretched out in the sunshine. "This is Marv. He weighs one hundred and eighty pounds." She pointed at the line painted about forty feet away. "He needs to be over there. Drag him by his shoulders. Carry him if you prefer. Do not let his head touch the ground."

Reyna squatted to wrap her hands under Marv's shoulders and grunted when her first jerk resulted in nothing, no movement. She shook her head and repeated it. Marv shifted and Reyna kept moving. The momentum helped. And when she reached the finish line, it was like she'd climbed Everest. As soon as Marv's feet cleared the finish line,

Reyna gulped for air, and in an instant, Marv was slipping out of her hands. The gloves didn't help here, either.

Watching the dummy's head bounce on concrete was horrifying, but Reyna couldn't stop and worry.

Alvarez waved it off. "Technically, that task was complete…" She pointed at the last event. "Drag this charged hose back to where we started and then walk to the finish line."

Head down, Reyna moved to the hose. Bundled up, the hose was heavy. Filled with water and at the end of the test…it seemed impossible to shift.

Reyna had to stiffen her knees and fight the fatigue.

As soon as she crossed the line, she carefully set down the nozzle and strode to the finish line.

When she crossed it, she sat slowly down on the concrete. Full sun. Full gear. She didn't care. If she didn't sit down, she'd fall down.

A shadow fell across her eyes.

"It's easier to breathe if you take off the face mask," Alvarez said as she knelt and helped Reyna struggle out of her mask, helmet, and canister.

Reyna immediately suspected she would live.

"Good news is you passed the test," Alvarez said with a sigh. "Bad news is Marv's gonna sue for the concussion you gave him."

Reyna grinned. "Gloves. I gotta get better with gloves."

"Yeah. You'll get lots of chances." Alvarez stood and offered her hand to Reyna to help her stand. "Return the gear to the start. You're all done."

She wasn't ready to stand, but pride made it possible. Reyna picked up her equipment and headed for the tower. "What was my time?"

What did it matter? She was only competing against the standard and she'd beaten that.

Alvarez tipped her head back. "You gonna rerun this one, too?" She shook her head. "Sid Fields made sure we all got the story about how you took his little test a second time so you could improve your speed with the gear."

That felt good. Sid had been impressed

enough to tell other people about her determination.

"That kind of sucking up to leadership will lose friends and alienate people if you aren't careful," Alvarez drawled. "Especially because you're in the boys' club most of the time, Montero."

Reyna hung up the coat and tried to brush off the disappointment. "That's okay, I've spent a lifetime in the boys' club. Sometimes I listen to advice like that…"

"Most of the time you ignore it, though." Alvarez sniffed. "I know another woman like that." Then she grinned. "Glad to have another on the team, Montero. I'll be sure to let both Fields brothers know you passed your exam."

Balling up her fist to shove it up in the air in victory was Reyna's first response. Playing it cool would be smarter. "And my time?"

"Eleven minutes and twenty-nine seconds. Respectable." Alvarez pointed at the building. "Go around to get back to the front door. Your results will arrive via email in forty-eight hours." Then she spun on one heel and headed for the next wannabe fire-fighter.

Since she had no audience, Reyna braced her hands on her hips and sucked in as much air as she wanted. It was sweet.

Then she straightened her shoulders and prepared to pretend the test had no effect on her. She made it back to the office and was almost to her SUV when she saw Pulaski sitting on her bumper.

"Let me guess. Eleven minutes and a little bit?" He held up his finger and thumb to show a small gap.

Reyna crossed her arms over her chest. "Let me guess. Something barely under eleven minutes?" Then she mimicked his hand gesture.

He grunted and stood. "Little bit more than that under eleven but yeah."

"You're still faster. I'm still smarter." Reyna shrugged. What more was there to say?

"Did mine clean. No warnings. Can you say the same?" Pulaski asked.

The vision of Marv the dummy's head bouncing kept her quiet.

"Stuff like that goes in the proctor's

summary of your test, you know." Pulaski smiled. "Good luck with whatever house you end up at—it won't be Sawgrass." He held up a hand and moved to slide into his truck.

Reyna realized she was wasting precious minutes of air-conditioning by staring him down as he backed out of the parking spot. As soon as she slid inside her SUV, she started it and turned all the vents her direction and the fan on high.

By the time she made it back to Concord Court, she was half-frozen and half-melted and completely irritated at Ryan Pulaski and the world in general.

But mainly at gloves. How could she have dropped Marv? And missing the step!

She was most angry with herself, though. In the real world, someone could have gotten hurt because of her errors.

Sean pulled in to park right beside her, unaware that she was prepared for a fight.

"What happened to the birthday party? The one that meant you couldn't help me today?" she demanded as she stepped up on the sidewalk.

Sean wiped sweaty hair off his head as he slowly followed. If she'd been melted, he wasn't far off that. Whatever he'd been doing, it had been hard work, too.

"It's setup. I've been 'setting up' since dawn." He enunciated every word carefully. "Now I have to go take a shower so that I can be back in Coconut Grove in time to man the grill." He shrugged. "That okay?"

Reyna tipped her head back and forced herself to calm down. "Sorry. I'm mad at someone else and taking it out on you." She went to walk up the stairs but turned back. "I don't understand why men have to turn everything into a competition. We could be helping each other, but no, he wants to shove the fact that I'm slower than he is in my face." She kicked the bottom step hard and then had to shake off the pain.

"Breaking your toe will show him." Sean had followed her up her steps. "Today was the test. You passed, but there was a jerk around. Do I have this correct?"

Reyna closed her eyes but let his hands on her shoulders turn her slowly.

"Yeah. Sorry. I know it's not all men. You aren't like that." She hung her head. "While I am too much like that for my own good."

He snorted. "Some of us learn how to

come in second early in life. You're catching up." He squeezed her shoulders. "You passed. That's all that matters."

Reyna wrapped her hands around his forearms and tried to let it sink in. He was right. "I wanted a spot close to home, over at Sawgrass. I won't get that, so I may have to move. I just…" She shook her head. "I should have worked harder on conditioning. And letting the dummy's head hit the concrete was…" She groaned out loud. "That'll be waking me up in the middle of the night."

His laughter wasn't what she wanted, but even she had to agree it was a silly thing to say. Marv was a dummy. His concussion was never coming.

"You've got to go." Reyna sighed. "Do you think you'll be back at the pool tonight? I might want company, if I wake up screaming about Marv's plastic brain damage." Would the group let her join them? She'd kicked them out of the pool area so many nights, they might want payback.

He dipped his head. "You? At the pool? But that's breaking a rule."

"Sometimes you need something more than the rules. I'd like to be around people who are not me." She was going to re-play her test. She was going to estimate how many seconds she might have shaved off each event.

And she was going to get madder at Ryan Pulaski if she let herself.

Standing here, looking up into Sean Wakefield's face was improving her mood. He almost made it possible to laugh at herself.

Sitting out at the pool, drinking cold beer and listening to other people talk could be the same escape a country-western bar in South Korea had provided when she needed it. A time and a place where she didn't have to think.

Sean wrinkled his nose. "I have another idea." He stepped back from her and ran a hand through his hair. "I'm not sure what time this birthday will be over. Mimi is a night owl." He opened his mouth but hesitated. Then he committed. "Do you want to come with me?"

"To your grandmother's party?" Reyna asked. Every family party she'd ever been to had involved place cards and salad forks. They weren't places where guests could invite whoever they wanted at the last minute. "She won't know me."

He nodded. "I know you think that's a problem, but it would earn me points." He waved a hand. "Mimi counts success by the number of bodies at her party. It takes up the whole block of her street. You have to see it to believe it. Do you want to?"

Reyna tried to imagine how that might look, but she couldn't. Instead, she smiled. "That's perfect for tonight."

"One hour." He held up one finger. "Dress to dance." Then he was trotting up his steps and going inside his town house. Reyna held up a hand as if she was going to change her mind, then realized there was no one there to listen.

She didn't dance.

And she had no plans to start tonight.

CHAPTER NINE

As soon as he and Reyna were buckled into his Concord Court–provided truck, Sean wondered if he'd made a mistake. The vibe was entirely "first date" or "blind first date" or even "coworkers who don't know each other but are stuck together for a long ride." It could be a difficult, uncomfortable evening for them both.

Sean cleared his throat, but no easy conversation starter came to mind.

Reyna twiddled her thumbs.

"It's not too late to turn back," Reyna said and motioned over her shoulder with one thumb. "I can't tell. Do I smell regret in the air?" She sniffed loudly.

Trust no-nonsense Reyna to slice right to the heart of the problem.

"I was having flashbacks to an awkward first date. Met her through one of those apps." He turned to smile at Reyna. "It was enough to make me dump the app from my phone."

Reyna grimaced. "No dating apps for me. I do not need more awkwardness right now. My father has threatened to set me up. Can you even imagine the awkwardness there?"

Sean would have liked to say something encouraging, but the threat of being fixed up by family was intense. Change of subject, please.

"I was considering ways to warn you about Mimi's birthday parties." Sean checked traffic and made a left turn, happy that one icebreaker was all it had taken to ease the weirdness. It would work out. It was like a date in that way, but not in any other way.

"I've warned other people, but no one can grasp exactly how big Mimi goes with the event." Any description of his grandmother would fail because she was larger than life.

Reyna pointed at a sign. "Where are we going in Coconut Grove? A couple of my favorite restaurants are there, but I haven't been in years." She was watching scenery pass by the window.

Sean tightened his hands on the steering wheel. He would bet good money that the Monteros had never partied the way his Mimi did. To Reyna, a birthday party took place at a stuffy restaurant or at her father's club, with cloth linens and polished silver.

Mimi would never.

"I guess you'd call it a street party. Mimi still lives in the three-bedroom bungalow where she raised seven daughters."

Reyna whistled. Sean was impressed with the volume.

"Seven daughters. Three bedrooms," she said slowly.

"And only one full bath," Sean added in his spookiest voice. "Hard to imagine. I think she and Bud were the first in the neighborhood back when it was built in the fifties. His real name was Howard, but everyone I know called him Bud. Mimi and Bud."

"Wow." Reyna shook her head. "The fights would have been epic if Brisa and I were forced to share a bathroom growing up. Multiply that by…"

Sean waited for her to do the math. Two sisters to seven. It was a difficult equation.

Fractions were hard. "Yeah, multiply it by a lot."

They both relaxed and he was struck by the swing in the atmosphere. In that minute, it was like they'd been doing this forever, riding side by side and trading stories.

It was too far the other direction for comfort.

"Since Mimi has adopted every family and child born and raised on the street for sixty years, her parties are truly epic. Every house contributes decorations and food. There's a competition for who'll make the birthday cake." Sean shook his head. "You have to see the whole thing." Then he turned to face her. "It's still not too late to turn around if you'd like. This won't be your kind of party. No white tablecloths. No valet on duty." He studied her a second before returning his gaze to the road. If she wanted to go home, he'd take her. He might even be relieved.

But he was afraid they'd both miss out on something important.

His impression of Reyna was changing.

He wanted to show her his family.

"Interesting. You're trying to get rid of

me now?" Reyna crossed her arms over her chest. "Can't wait to meet Mimi. Anyone who can inspire people to celebrate her like that has to be special." She wrinkled her nose. "What's she going to think about you bringing a strange woman around?"

"I'd guess it largely depends on the strange woman herself and what constitutes strange, but she's going to like you." Mimi would.

And Reyna would be in love with his grandmother before her night was over.

"Good." Reyna tapped his arm but withdrew her hand quickly as if she was crossing a boundary. He would have encouraged her to cross that boundary whenever she liked, but he'd reached the street leading into his grandmother's neighborhood.

The cars lining both sides of the street were exactly what he expected.

"I'm getting the picture," Reyna said. "Mimi's a celebrity and this is her theater, right?" She brushed her hands over her skirt. "Am I dressed correctly?" She gestured at his jeans.

He didn't have to check out what she was wearing. The red dress she'd put on for the occasion was burned into his brain. Reyna

Montero had two speeds: business casual and stop-a-man-in-his-tracks. This dress? It was casual, comfortable, but on her, it was also memorable.

Not that he could say any of that to his boss.

Another way this was nothing like a date: compliments on her dress were inappropriate.

"You are going to see every fashion under the sun." Sean watched her fidget. Was she nervous here, too? He'd gotten so comfortable with her taking command of whatever came up at Concord Court. This was another side to Reyna Montero. "Mimi will change her outfit at least once this evening."

She raised her eyebrows.

"It's true. Mimi has a real flair for celebration." He smiled. "You won't be able to say that I didn't warn you."

She tilted her head to the side. "You roll with it, don't you? Whatever Mimi asks you to do, the emergencies at Concord Court… You take each day as it arrives."

Sean couldn't tell if she thought going with the flow was a good or a bad thing. "I know I can handle whatever comes."

Reyna blinked and then relaxed against her seat. "Yeah. You can."

Sean turned quickly because he wanted to see her face. Her tone… It was…admiring?

The true hero between them thought he could handle whatever came.

Before he could stop her, Reyna had opened her door and slid out of the truck.

Sean hurried to catch her. "Be careful out here. Sidewalk's uneven." He held his hand out to make sure she was steady. Reyna shocked him by wrapping her arm through his.

"You don't have to worry about me. I'm pretty good at handling whatever comes my way, too. When we have a minute, remind me to tell you about performing my go-to karaoke song at a bar in Pyeongtaek." She stumbled when he slammed to a stop. "If I'd known your walking was uneven, I would have taken my chances on the dark sidewalk." This far from the party, it was dark, but he could see her eyes as she stared up at him.

He could also sense that she thought holding his arm was a mistake.

But it wasn't. Reyna holding him, making jokes with him here on the quiet street, was perfection.

Sean put his hand over hers to stop her retreat. "I can't wait." He would stand there, like that, just the two of them, for as long as she would.

She huffed out a breath. "You know I don't love a stage, but..." She waved a hand. "Sometimes, you have to take a shot. We'd flown a rescue op, but it turned into recovery. The team we'd been sent to provide cover for had been ambushed. All we could do was bring their bodies home. My whole team was there, and the bar was silent. Tense. So the bartender, this funny guy who had a different cowboy hat for every day, jumped up on the bar and demanded I sing." She dipped her head. "You'll never guess."

How simple her story was, a description of a terrible day that had stayed with her and her crew. He understood the dangers of war. How many other people would see how that could change a person?

But tonight, she was choosing the part of the memory she wanted to keep. There was wickedness in her stare that washed straight through him. Any man who could find a woman who looked up at him like that was destined for adventure.

"I can't stand it. Tell me," he said, surprised at how husky his voice was.

"Dolly Parton. 'Nine to Five.'" She wagged her eyebrows. "If you ever need to lighten the mood, that's a winner. As soon as the music starts, your audience is in. Lay on the drawl and it doesn't matter how bad your voice is." The faint breeze stirred her hair, tossing one strand over her eyes, and she shook her head to brush it away.

Her teasing eyes, how her hair moved in the breeze, the weight of her hands on his skin and the faintest scent of roses in the air created a moment he'd remember.

She said, "Life goes on and everyone has to sing along."

That was the only thing that put Sean's feet back in motion.

"I would bet all the money in my wallet that Mimi's DJ will have that song in his repertoire. If this party starts to drag, you're up." He tangled his fingers through hers and started walking again.

"I never sing alone. Be prepared to duet," she answered in a singsong.

"Lucky for us both and everyone at the party that I can carry a tune." His hand on hers. The quiet street. The flirty edge between them in that instant.

The resemblance to a good date was growing stronger.

They turned down Mimi's block and Reyna gasped. He'd been the one sweating in the midday sun to get the decorations up, but tonight, he had to admit, it was beautiful. He'd assembled a small stage where Mimi was holding court at the end of the street.

And leading up to that stage, strands of white lights draped posts and fences and mailboxes and one car that had been left on the street for too long. The antenna was a sparkling arrow pointing to the sky.

"Is that a disco ball?" Reyna asked. She held out her hand and watched sparkles of light dance across her palm until she laughed out loud. "Excuse me. Are those disco balls?" She drew out the *s* to make sure he understood her question.

"Mimi enjoys country music, but she's more of a dancing queen. I hope you like or can at least endure disco for the evening." Sean shoved his hands in his pockets. This was a lot. "I told you. I could have warned you, but you would have doubted whether I was telling the truth. Disco is alive and well in Coconut Grove tonight."

"I've never seen anything like this." Reyna's eyes were huge as she swiveled one direction and then the other. "I love it." Then she pointed. "Mimi is waving us over."

Sean would have asked her how she knew it was Mimi, but the tiara perched on top of his grandmother's white curls was the best clue.

"Let's go introduce you. Then we'll find you a beer. It'll all make more sense after that." Sean waved at the cousins and neighbors and various family members sitting or dancing or standing along the street. His cousin Manny Jr. waved a pair of tongs from his spot at the grill.

Mimi was swaying along to the music. "My grandson. You made it!" She held out both hands, so Sean leaned forward to kiss her cheek. He didn't let go of Reyna, and Mimi's stare locked onto their hands like a homing device. "And you brought me a new friend. How did you know exactly what I wanted for my seventieth birthday?"

When Reyna met his stare over his grand-mother's tiny frame, he mouthed, "Eighti-eth," and then held a finger up to his lips. Mimi's real age was the worst-kept secret in the world, but she enjoyed the game.

"This is Reyna. She's my boss." Sean realized as soon as he said it that it was a mistake. Reyna straightened and pulled her hand away at the reminder of what they were to each other.

Mimi immediately hugged Reyna tightly. "So beautiful. And what a hero. Sean has told me all about your service and what you're doing at Concord Court."

Sean pulled his ear and studied the crowd. Had it been a mistake to tell Mimi so much about his job? She was an expert interroga-tor, so it couldn't be avoided.

"Happy birthday, Mrs..." Reyna shook her head. "I only remember Mimi. I'm sorry."

Mimi rolled her eyes. "That's all I remem-ber, too. Call me Mimi. Everyone does. I'm your grandmother, too. Unless you have a grandmother who is mean. I don't wish to fight unless I can win."

Sean watched Reyna relax again. The twinkle in his grandmother's eyes had melted away some of her concerns.

"No grandmother, although my father is something else." Reyna wrinkled her nose.

"And what does he signify?" Mimi speculated. "Nothing, that's what. We're family now. Him, I will fight."

Reyna's smile, surrounded by glittering, sparkling lights, knocked him off his game.

He'd known that smile would be memorable. It was rare. That made it more valuable.

"Get her some food." Mimi snapped her fingers in front of his face. Had she been forced to repeat herself? "Then we dance. Do you know how to hustle, Reyna?" A sly grin curved her lips. "Sean knows how to hustle." She wagged her eyebrows and then straightened her tiara.

He and Reyna watched her descend from her stage. Then he noticed Reyna had covered her cheeks with both hands.

"Do you wish I'd taken you back home?" Sean bent his head so she could hear him.

Her eyes met his—a kiss would be so

easy. But she said, "No, I was wondering if Mimi would adopt Brisa, too. My sister would love her. I love her."

Sean made a mental note to ask someone smart why finding out that a woman loved the same person he loved more than life automatically made her the most beautiful person in the world.

Because Reyna was. Her eyes sparkled. Her red dress flowed around those legs that always amazed him. And there was no doubt that her love for Mimi was genuine and born between one heartbeat and the next.

"Thank you." This smile was subdued, but Sean read emotion in it.

He'd thought she was stoic.

Instead, what Reyna felt, she felt deeply.

"You're welcome. Come meet Manny. We'll get some food. You're going to need it. The hustle is only the beginning."

Sean watched her skip down the steps he'd built. The whole place had required a ton of sweat and many curse words when no one was nearby.

But this was his thing, the thing he could do. He could build things.

And tonight, two women he admired were enjoying it.

Tomorrow he'd get his head on straight. No one fell in love under the glitter of a disco ball.

CHAPTER TEN

REYNA SETTLED BEHIND her desk the next Saturday morning with purpose. Brisa watched her closely from across the desk, and it was important to Reyna to show her sister she had things under control. They had spent the week going over the ins and outs of Concord Court. They'd argued about the proper way to set up agreements with consignment shops and local vendors who might help with Brisa's Back to Business program. Whether or not Reyna liked the title (she didn't), she had to admit that Brisa had made impressive headway on developing her own program.

When Jason Ward, the new coordinator of their job counseling program, had come into the office on Friday to discuss ways of working in a short presentation on business casual attire to his group meetings, Reyna had decided to make her escape. Her opinion hadn't been requested anyway.

That hadn't stopped her from giving it freely to Brisa before, but space was a good idea. Sean had taken to standing in his doorway whenever they started talking, like a bouncer in a bar prepared to break up a fight if it got out of hand.

And since she hadn't figured out how to settle back into their normal relationship after he'd spun her in circles under a glittery disco ball and introduced her to his adorable grandmother, her mouth was bone-dry from the anticipation of coming up with clever conversation when he appeared.

It was like the early days, when his good looks had stopped her cold when he showed up unexpectedly.

Enough was enough. Reyna wanted to be her regular self again. He had the day off today. This was the perfect opportunity to focus on work.

Easy. It was the usual to-do list.

Brisa had spent some time making herself at home behind Reyna's desk. Some of her things had been rearranged, but it was easy enough to return them to the proper spot. Reyna moved her stapler up by the phone.

Number one on her list of things she

wasn't going to do: stutter, blush or trip the next time Sean crossed the lobby. At her age, it should have been impossible to be flustered by a man.

Number two: she was definitely not going to waste time worrying about why she hadn't gotten a call about the applications she'd submitted to join Sawgrass or any other station. It had only been three days. Haunting her email inbox was not helping with her anxicty over finding a job, even if it had paid off when the results of her physical aptitude test arrived.

Firing off applications the same day had seemed proactive.

"Thank you for offering to work my Saturday, Reyna. I appreciate it," Brisa said, her legs crossed and her hands tightly knotted on top of her knee.

Reyna slumped in her chair. "Of course, Brisa. Now that I have no classes and no new job, I have all the time in the world." Her little sister deserved some flexibility, too. "The best thing about having both of us on staff is this flexibility. Running Concord Court requires different things on different days. It happens." She added an airy wave of her hand to show how unconcerned she was to be working on Saturday.

"Good. Good." Brisa nodded.

Reyna watched her little sister bite her lip, a sure tell that there was a comment coming.

"So…" Reyna drawled. "Is that it? Bills won't pay themselves." She moved her mouse to wake up the computer.

"I took care of that yesterday while you were giving the tour to that sailor's family." Brisa smiled sweetly. "And I contacted everyone we have referrals on. If you'll check your calendar, you'll see the appointments next week. I'll be happy to take care of those in addition to the guy who is coming in to show me his suit and tie options. He has an important interview. Dream job. Just wants a boost of confidence." Her sister wagged her eyebrows in an "I told you so."

Reyna frowned as she pulled up the calendar. There, in a staggered line, were four different appointments.

"I know you haven't had a chance to look over the details of the referrals, but—" Brisa uncrossed her legs "—you aren't going to reject them without a meeting, so I moved ahead."

Reyna studied her sister's face. Brisa was right. In the time she'd been running Concord Court, she had never rejected a referral outright, even if her concerns about the requirements of the vet were beyond the Court. Evicting Charlie had been hard, but so far, he'd been their only problem. Everyone else was moving forward with the rules of the place. Until that became an issue, she'd prefer to let the vets have a shot.

But she'd never told her sister that. How had Brisa picked up on it?

"Well." Reyna wasn't sure what to say. With all that done, what would she work on today and tomorrow?

"I know you want to give everyone a chance, sis. I do, too. That is one policy we agree on." Brisa's bright smile suggested she understood Reyna's problem. "I know this takes some adjustment for you. It's almost like you could take a day off today and the whole place would continue to stand." Brisa rested comfortably in her chair. If she had any nerves about being in charge, they didn't show.

"I could, or you could. Have you had a day off since you started?" Reyna asked.

She knew the answer. This was a stalling tactic and not a great one.

"I have. Monday. As we agreed in the beginning." Brisa covered her heart with a hand. "Some of us understand the value of rest."

Rolling her eyes was childish, but Reyna did it anyway. Her little sister could bring that out in her sometimes. "I like to work. This is a nice place. Sue me."

"As long as you aren't changing your mind about my role here. Go sit by the pool. It's nice out there, too. Work on your tan." She pointed at the door. "Since you need to be thinking about getting a date, you could go shopping or get your hair done or…" She snapped up straight in her chair. "A manicure. That's it. Go do that." Brisa nodded firmly.

"I am not thinking about getting a date, not to keep Dad off my back, so there's no need for any of that." Reyna frowned at the way the memory of dancing with Sean and her chatting with his grandmother popped into her head. It hadn't been a date.

Besides, she'd rather do almost anything

other than get a manicure. Was that required for dating now?

"Fine. Don't listen to your brilliant little sister," Brisa said and slumped back in her chair. "I wish you'd do something for yourself."

"You mean, other than sneaking around to take classes for a career that I want and making other people cover this awesome job my father created for me?" Reyna asked. "That's enough for a long time."

Brisa sighed. "Experiencing guilt because you're crushing classes for a career in public service again. With a sister like you, is it any wonder I have issues?"

Reyna pointed at her sister. "You have issues, all right, but I take almost no responsibility for those. Being a Montero is my burden, too."

They were quiet for a long minute. Neither of them had to make a list of what those issues were. Reyna hoped that Brisa understood that the need to measure up to someone else came from Luis Montero, not her.

"Have you gotten calls from any of the applications you put in?" Brisa asked, then shook her head. "Sorry. Of course you haven't—it hasn't been long enough—and now I've reminded you that no one has snapped you up within the first twenty-four hours of passing the physical aptitude test and so you are destined for the trash heap." The corner of her mouth quirked. "Am I right?"

Reyna cleared her throat. "Maybe."

When Brisa groaned out loud, Reyna bent forward to press her forehead against the desk. It was silly to feel that way. She knew it. Things took time in the real world.

If only the memory of Marv the dummy's head thudding on concrete didn't pop up every time she reminded herself of that.

Brisa tapped her on the back of the head. "Hey. Sit up. No Montero shows weakness like this." She'd tried to copy her father's delivery. It was pretty effective.

Reyna collapsed back in her chair. "You're pretty good at that."

"I know." Brisa sniffed as if it was beneath her to acknowledge the little people. "Take a day off. Go do something fun. If that's re-grouting the bathroom for you, go do it."

"I don't do home improvement. You know

that. Do you remember the time we decided to paint your bedroom with stars without asking permission?"

Her sister's grimace was confirmation she did remember it. "How long were we in the doghouse?"

"Three weeks—one week for every coat of white paint it took to cover up the neon pink stars. Dad was mad about property values and the decorator was horrified. You were usually so good at crying your way out of punishments." Reyna had never been able to tell her little sister no when she'd blinked up through tears. Their father was only marginally better.

"While you resorted to logic." The disgust in Brisa's tone made Reyna grin. "The two of us are hard to beat."

They both laughed. It was nice to remember some of their rebellions against Luis Montero.

"We make a pretty solid team when we work together," Brisa said.

"Thank you for helping me get around Luis this time, BB." Reyna hoped her sister understood that she knew well what Brisa was risking.

"Thank you for finally coming home. I've missed my partner in crime, Rey." Brisa straightened her shoulders. "And that's why I order you to get out of this office. This new world is about work-life balance, not 24/7 service."

Reyna fiddled with the edge of the stack of papers she'd had lined up on her desk since about two seconds after getting her test results. "I've been thinking about mailing out more résumés and copies of my certificate." She looked at her sister. "But if I do this in Montero fashion, I should get in my car and hand-deliver them, shouldn't I? No one tells a Montero no to their face."

"If they do, they don't live to tell the tale," Brisa said fiercely before breaking down in giggles. For a period of time, they'd imagined their father was a mobster. Too much television had convinced them there was no way he could be rich off "investments." They'd spent a full summer like teenage sleuths, searching for clues, and never turned up anything but old copies of the *Wall Street Journal* and spreadsheets. So many spreadsheets.

"If that's what it takes to convince you

that you've done everything you can, I say go for it." Brisa pointed at the stack of résumés. "You aren't quite as charming as I am, of course, but you inspire confidence in a person. That's hard to translate into words on paper."

Reyna pursed her lips as she decided whether Brisa was complimenting her or insulting her. Since there was nothing but truth in her words, it was hard to argue. "Fine. I'll do it. Then I'll come back. I was thinking one of the things we could do to help Sean get his program going is to identify grants that could cover the costs of training." Reyna started to jot down a list and realized her sister was glaring. "What?"

"You haven't even agreed to continue with the dress for success program, the one you said would be a test, and you're already planning how to swoop in to save Sean's." Brisa crossed her arms over her chest. "If you were going to move ahead anyway, why make it conditional on my business attire program?" She tipped her head to the side. "How else would you put me through the hoops to prove my commitment, right?"

"Trust me, I'm aware of all the progress

you're making. We've been fighting over the proper way to build Concord Court and the programs, remember?" Reyna exhaled slowly. "Honestly, I wanted a project to throw myself into. I'd be useless on yours. His? Money is the easiest piece of the problem."

Brisa smiled sweetly. "It really is."

Something about her tone caught Reyna's attention.

"You've already started solving the money problem?" Reyna shook her head as Brisa rounded the desk and pulled out a binder. She flipped it open to the first page, where Reyna read, "Targeted Grant Programs— Phase One." She flipped through the pages slowly. It was a bare-bones outline of the steps they'd need to follow to get Sean's program up and running. "I told you to put it on the back burner."

"You don't get to decide what I go for, Reyna." Brisa squeezed her eyes closed. "I haven't done anything but research. When it's time, I'll present something to you and Dad and whoever it takes."

"Does Sean know you've been working on this?" Reyna asked. Why did she want to know if Sean had been keeping it from her…? Well, she wasn't going to spend much time thinking about that.

"No, but I have to have something to work on while I'm sitting at this desk or I'll die of boredom. I have another, bigger plan, too, but I need to work on it more before you shoot it down." Brisa smiled sweetly at her.

"You want me to leave so you can sit at this desk and work on your projects, don't you?" Reyna asked.

Brisa nodded.

Naming the emotion that squeezed in her chest took a minute. Hurt. Reyna was hurt that her little sister didn't want her help.

Some things had changed while she was gone.

That was a good thing, even if it would take her some time to adjust.

"Okay, that's what I'll do." Reyna stood uncertainly before brushing her hands down her khakis. "I'll go and apply in person. That will make a difference."

"Probably won't hurt," Brisa agreed.

Probably. That didn't boost Reyna's confidence, but she wouldn't admit that, so she picked up her stack of papers.

"You'll call me if you need me?" Reyna stepped out from behind the desk and tried not to mind when Brisa slipped right into her chair as if she had been anxiously waiting for Reyna to move out of the way. Brisa immediately moved the stapler back under the computer monitor. "But you won't need me."

Brisa widened her eyes. "Can't imagine it."

Right. On that note, Reyna pasted on a smile, waved as if she didn't care that she could so easily be replaced, and stepped out into the heat. Mira and the rest of the running group were finishing up their morning jog. Sean was in the middle of the pack as they slowed to a stop near the pool. She hadn't come up with a good solution on how to act as if everything was normal between them. Mimi's birthday party had changed things, but it shouldn't have.

Once you've seen someone do the hustle, you don't ever look at them the same way.

And a handsome guy who loved his grandmother, danced like no one was watching, and was currently watching her while he wiped sweat off his face with his balled-up T-shirt…

It was a lot to adjust to.

"Morning, Reyna," Mira called. "You missed our run. Next time, join us."

It was impossible to think of anything she'd like less than jogging in the Florida heat. "I'm strictly treadmill, Mira. Years of running in the elements has convinced me to take it easy these days." *When* she ran. She hated running with a passion.

"Smart. Running is stupid," Sean muttered as he sat down in the deep shade on the parking lot curb. "I only do it because I'm afraid of Mira."

"And don't you forget it." Mira shook her head as she met Reyna's stare. "These men. You'd think I forced them to run at gunpoint."

The charged silence as response suggested they had nothing but complaints but were unwilling to share them. Sort of like every forced run she'd ever been on.

"At least it's over," Sean muttered before turning to Reyna. "Where you headed to?"

Reyna studied the rest of the group, who had taken some unseen cue to drift away. "Did you tell them to do that?"

Sean glanced around before snorting.

"Nah. They have it in their heads that we're going to fight or something."

"Why?" Reyna had never been one for public confrontation. Now was no time to start.

"They think I poke at you too much." His lips slid into a grin. "Doesn't mean we have to fight, though."

Reyna agreed. "You do poke. Why is that?"

Sean slowly stood. This close, all Reyna could see was tanned skin and his lazy grin. She couldn't have turned away from him if someone offered her a fortune. Sean Wakefield was strong and tall and too handsome for this time of day…or any time of day. Reyna cleared her throat and met his stare. It would do no good to let him know she thought so.

"I like to get your attention, Reyna." Then he raised his eyebrows. Then he crossed his arms over his chest.

As if he was waiting for her to… What was he waiting for her to do?

Reyna waved her stack of papers. "I'm going to go see if I can hunt down someone who doesn't care that I'm bossy and a Montero and that I dropped the dummy on his head." She shrugged. When she put it like that, the task grew harder—*much* harder.

Sean took the papers from her hand and scanned the top, her résumé of accomplishments in the Air Force. His whistle was long and low. "You know, I joined the Marines because I thought I could be a hero like this. Decorated for military service." His smile slipped as he handed her the stack. "Not everyone can manage it."

There was something there. Sean's face had changed. His eyes were darker. The smile reappeared. "They don't hire you, they need their heads examined. Tell them I said so."

Reyna laughed because he wanted her to. Why didn't she know how to answer him?

"Thanks. I needed a pep talk." Reyna shifted on the sidewalk. "You're good at that."

He folded his hands and bowed. "We can't all do what you do, but I have my talents." He moved to walk through the pool area, but Reyna held out a hand. She wanted to say something, but what? His eyes bothered her.

"You don't talk much about your time in the service, Sean." She cleared her throat.

"If you need someone to talk to, I'm happy to listen."

He studied her hand on his arm. "Thanks." He waited until her hand dropped. "It wasn't that long. Just long enough to leave me with nightmares for the rest of my life, I guess." He tipped his head up to study the brilliant blue sky. "Fire wakes me up at night. And you want to volunteer to run into the flames." He shook his head. "Couldn't do it. Another way Reyna Montero beats me."

Something funny would be good. She could toss it out, release some of the building tension between them and get back to her plan for the day.

But it wouldn't come.

Because that wasn't her talent. It was his.

Eventually she squeezed his hand. "Hey, those nightmares? Imagine how many of them your dogs will chase away for vets all over Florida. That's a pretty cool superpower to have, Wakefield. Don't forget that."

His eyebrows shot up. "Superpower?" He held a hand to his chest. "Little ol' me? You'll turn my head, you will, Ms. Montero." His drawl was cuter than it should be, but he'd managed to set them back on level ground.

Reyna turned to get into her car, the warmth of his stare following her. When she started the engine, Sean had braced a shoulder against the wrought iron fence around the pool, and he was staring at her. She could skip this errand. If he was going to be at the pool, she could join him. Sean would make sure she was distracted from all the worries that chased each other around in her head.

He answered her wave with a lazy one of his own and she forced herself to back out of the parking spot. He was an employee of Concord Court. She was still in charge of the Court for...possibly forever. No one needed the complication of a flirtation between them—not her, not him, and not Brisa, who would get caught in the fallout for however long she was here. And if things went badly, Sean could lose his job. Luis Montero wasn't above using Reyna's feelings to get what he wanted.

Better to get some distance, so she pulled out of the parking lot and drove to the first fire station she could think of. She'd applied for positions in Miami and in the neighboring towns. Sawgrass Station, working for Mort Fields and being close to home—that was her goal, but she was trying to be realistic. More stations meant better chances of getting a job. There was no way she could get to all of them in one day, so she might as well make these visits count.

Logically, Sawgrass Station made perfect sense. She'd work the three-on, three-off schedule required, and she'd plug in whenever she could at Concord Court. Then she would have it all. Her father couldn't argue if she was on-site overseeing everything, even if it was part-time. She would continue to be able to help with whatever Brisa needed.

If she needed any help at all.

Reyna was still adjusting to the fact that her little sister had completed every task on the to-do list Reyna had made up in her mind.

There was no actual list on paper lying around that Brisa could see and follow. Her sister had come up with her own tasks and checked them off without supervision. What if this period of time, when she'd been forced to ask Brisa for help, turned out to be exactly what Brisa had needed all along?

Reyna almost drove past the station because she was trying to imagine a world where Brisa was settled and confident and prepared to stand on her own. It would be amazing. It might also kill their father.

With a hard brake, Reyna whipped her SUV into one of the station's visitor parking spots. She checked her hair and realized she hadn't gone home to change out of the Concord Court polo. Should she come back?

Would she give this another shot if she didn't seize her chance right then and there?

It was hard to say, but Reyna was afraid she knew the answer, and she'd be disappointed in herself if she didn't get out of the SUV and go inside.

She managed to slide out of the SUV and shut the door without hesitation. Then she paused to check her reflection in the window. Hair—fine. Nerves—written all over the grim expression on her face. If there was one thing she'd learned growing up a Montero and then solidified in the military, it was to never let them see her sweat. Who was them? All of them. Her father, her sister, the men and women she fought beside and those who reported to her. The only thing constant in military service was change. That shook up most people. Reyna wasn't immune to nerves but she'd learned to convince other people she was. They respected that.

She straightened her shoulders and walked toward the glass door leading to the modern building. On the right side of the building, four doors were up, revealing two ladder trucks and one engine. This was a large station serving an urban area. If she could get on here, Reyna would be part of an important team.

She paused and pulled to open the door before remembering it pushed open. Irritated with herself for missing the reminder on the door, Reyna hurried inside. Pulling instead of pushing was an easy mistake. People made it all the time, so if someone was watching her, she'd pretend it didn't bother her.

Then she realized no one was paying her any mind. She'd stepped inside chaos. Before she could get up to the counter, she heard, "Don't let her out the door!" The male shout urged her to action, so Reyna stepped in front of the door, prepared to be the last line of defense.

Instead of a gun-waving robber or whatever she'd imagined in that split second, a large white dog with black splotches came galumphing around the corner of the desk. Before Reyna could relax, the dog had two front paws planted on her abdomen, and a tongue swiped across Reyna's cheek.

If someone had shot her right there, Reyna wouldn't have been more startled. She was frozen in place.

Then Pulaski bounded into the small reception area and slid to a halt in front of her. "Good thing you didn't let her get away." He tugged the dog back down on all fours. "Excellent timing, Montero."

Reyna had to catch her breath. It was easier now that the dog wasn't leaning on her stomach, but she hadn't recovered by the time six firefighters filed in behind Pulaski, as well as Mort Fields. "Not looking good for your assignment, Pulaski. Thought you were going to teach Dottie some manners."

Reyna was happy to have arrived for this

moment, even if she'd be wiping dog kisses off her face when she got home.

"She's out of control, sir," Pulaski answered.

Reyna said, "You mean the dog, right?" She pointed to herself and raised her eyebrows. The smiles on the firefighters' faces were reassuring. They got her joke.

Pulaski's fake laugh was satisfying, too. "What are you doing here, Montero?"

"Came to see the chief," Reyna answered.

The chief braced both hands on his hips. "Reyna Montero. Didn't expect to see you here today. Most people wait until I call them to come talk about a job."

Had he meant to call her? Was that what he was saying?

"Sir, do you have time for a quick meeting?" She waved the résumé she'd brought in. "I won't take much of your time."

He motioned with his head to an office nearby. The walls were glass. His desk was spotless. Chief Fields was a man who liked order, apparently. How did Dottie fit into this equation?

As if she'd been summoned by the thought, the dog wiggled in a wild dance over to sit at Reyna's feet. There was no word that described the dog's expression other than *adoration*. Since she'd never had a dog, Reyna hadn't expected to fall in love in a heartbeat, but it was impossible to look down into the dog's eyes and not understand that she loved Reyna unconditionally.

Was this what Sean went through with his rescues?

"Pulaski, go find something to clean. We'll return Dottie in a few minutes." The chief held the door open, waited for Reyna and the dog to enter, and shut it behind them. Reyna slid the paper onto the spotless desk and then brushed away a white hair that floated down onto the shiny surface.

"Yeah, the hair gets everywhere." The chief sat down and nodded as Dottie came over to spread more kisses around. "It's worth it, I guess." He scratched the dog's ears. Dottie sighed happily and they both looked at Reyna with a question.

The problem with starting here was that Mort Fields already knew the list of qualifications she'd rehearsed in her head. He'd already hired Pulaski, who had won their relay in front of the chief fair and square.

But she was here. She had a chance to

make a case. She owed it to herself to take her shot.

"I had hoped to discuss my qualifications with you, sir. I don't know if you are looking for more firefighters to fill out your crew, but if you are, I hope you'll consider me. I served for two decades in the United States Air Force. I understand the requirements of service. I would like to continue that commitment here." Reyna forced herself not to go on about her skills. She wouldn't be bossy. She'd try to be friendly. If the dog would leave the chief, Reyna would talk only to Dottie for the remainder of her visit. The chief was politely listening to her pitch, but he'd already filled the job. Waiting for him to dismiss her would be easier if she could stare into Dottie's eyes.

But Dottie wasn't leaving his side. She stared up at Mort with devotion.

Dottie loved well, and she wasn't stingy with her targets, either.

"I thought firehouse dogs were supposed to be purebred Dalmatians," Reyna said and quickly added, "sir." Dottie was large. Reyna couldn't identify the dog's makeup, but her best guess was there might be a Great Dane in the mix.

He sighed loudly and patted Dottie on the head. "Yeah, but my daughter insists on rescues. My station has always had a dog. Helps with outreach and kids love them. Had a photo booth once and the station dog, Smokey, earned three times more than any man or woman working it." Mort nodded at the dog. "And sometimes, when we're away from home, a dog around here lightens the load. I wasn't quite ready for a deaf Dalmatian-slash-horse like this one. You know? In your head, it's all those great pictures of the dog posed beautifully on a fire engine. In real life, it's…" He motioned at Dottie, who was gnawing on a corner of his desk. "It's a lot less regal in real life."

"A pretty rescue for community outreach." Reyna smiled. "That's a great human interest story. You've got Pulaski working with the dog?"

"Kid's only been here two days. You might cut him some slack," the chief drawled. "Crew's pretty full up as it is, Montero. Although…"

Reyna did her best to ignore the deflation she experienced.

It was time to move on to the next station.

"Thank you for your time, sir." Reyna stood. "I can get you the name of a good dog trainer or obedience class if you'd like." She paused to stare into Dottie's beautiful eyes and then scratched under her chin. "Those little kids are going to love you, girl."

She could elbow her way into Sean's service animal project. More time with dogs could be good for her.

The chief said, "Well, now, Montero, it's real interesting you stopped in today. Did you know Pulaski's dad was a firefighter, too? And the kid just got out of the army. You two have that in common, even if he doesn't have your service record." He leaned forward. "I knew his dad. Good man. Snapping his kid up from the academy was a priority of mine." He didn't smile, but Reyna understood he was enjoying himself. "I have one more slot I want to fill, though. My brother, he lobbied hard for his hotshot. He also said you have some trouble with people. That true, Montero?"

Reyna raised her chin. "No, sir. I'm good

with people." He would believe it if she said it confidently enough. She'd learned that lesson early on.

"Say you were offered a probationary start, Montero. Six months training. Would you take it?" The captain stood.

Reyna immediately nodded. "Yes, sir. I would. I have considered the highest and best use of my time, and I want to serve as a member of the Miami Fire Department and Sawgrass Station." She waited tensely for his reaction.

"Highest." He whistled. "And best. Well, it ain't every day I find someone talking like that." He propped his hands on his hips. "Good news, Montero. You're hired."

Reyna swallowed the victory shout bubbling below the surface and offered him her hand. "Thank you, Chief. You will not regret this."

He shook her hand, then grimaced. "No, I won't, but you might. Dottie belongs to the newest member of the team. Today, that's you."

Reyna looked down at the dog, who'd returned to evaluating the corner of the chief's desk with her teeth. Mort brushed her away. "You don't have a problem with that, do you?"

Reyna shook her head no while she considered explaining that she knew nothing about dogs, her townhome didn't allow them, and her father would be incensed if and when he found out about the job and the dog policy she'd flagrantly broken.

But this was her chance, the key to making her plan for her life and Concord Court work.

He clapped his hands. Dottie didn't react, but her tail was wagging wildly as if she knew something had changed. "Take her home. Teach her some manners. I'll get you on a schedule. Soon as we can, we'll start sending you and Pulaski out to deliver fire safety talks at the schools." He shook his head immediately. "No complaints, please. It's part of the job. It'll be yours until the next rooks come in. That's how we do."

Reyna tipped her chin up. "Thank you, sir. I look forward to serving."

He grunted and pointed at the door. "Get Dottie's leash and food from Pulaski. Make the kid carry it all out to your car. If he complains, let me know. Dottie loves him, too. He might be back on the hook."

He patted the dog as they left his office. Pulaski was hovering near the door. "Well?"

Reyna wanted to gloat.

But she was about to take home a Dalmatian Dane.

Who was really winning?

She didn't have anything to celebrate yet.

"Dottie's coming with me. Since you can't train her, Chief wants me to give it a shot so we can head out to the schools when they start back up." There. That sounded almost like he'd been demoted when she was hired.

Pulaski's slow grin convinced her he wasn't falling for it.

He held out her leash. "Here you go. I'll meet you at your car with her food. Can't think of a better person for the job, Montero."

Reyna held her head high as she remembered to pull rather than push the door open from inside. Dottie was loaded into the front seat of her SUV by the time Pulaski brought out her food. And then Reyna was headed back home.

With the job she'd wanted.

And a dog.

CHAPTER ELEVEN

THE HEAT WAS always what managed to bring Sean out of the nightmares. Stifling under the sheets wrapped tightly around him, Sean kicked one leg out. Air-conditioning automatically chilled that skin, but the rest of him burned. That feeling, the certainty that he'd never be cool again, always took time to fade.

Sean wiped the sweat off his forehead and stared up at the ceiling. No matter how often he did this and no matter how many successful nights of sleep fell in between, he was always shocked at how clear the memory of the explosion outside of Kabul remained.

Time was supposed to soften the hard edges, but orange flames against black night remained stark in his dreams.

The shrill hum of noise that had replaced his normal hearing for what seemed like forever after the explosion faded almost as quickly as he opened his eyes, but the prickle of burning skin across his cheeks and nose was harder to chase away.

He reached down to pet Bo, but the dog had gone to his new home.

Sean should have anticipated the nightmares because of that. They came like clockwork on the first night after his dogs moved to their new homes. That was a side effect of this fostering plan that he needed to warn his volunteers about.

The walls closed around Sean, and he struggled to the side of the bed. There was no way to sleep. Getting up was the only way to survive.

When he stood, air ghosted over his skin, so he changed into a dry T-shirt and shorts. Then he paused at the doorway. He needed to get out, but the pool group had disbanded hours ago. Didn't matter. He couldn't stay here.

Television. It might distract him. If Bo were here, he could lie on the couch, a loose collection of bones and fuzzy ears stretched out beside him. Sean wouldn't sleep, but the night would pass.

But without Bo…

Sean ran his hands through his wet air and forced himself to focus. He was fine. There was no danger. Eventually his heart rate would slow down to normal, and the panic would recede. He could wait this out.

Therapy had taught him to try focusing on his body in that moment. Sean inhaled slowly and pressed his feet firmly into the ground, feeling the connection. The air was cool. The silence was so complete it had its own texture. He was thirsty but not hungry.

And every second, he was coming back to himself.

Sean bent to pick up the remote control but tossed it back down.

Walking around the apartment complex was a terrible solution, but he could tell himself he was moving, doing something, and hope it was true.

Sean was reaching for his running shoes when he heard Reyna say outside his door, "It's time to do your business."

Sean frowned at the door while he tried to decipher what kind of message his subconscious could be sending him, using those words and making him think Reyna had spoken them.

Then she added, "Please, Dottie, do not make me call the emergency vet tonight."

There was no possible hidden message there, Sean decided, so he pulled open his door. Reyna and an oversize Dalmatian were standing on the grassy area in front of their townhomes. "Am I hallucinating?" Sean asked. "That's a new side effect of PTSD. Usually it's nightmares." He sat down on his top step and caught the dog, who'd launched herself at him. "Nope. Dottie is all real." He glanced up at Reyna. "You're real, too, right?"

Reyna groaned and dropped down to sit beside him. "I had hoped I was in a nightmare, but if you're here, this must be real." She closed her eyes. "Did we wake you up?"

"No." Sean scratched the dog behind her ears. "Were you trying to?"

He expected an immediate argument. Instead, Reyna answered, "No. Maybe." Then she kicked out one leg, her bright white tennis shoes gleaming in the moonlight. "Probably. I knocked on your door this afternoon to beg for help, but you didn't answer."

She'd come to ask him for help. Suddenly, his mood lifted. Nightmares had broken him, but this woman, one of the most impressive people he'd ever met, had come to him for help. The knotted muscles across his shoulders eased.

Sean watched the dog sniff around the bottom of the steps, prepared to move his feet quickly out of the way if she took aim. "Bo went home today. I had to drive him over to meet his vet, and we worked through some of his concerns. It took longer than I thought it would."

They both watched the dog, who had decided that rolling in the grass was the perfect way to celebrate being awake at three in the morning.

"You gonna tell me the story?" Sean drawled. Whatever he'd imagined might help him outrun his memories, this would never have made the list. And if he'd dreamed it up, he'd never have guessed the relief or comfort or peace or whatever this emotion could be called would roll over him this way.

"I got the job today, starting with lots of on-the-job training and serving as part of Sawgrass Station's community outreach, but only if I can manage to teach Dottie here some manners." Reyna tipped her head back. "I've never had a dog, much less a dog who can't hear me desperately calling her name or one the size of a small pony, and I have no idea what I'm doing. All afternoon, I studied training articles and tips, but she's…" Reyna waved her hand at the dog, who'd stopped wiggling, all four feet up in the air. "Is there something wrong with her?"

Sean sighed. "Hard to say. Right now, I'd say she's afflicted with typical puppy syndrome. How old is she?"

"I'm not sure. She was a rescue." Reyna touched the dog with her foot. Dottie immediately sprang up to come over. The dog licked her chin and Reyna let out a watery sigh. "She ate my mail. Is she going to die?"

Sean blinked. "From eating paper? I don't think so. I once had a dog who pulled books off a shelf and destroyed the covers. Although that was more ripping than eating." The dog had moved on to eat part of the lowest shelf, but telling Reyna that Dottie could be chewing on literal wood next wasn't a good idea.

"Yeah. That's what happened all over my living room. I made one phone call to find her an obedience class and came back to Mailmageddon. It snowed little wet chunks of paper all over my sofa." Reyna rested her cheek on Dottie's head and stared up at him. "Is this how it's supposed to happen?"

"What?" Sean asked as he held out his hand to the dog. She sniffed delicately and inched closer to him.

"Falling in love." Her eyes were steady on his. There was no way Sean could look away. "I've known her less than a day and I think I might die if something happens to her."

That was something he understood. Dogs brought it out in him, too.

What was less clear was what was happening the closer he got to Reyna.

Her hair was a mess, rumpled and sticking up. She was dressed a lot like he was, in shorts and a T-shirt.

But it was impossible to look away from her. The worry in her eyes, the glimmer of tears... He had to do something.

"Stay here." Sean stood. Dottie's head lifted as she tracked him. "And take away whatever that is hanging out of her mouth. I'll be right back."

Sean trotted to his refrigerator and yanked open the door. At some point, he would love to be able to prove his worth to Reyna Montero in a spectacular way.

Tonight, he'd have to use leftover hot dogs. He cut a couple into tiny pieces and scooped them into a plastic bag. He grabbed two bottles of water and closed the fridge with his hip. As he turned to hurry back outside, he realized a big goofy grin had taken over his face.

He inhaled slowly, relieved to have found the key to making it through another night. Then he realized that key was Reyna Montero, world's worst disco dancer and owner of the most beautiful smile.

Sean waited for the panic to return. This…joy at sitting outside his apartment with a woman and a dog… It had to mean something scary, didn't it?

He walked slowly back out to rejoin them because he couldn't change it, whatever it meant.

"It was my shoestring," Reyna said when he sat next to her. "She chewed through my shoestring while I was wearing the shoes."

Sean laughed. It felt good. Reyna's tone

wavered beyond despair and disbelief, but the giggles that trickled out were cute.

Reyna Montero? *Cute?*

"Don't look now but she's got her leash in her mouth," Sean said and offered Reyna the bag of treats. "Let's distract her."

"Right. If she chews through her leash and gets away, I'll never catch her. She's fast when she's on a tear in my living room." Reyna held up the plastic bag. "Do I want to know what this is?"

"That is the key to success with a dog. Any dog. All dogs." Sean picked up the bag and waited for Dottie to turn his direction. Training a deaf dog might take creativity but it couldn't be that different. When the dog came closer, Sean took out one of the tidbits and offered it to her. "Food. Give any dog food early and often when you start training. Life gets so much easier for you, and the dog loves it. Eventually they learn to keep their eyes on you and do what you want them to."

Dottie delicately took her treat, and Reyna giggled again at the way Dottie immediately locked eyes on the treat bag.

"You try it." Sean braced his elbows on

his knees. "Give her a couple so she knows you've got the good stuff."

"I read a dozen different websites about training puppies this afternoon, between cleaning up messes. Can it be that simple?" Reyna followed his directions, Dottie inching ever closer until her chest bumped Reyna's knees.

"Okay, now..." Sean thought for a second. "We should train her to watch you for commands."

"Holding out my hand to get her to sit was suggested on one of the articles I read this afternoon." Reyna held her hand out over the dog. Dottie was already sitting so it was hard to judge the effectiveness.

"Do the hand signal with the verbal command, and follow with a treat. Right now, that treat is the critical piece." Normally, he'd be itching to take over, but everything Reyna did fascinated him.

"Say the command even though she can't hear me?" Reyna asked.

Sean shrugged. "That part's more for you than her, but I don't think it can hurt to reinforce the command. She'll be watching your face, too."

Watching her was pretty fascinating all on its own.

"Sit, Dottie." Reyna held out her hand and then gave the dog a treat. "You think this will work?"

"I'm certain. As long as the hot dog holds out, Dottie will do her best to please you." Sean tipped his head to the side. "Work on sitting, but you should also work on 'watch me.' Since Dottie can't hear you, she needs to watch you for commands."

Reyna considered that. Then she pointed at her eye. "Watch me, Dottie." The dog accepted her hot dog and wagged her tail.

"When you go inside, practice in the new surroundings. You can also teach her that a wave and 'okay' means she's free." Sean straightened. He'd done what he needed to do. Spending any more time out here with the two of them was only going to drag him deeper into this fascination with Reyna.

"I'm keeping you up. I'm sorry." Reyna squeezed his arm and Sean felt the tingle zip across his skin. "I knew you would be able to help. Thank you."

He studied her face. A weak breeze ruffled the hair around her face, which was pale in the moonlight. Beautiful.

"Thank you for chasing away the nightmare." He should stand.

He'd let them go inside first. He wasn't going to get any sleep, anyway.

"Want to tell me about it?" Reyna tugged the leash Dottie had in her mouth. "Watch me, Dottie." The dog wasn't sure what Reyna was asking but she understood hot dogs, so she spit the leash out and accepted her treat.

Their chuckles floated on the breeze. The three of them might be the only creatures on the whole planet. It was peaceful. That made it easier to tell her.

"It's a memory. A night operation in Kabul." Sean rolled his head on his shoulders, the tension there hard to shake. "Insurgents had taken over an elementary school, so we were sent in to clear it, remove the hostages." No one ever expected them to bring enemy combatants peacefully in, but that had been their directive. Keep casualties low, but do what it took to eliminate the threat. The plan had been scheduled at night because it gave them some cover, so they'd moved in and waited for the order to approach. "Part of my team had cleared the outer doors when the building exploded."

Reyna reached over to grasp his hand. Her warmth took some of the pain.

"I was thrown back by the blast, but never in much danger. I remember the way the flames burned against the dark sky, the horrible ringing in my ears, and the horror that we'd lost some of our team and however many kids were inside."

Reyna didn't speak, but her grip tightened.

"Eventually we found out the whole group, even the hostages, had been relocated the night before, so it was a trap to take out US marines." Sean traced his thumb across the back of Reyna's hand.

"My hearing came back, but my nerve never did. Soon as my chance to come home arrived, I grabbed it and returned to safe ol' Georgia." Sean watched Dottie nose the treat bag. This dog would get Reyna straightened out. "Anyway, that's my story. I joined because my father did, and everyone told these great stories about him. I never met him, but

I wanted to be like him. Guess we can't all be heroes."

Reyna's snort wrinkled some of the peaceful atmosphere.

"Are you snorting at me? At my pain?" Sean drawled, determined to play off the sharp ache in the region of his heart at her dismissive sound.

"Never at your pain, but your definition of hero is kind of small." Reyna took the leash from Dottie's mouth again. "Chew toys. That's my first purchase in the morning."

Sean turned to face her. "What does that mean? About my definition of hero?"

Reyna stared straight ahead, her focus on the parking lot instead of the dog chewing on her other shoestring. "You're the guy who rescues dogs and vets and women who need help in the middle of the night and friends who need a laugh and old guys named Charlie who have no one else to turn to and grandmothers who love disco. I've known a lot of men and women who flew dangerous missions, but I've never met anyone else like you. You have time for what matters, for what people need—you have time for the people who can get lost too easily."

She kept staring straight ahead and didn't look at him. Though he wanted her to.

"So don't tell me you aren't a hero. I abandoned my sister because I needed to get away from being a Montero. You wouldn't have done that."

Whatever he'd wanted to say was gone when Reyna waved her hand. "None of that's important. You're a hero, so don't say anything silly like that to me again." She stood and brushed off her shorts. Her untied shoe flopped down on the sidewalk and Dottie immediately scooped it up in her mouth. Reyna bent down and wrapped an arm loosely around Sean's neck for a hug before seesawing back up the stairs, one sneakered foot and one bare foot. "And I think I've changed my mind."

Sean couldn't have figured out what she meant even if the conversation had followed a recognizable pattern. He was stuck on the scent of roses that followed her. It suited her perfectly, especially in the dark night, just the two of them.

"Your service animals..." She touched Dottie on the head. The dog stared up at her with her mouth clamped around the shoe.

"They're important. If you'll help me train Dottie, I want to go ahead with your plan. We'll start with the volunteers you've identified, and roll out the full program after we work through this first class of dogs. Brisa will be happy, too." Reyna offered him her hand. "Deal?"

Sean stood and took her hand. "What about your father?" He didn't let go. "I'll help you no matter what, Reyna."

She snorted again. "See? That's what I mean. I'm offering you the perfect opportunity to get whatever you want, but you're going to insist on doing the right thing, even if you lose your leverage."

Sean studied her face. "You might have a point."

"We're going to do this—we'll get your program up and going. Dottie is going to become the station's perfect mascot, and I will earn my spot on the crew." Reyna shook her head. "But when my father finds out, there will be consequences." She shrugged. "Like the last time I refused to follow his rules."

Sean hadn't let go of her hand. He didn't want to. She'd disappear inside when he did. "Consequences for me?"

"Possibly. Brisa and I have a little protection, but you... Your job..." Reyna stared up at him. "Just make sure you understand that my father won't hesitate to put your job on the line to pull us all into what he wants. When I left home the first time, Dad tied the strings up tightly for Brisa, so she's been here, dealing with him alone. I did what I wanted the first time around. I don't want the consequences of my decisions to overwhelm either of you this time."

"I was looking for a job when I found this one, Reyna, and honestly, I've seen you and your sister face off. Surely your father is smart enough to avoid the heat y'all bring." He couldn't contain the smile as she rolled her eyes. "It's going to be okay. I'll set up the training and let you know when we start."

"Okay." Reyna pulled her hand free. "See you in the sunlight, Sean." She was behind a closed door before Sean was free of the spell.

"See you in the sunlight," he repeated. It was almost poetic, something he'd never associated with Reyna Montero, but the sentiment made perfect sense.

Both of them wore masks during the day.

Hers said competent, confident, a leader. His was confident, too, but also easygoing, laid-back, with a joke always on his lips.

But tonight they'd both been who they were underneath all that.

Not quite as strong or confident, but real.

It had taken the miracle of falling in love with a puppy to bring this side of Reyna out. He was reminded of that instant when she'd asked if love was supposed to happen like that. The thread between them had snapped into place.

In the sunlight, she'd be on her guard again, her protective facade in place.

He could fall for the other Reyna, the one she protected. The problem would be finding her again.

CHAPTER TWELVE

AFTER A WEEKEND of doing her best to teach Dottie some manners while carefully avoiding making a bigger nuisance of herself to her next-door neighbor, Reyna was excited to return to Sawgrass Station for her first official day.

When the chief had informed her that the first order of business was taking the ladder truck for a drive, Reyna was nearly certain she'd hit the jackpot. The academy's lessons on the big ladder trucks and smaller engines that pumped water had been minimal. Starting them up, which was complex; working the electronics, also a challenge; and getting comfortable with the height had been the focus. They'd done most of their practice in a simulator.

But today, this morning, Reyna was sitting behind the wheel of an actual fire truck and the adrenaline was sweet.

Almost as sweet as facing down the runway in a jet.

"Your buddy Pulaski is not a big fan of the truck?" Baptiste asked as Reyna snapped the lap belt closed.

"Took out a school bus in my first run through the driving simulator. Never been the same since," Pulaski answered from his spot on the jump seat behind Baptiste. He was wearing headphones to monitor communication in the cab. "The horror of fake kids screaming takes a minute to forget."

Baptiste raised his eyebrows at Reyna. "Ain't never heard that before."

"Pulaski went first but everybody in the class learned a lesson from his run. We all slowed down." Reyna shook her head. "I only sideswiped a light pole."

"That could happen today, too, but let's hope there ain't no buses running," Baptiste drawled.

"Second-guessing the chief's assignment, Baptiste?" Reyna asked as she turned the switches and pressed the buttons to start up the truck. The immediate thrum of the engines was like magic—every one of her senses was alert, prepared for anything.

"Never. For me, riding in the truck never gets old." Baptiste shook his head. "Might wish I had a helmet, but I'm prepared to die."

Reyna rolled her head on her shoulders to loosen the tension in her neck. "Where to?"

"We're gonna take a practice turn around this parkin' lot first." He pointed. "Take me in a circle, nice and slow."

Reyna followed his directions and then did the same thing in reverse to show she could.

"All right, now let's head for the open road." Baptiste sighed. "But let's stay off the interstate."

Reyna enjoyed the spark of anticipation. Driving this big red beauty on a call would be thrilling. Even today on a sedate run on the city streets around Sawgrass Station, her senses were sharper than they had been since she'd retired. She was focused and she followed Baptiste's directions perfectly. Warning lights, check. Light bar, check. Siren blast, check. Horn at the intersection, check.

And it was over too soon. Reyna fought

the sinking sensation as she made the wide turn back into Sawgrass Station.

Baptiste said, "Think you might have found your calling."

Since she was already considering how to convince the chief to send her for the specialized driving course, Reyna thought he might be right.

"Let's back it into place, then." Baptiste stretched to look one way and then the other, and pointed at the middle opening. This was a test.

Reyna checked over her shoulder to see Pulaski's concerned expression. If they knew some of the places she'd maneuvered in and out of...

Focusing hard, Reyna enjoyed the sizzle of a challenge. Then she backed forty-plus feet of ladder truck into the middle bay of the station in one try.

The urge to celebrate was nearly overwhelming, but she tamped it down.

Baptiste whistled loud and long. "You absolutely just did that." Then he held up his hand for a high five and Reyna smacked it hard.

Sliding out of the high seat was sad but exhilarating, especially when Pulaski rounded the truck to meet her.

"Guess that Air Force training comes in handy sometimes." Reyna smiled sweetly at him.

Pulaski followed Baptiste's lead and held up his hand. Reyna smacked his twice as hard and had to fight the urge to strut into the station. Up to that point, she hadn't been sure that this plan was the best for her life. Running Concord Court was an awesome calling and responsibility.

But today? She was alive and she could not wait to climb back up into that driver's seat.

"Come on," Baptiste said, already heading inside. "Meeting's in a few."

She walked into the room of unknown firefighters whom she was going to have to connect to, a much harder job. Reyna braced her shoulder against the paneled wall of the common room at Sawgrass Station and tried to pretend she was perfectly comfortable. Her new uniform? The navy T-shirt and twill station cargo pants were fine. Pretending that she didn't notice or mind the surreptitious glances from everyone in the room? That was disconcerting. The key to that was forcing the muscles in her face to relax. Since her normal expression in such situations might be called "Resting Worried Face," it was something she worked on now and then, especially around new groups. That only meant she was thinking.

Reyna scanned the firefighters and realized no one was paying a bit of attention to her at that moment.

Dottie was snoozing in the captain's chair and all eyes were on her.

"I understand we have a couple new distractions, but focus up, people," Mort Fields snapped. A small rustle filled the space as everyone turned back to him. "This week a crew will be cleaning and doing maintenance on Engine Three, led by Rashid. Training will continue with our new recruits, Montero and Pulaski. They will also be shadowing several of you for the next few weeks." Fields waved at them. "Many of you know Pulaski's father, heretofore known as the first Pulaski. This Pulaski's an army veteran, aced his physical aptitude and has no natural talent for working with dogs."

Pulaski dipped his head to acknowledge the comment but didn't argue.

Fields waited for the rumble of welcomes and trash talk to die down. Reyna straightened up. Her turn was coming.

"And Montero here comes to us from the Air Force. Decorated officer. Has trouble with her gloves, so don't let her drop you on your head." Fields stared at her over his clipboard.

Reyna tipped her chin up. She'd wear gloves twenty-four hours a day for the rest of her life if that was what it took to never drop anything again, just to show them. She definitely needed the practice.

"Montero speaks Dottie's language, so for now, she's training and caring for the dog. She and Pulaski will take most of our school visits when the school year kicks off and most of our community outreach, but I'll still require volunteers when I ask for volunteers." He dropped his clipboard. "Do I need to give my speech on the importance of community support to you, to me, to first responders all over this city?"

Reyna bit back a smile at the solemn head-shaking that went around the room. He'd obviously given the talk more than once. They did not want to sit through it again.

"I didn't think so, and your next opportunity is coming up. Back to School Blowout, the citywide festival that'll be taking place at Bayfront Park, is in two weeks. Montero will be Dottie's handler. We'll have a photo booth along with several police K9 units. Baptiste will be cooking jambalaya for sale, which is always a moneymaker. The volunteer group is planning to sell baked goods. I need guys to operate the engines, sit in the dunking booth, and make up the volleyball team that will defeat whatever losers the cops put out on the court." Fields stared over his reading glasses. "Pulaski will be in the dunking booth, for sure."

Reyna turned to see what Pulaski thought of the decision. His lips were a tight line, but he nodded.

"I knew I could count on you." Fields waited for the rest of the slots to be filled by volunteers. Reyna almost volunteered to captain the volleyball team, but Fields added, "This volleyball game needs to be good. Otherwise, we're looking at some new volunteers for extra kitchen duties."

She'd clap from the sidelines this time. She hated cooking, and dishes were worse.

No one in the room groaned or argued. Reyna understood why there was no response.

Fields had his guys trained well.

And she'd gotten off lucky. How hard could a photo booth with Dottie be?

As if she'd heard her name, the dog came trotting out of the chief's office with a file folder in her mouth.

The dog loved paper. Reyna would have covered her face with her hands, but Dottie dropped the file immediately when she realized everyone was staring at her. Then she sat beautifully and wagged her tail. The response was immediate. "Aww" was the general consensus. Around the room, people tried to get her attention. Reyna noticed even Pulaski got into the game as he knelt down and snapped his fingers.

That much distraction made Reyna nervous. They'd been practicing the sign language for "watch me" and "sit" for a couple of days, but Dottie was a work in progress.

Luckily, Reyna had discovered that cheddar cheese, little bites of it, were Dottie's obsession. She'd convinced the dog to drop her credit card bill by walking toward the refrigerator on Sunday.

"You won't know if you don't try," Reyna muttered to herself. She waved to get the dog's attention and then raised her hand to touch her cheek below her eye, the signal she'd been using for "watch me." Dottie's ears lifted. They hadn't done anything with "come" yet, but Reyna had already decided patting her leg would be the symbol. Dogs instinctively knew that one, right?

Reyna gave it a shot. She patted her leg and Dottie trotted over before plopping down in a lounge. It could use some work, but Reyna pulled out a bite of cheddar—apparently she was going to be carrying cheese around in a plastic bag in her pocket for the rest of Dottie's life. The dog took her treat and everyone in the room applauded as if she'd accomplished something outstanding.

"That dog was a beautiful menace last week," Baptiste said with a whistle. "Good thing Montero came along, huh, Pulaski?"

Good thing Sean Wakefield couldn't sleep at night was more like it, but Reyna loved seeing Pulaski's grimace so much that she'd never admit to having help.

"That will be all for today." Fields motioned everyone out the door. "Pulaski, Montero, we'll be training Wednesday, Thursday and Friday this week. You're off duty until then. I appreciate you coming in this morning."

"Glad to do it, Chief," Reyna said as she picked up the end of Dottie's leash and the folder she'd dropped. "We've still got lots of work to do."

"Baptiste was right. Good work with the dog." Fields bent down to press a kiss to Dottie's head. "Make sure she's good with crowds. Disappointing kids is something I'll never be okay with, so a dog that's scared of kids is going to be a problem."

Reyna nodded, even as she wondered how she'd find kids to test Dottie's response before her upcoming appearance at the big Back to School Blowout the city had thrown for as long as Reyna could remember. All the city services had booths there, along with entertainment, food and lots of fun for kids. Police, fire, EMT... They all collected donations that supported a variety of programs. The fire department had always collected to fund academy scholarships for kids who wanted to become first responders.

"You get the dog. I get the dunking booth." Pulaski sighed. "That's fair."

Reyna almost tripped over Dottie as she turned to study Pulaski. Was he being nice?

"I'm a better swimmer than you are," he added before his lips curved in what might be a smile.

Reyna snorted. "Don't dare me, Pulaski. I know where there's a pool open for a race right now." She stopped as he bent to talk to Dottie.

"What a pretty girl," he murmured before rolling his eyes. "She can't hear me. I guess I *don't* know how to handle dogs. Never had one growing up."

"I didn't, either." Reyna shook her head. "Whatever she can and can't hear, she can definitely see your face. So I think she gets what you mean. She's pretty smart." When Dottie glanced up at her, Reyna gave her a piece of cheese.

"What is that?" Pulaski pointed at the bag of treats.

"The key to success." Reyna grinned and

slipped the bag back in her pocket. "Be nice to me and I'll share it." Her phone vibrated to indicate she had a text, so Reyna pulled it out of the other pocket, relieved she'd remembered to put it on silent before the meeting. If she hadn't and someone had texted ten minutes earlier, she might be the one sitting in the dunking booth.

Are you coming into the office after your meeting? The text was from Brisa.

Reyna typed, Headed in now. Gotta stop to change clothes. Be there in fifteen.

Her sister's thumbs-up emoji was a quick response.

Pulaski held the door open for her and Dottie. "I'm pretty glad to be in the dunking booth. Kids are a lot."

Reyna wrinkled her nose. "You think?" She should reevaluate her gloating. Kids were a lot, but wouldn't their parents keep them in line?

"Hope you can find some to practice on." Pulaski trotted off toward his truck.

Reyna opened the passenger-side SUV door for Dottie, who jumped in as if she'd been born doing it.

The need to test Dottie's response to a large group of kids was becoming clearer.

Where was she going to find kids to practice with?

As she slid behind the wheel, Reyna realized the easiest answer to her new problem was Sean Wakefield. Whether he knew kids or not, she had faith he could help her find a solution.

What did it mean that he popped into her head the second she needed help?

She'd tackled bigger missions than this with all eyes on her, no safety net in place. Now that she'd relied on him one time, it was tempting to make him her go-to for everything.

But that wasn't right. He hadn't signed up for that.

Reyna glanced over at Dottie, who had pressed her nose to the air vent in a not-so-subtle hint that she'd like some air-conditioning.

"Smart girl." Reyna touched Dottie gently on the back—she'd been reminding herself to do so ever since she'd startled the dog by touching her face without warning the first day they were together. Then she scratched the dog's ears and started the SUV.

Back at Concord Court, she made a wardrobe change, spending entirely too long staring into her closet at options other than the approved Concord Court polo, before heading into the office.

"You have a dog. You actually have a dog?" Brisa said as Reyna walked in. "Sean told me things had changed over the weekend, but I said there was no way my sister would make such a drastic decision without letting me know." Brisa knelt slowly, her hand held out for Dottie to sniff.

"You told me to go out and get my job." Reyna pointed at the dog. "This is how I did it."

Brisa spared her a second's long stare before returning her gaze to Dottie. "He also tells me there's been a change in our position on his service dog program."

Sean had stepped out of his office. He grimaced. "Sorry, boss. I should have let you do some of the talking, but…" He shrugged. "I'm glad to get started."

Her instinct to smile and tell him she understood was weird. Reyna had always been known for her reserve.

Sean Wakefield entered the room and she was half a second from grinning.

When she noticed Brisa watching them carefully, Reyna cleared her throat. "No, it's fine. I'm glad you two talked. Brisa is ready to get started, too."

Brisa nodded enthusiastically. "Yes, in fact, I got a call this morning from someone I contacted last week." She held up her hand. "I don't want to listen to any complaints about how I should have waited until you gave me the okay. The deadline was so close for this grant money that I had to go for it. Do you know Julius Stewart?"

"The dog food king?" Reyna asked. "Never met him." Stewart Foods operated in lots of different areas, but one big line of the business was pet food and treats. Every list of donors for Miami's philanthropy featured Julius Stewart's name near the top, but somehow, he was outside of the usual Montero circle.

Brisa chuckled. "I didn't mean *know* know. He's not a member of the Cutler Bay Club, so he's not part of Dad's crowd. I was afraid to approach any of the usuals for donations because it would have gone straight back to Dad." Brisa was packing a leather bag as she talked.

Reyna exchanged a look with Sean—she was impressed. Brisa was thinking ahead. She was steps in front of even Reyna.

"But you've heard of him," Brisa said. "His offices are here in Miami and he's got a grant for organizations that work with rescues. The deadline was last Friday, but I called him to beg for an extension, and mentioned my military hero sister who was running this program for vets." Brisa stood and made the "so you get where I'm going with this" motion. "He was out of the office, but this morning he returned my call personally and told me he'd love to find out more, but we'd have to go today. He's headed out of town for some business meetings or something."

"How did you manage to get directly to the head of a huge corporation?" Reyna asked. "Not to mention talk your way into a one-on-one meeting and an extension?"

Her sister was amazing.

The flash in Brisa's eyes was a clue she

was also annoyed. "We don't have time to go into how I do what I do, Rey."

Reyna nodded. "You need me to cover the office. I'm here. Go. Both of you should go."

Brisa sighed. "This is where the fundraising kicks in, Reyna. He wants to meet you. His grandson is Navy and he's very proud of him. It's your service that opened this door."

Reyna glanced at Sean. Was he ready to make a pitch like this? He understood her concern, because he shook his head. He wasn't sure.

Brisa was watching them again. Had they developed the ability to communicate without words somehow? "We're going. We're taking Sean's slideshow. Sean will cover the office." She nodded while she waited for them to get on board. "And we have to go…" She stared hard at the large clock that had appeared in the lobby without Reyna's input. Brisa was making herself at home. "We need to go now." She slung the bag over one shoulder and stood, ready to launch into action. That was Reyna's little sister. She'd always been one to leap before looking.

"What do you think?" Reyna asked Sean.

"This is your program. One of us needs to stay, but…"

"I've got a couple of companies out quoting the landscaping. I need to wait on them anyway."

Reyna frowned. "We're going to use Marcus Bryant's company, as we've been doing." He was a Concord Court vet who was about to launch his own landscape design business. Reyna had done her best to support his goals by being a sounding board, even when she couldn't help with much else.

Sean stared at Brisa, who cleared her throat. "Well, about that…"

Reyna scowled at her sister. "We're going to support our vets, Brisa."

"I wanted a comparison. We need to know how much it's costing us to go with Bryant's company versus the competition." She crossed her arms over her chest. She wasn't going to back down. "Let's get this grant. We can argue about who makes what decisions later," Brisa said softly.

"Fine. I'll drive." Reyna waited for her sister to leave, then turned back to Sean. "We're sticking with Marcus, but thank you for getting the quotes." She pointed at

Dottie. "Can I leave her with you? I've almost run out of fine leather shoes for her to chew at my place."

He smiled. "You bet." He held out his hand and Reyna plopped the bag of treats in it. "Good job, boss."

Reyna fought that weird compulsion to grin again. "You're sure you're okay with this?"

He nodded. "I wanted to do this through Concord Court so I'd have this help. Your sister's doing her part. I'll handle the dogs. You guys get the money." His hand brushed hers as he took Dottie's leash. "Go out and conquer."

Reyna straightened her shoulders. "I have my job because of you, Sean. Dottie did well this morning, and we're going to make this program a success."

"You have your jobs—" he hit the *s* hard "—because of you. I'm happy to help however I can. It's never a hardship to hang out with a beautiful lady." He scratched Dottie's ears, and Reyna ignored the deflation that hit when she realized he'd been talking about the dog, not her.

That was fine. Sean worked for her.

"Okay. On that note…" Reyna picked up the binder that Sean pointed at on the desk. In Brisa's hurry to make an exit, she'd left it behind. "I need to give Dottie some practice around kids. She's going to be manning…" Reyna paused. Could a dog "man" anything? "She's going to be starring in a photo booth. Chief expects lots of kids. Got any ideas?"

"One or two. Let's talk when you get back."

Relieved, Reyna nodded. Of course he'd help her. That was who he was. The knight in shining armor she'd always been certain she didn't need.

Reyna clutched the binder. "We'll be back with a check."

She glanced back at Sean and Dottie before she left. It was an adorable picture, the handsome guy and the playful dog.

"Hey, Reyna?" he said. At the sound of her name on his lips, Reyna froze.

"I meant you. You're the beautiful lady." He tipped his head to the side. "Although Dottie is stunning, too."

Even if she'd been able to think of a response, speaking would have been impossible. Her mouth dried up instantly and the best she could manage was a feeble wave. She tripped over the threshold on her way out of the office.

The grin that quivered along the edges of her lips broke through as she slid into her car.

"Took you long enough," Brisa muttered as she accepted the binder.

"Where am I going?" Reyna asked as she backed out of the spot.

"Downtown." Brisa studied her face carefully. "Are you grinning?"

Reyna shook her head. "Nope."

"Lies," Brisa muttered. "Between sisters."

"Getting the quotes was good initiative. We can decide what to do next with the information," Reyna said.

Brisa tipped her chin up to acknowledge that.

"And this grant opportunity? You're the only person I know who could have talked us into a personal meeting past the deadline. You're also the key to getting the money. I appreciate that." Reyna had to get it all out, right here.

Brisa's shoulders relaxed.

"You're doing a good job." She ignored the shock on her little sister's face. "Let's go downtown, into this big shiny building and get the win." She held out a fist for her sister to bump.

Brisa stared at her fist. "Other sisters might hug."

Reyna disagreed and acknowledged Brisa's tentative fist bump.

They were quiet on the drive and on the elevator ride up to the eighteenth floor. Marble tile and rich wood led into a lobby for Stewart Foods. Along the walls were framed photos, each one a person with a flag in the background.

A short man with a shock of salt-and-pepper curls straightened up from leaning against the receptionist's desk. "Like our wall of honor? Those are all Stewart Foods employees who have served in the military." Then he held out his hand. "You must be the Montero sisters." He pointed at Brisa. "If you ever need a sales job, please call me first. And, Reyna, it's a pleasure to meet you." He held out his hand. "Let's talk about how much money you need to get this service dog training program up and running."

As she traded an "is it going to be this easy?" look with Brisa, Reyna had to smile.

No matter how this worked out, whether she and Dottie navigated her probationary period at Sawgrass successfully or her father managed to strong-arm them all into doing exactly what he would prefer, Reyna was glad to have her little sister back. Together, they were going to accomplish big things.

CHAPTER THIRTEEN

SEAN SHOVED HIS feet into his shoes and tried to explain to his sleepy brain that he would be glad he'd gone running before the break of dawn—especially when noon rolled around and the streets were melting.

"Besides that, Mira knows where I live," he muttered as he pulled his door open. He wasn't sure why he was surprised to find Reyna sitting on her steps. The way she'd startled every time he walked through the lobby for the first months they worked together made more sense now.

For him, the shock of finding someone he couldn't stop thinking about appearing when he least expected it was taking some adjustment. He tried to convince himself it was all about Dottie, but himself wasn't buying it.

The day before, they'd danced again, this time with Brisa spinning in circles right beside them. Julius Stewart was going to be the first person to provide financial support to Shelter to Service.

And it wasn't through a grant provided by the Stewart Foods Foundation.

No, the Monteros had made a personal plea that convinced Julius Stewart to fully fund the first year's shoestring budget. He'd also given them an open door to come talk about future improvements.

Sean still hadn't come to terms with the fact that today was the day—the day everything started, the day that the program he'd been dreaming of would become a reality.

Celebrating that with Reyna had been sweet. It was easy to imagine other days when they'd dance to mark her successes.

Zero to sixty in one day. Brisa and Reyna shared that quality. Keeping up would be the challenge.

So finding Reyna before he'd expected to...

Sean slowly stepped outside and closed his door, schooling his face to pretend he was nothing but calm.

"Morning," Reyna said over her shoulder before pointing at Dottie. "She's better than a rooster as far as knowing when the sun is coming up."

Sean stepped down beside her and looked up at the pink sky. "Is she?" He made a show of turning one direction and the other. "No sun that I see." He bent to talk to Dottie, who paused in her exploration to say hello.

Reyna's quiet laugh was a solid reward. He tried to come up with something else funny but couldn't.

"When do babies start sleeping through the night, and am I close?" Reyna stretched back. Seeing her like this—rumpled from sleep, her hair out of control like it never was when Reyna was alert—reminded him he was coming to know her better than anyone else might.

"She needs more exercise during the day. Teaching her to kennel is a good idea, since you aren't sure about the situation at the firehouse, especially when there's a call, but finding her a place to run should be on your list."

Reyna nodded. She pointed to the grassy area lining the parking lot at the back of the complex. "Do you think that would make a good dog park? No trees yet, but we could plant some and build a gazebo or something." Amazed, Sean turned back to her. She must have noticed the silence. "What?"

"You've come a long way," Sean said. "A dog park? From 'no dogs is the policy' to a dog park?" He stopped. "Are you changing your mind about the firefighting? This sounds like a long-term planning suggestion, one management might make."

Reyna straightened. "It was mainly a 'this would make my life easier' suggestion, but I guess you're right. The current management would not be receptive to that." She tapped her chest. "And who knows what will happen next?"

Her shoulders slumped and Dottie immediately trotted over, her ears and eyes alert. Reyna smiled as she scratched the dog. "Do you have a temporary solution for my problem?"

When she glanced up at him, Sean had to lock his knees. Admiring competent, in-control Reyna was simple. It was impossible not to respect a woman who'd accomplished what she had.

But this vulnerable, beautiful woman whose request for help made him feel like a world conqueror himself? That was addicting.

"I do. Heartfield Park." Sean rubbed the ache in his chest and had to turn away for a minute. "In fact, that could be the answer to several of your questions." He held out his hands to tick off the points. "Dottie needs some exposure to kids. There's a great playground next to the dog beach. If we went this weekend, the place would be crawling with kids." He held out a second finger. "The dog beach has an off-leash area where you can let Dottie run and practice making sure she knows when to return."

Reyna smiled. "I like it. Is it anywhere near Punto Verde?"

Sean propped his hands on his hips. "The nursing home where Charlie is? Not really." He frowned as he studied her face. "But it's not too far out of the way. Why?"

She stood slowly. "You know how you have the nightmare about the fire?"

Sean nodded.

"My nightmares are different." She stared up at the pink sky. "People that I've failed show up. It's nothing dramatic, and sometimes I don't know their names. That rescue mission that turned into recovering bodies? I can sometimes see their faces, but it's like they're in photographs in this huge house I'm trying to escape. I don't know what I'm running from, just that I've got to get out." She cocked one eyebrow. "Symbolism, am I right?"

Sean understood the impulse to shrug it all off with a joke.

He also knew the pain that lived underneath that. He squeezed her shoulder and was reminded all over again how small she was to be bearing such a heavy responsibility. Almost like the world was hers to save.

"Anyway, Charlie was in the living room of that house last night. I recognized his couch." She snorted. "He didn't speak, but the couch was blocking the doorway. I tried climbing over the couch, but I woke up before I found out if that worked. Dottie the rooster had to go outside."

Sean fought the urge to pull Reyna closer. He knew the bounds of their relationship, but…

"I hate dumping my problems on you. Why am I doing it?" She looked up at him. "Something you did opened this door between us and I can't make myself close it." She closed her eyes. "And I'm your boss. It's awful, but I'm half a second from leaning on your shoulder." She put both hands on her forehead. "Go. Go for your run. Please."

Sean took one of her hands. "I want you to lean on my shoulder. Will you?" They could figure out the rest later, when the sun was up and they had business to do. Here, he wanted her in his arms.

She was shaking her head even as she stepped closer, wrapped her arms around his waist and pressed her cheek against his shoulder. "What am I doing?"

Sean ran his hands over her back. "Being human, I think."

They stood that way for a happy minute. "We'll go see Charlie. I take my dogs over there to practice around walkers and wheelchairs. It's good practice for Dottie, too." And he wanted Reyna to be the kind of person who checked on people like Charlie. A lot of the people at Punto Verde had no family close by, so they depended on good people to visit.

She sighed. "Good. Maybe he'll move his couch away from the front door."

They both chuckled. It was good to laugh

at the nightmares that visited. They had less power that way.

"If I don't go now, Mira will come looking for me. The runs when Mira is forced to come looking for me are awful." Sean pressed his nose into Reyna's shoulder. That rose scent that always brought the flash of memory of her necklace filled his head.

"Go." Reyna straightened. He hated the way the warmth of her body against his evaporated. It was the best kind of heat, this connection to Reyna.

"Would you like to go with us? Dottie might enjoy a jog." He looked down at the dog stretched out on the cool grass. If he was right, she'd gone back to sleep. That was the thing about dogs. They might get up at dawn but they recovered with eight or nine two-hour naps during the day.

"No. I would not. I'll build the dog park myself to keep from running anywhere but an air-conditioned treadmill." Reyna smiled up at him. "I'm fussy that way."

Fussy but cute.

"And smart. That's definitely the way to go, but Mira..." He shook his head slowly.

"Would you like for me to train Dottie to jog? I could take her this morning."

Reyna gasped and clapped both hands over her heart. "You're kidding. That's above and beyond the call of friendship." She bent closer. "I would pay you a jillion dollars."

"A jillion? How many zeroes is that?" Sean asked as he grinned at her. He made jokes. That was what he did. When she did it? His heart sped up and the weird, uncontrollable smile broke out.

Was that a bad sign? Or a sign that he had it bad?

"I don't know. I'll start writing zeroes and you tell me when to stop." Reyna clasped her hands under her chin.

"It'll definitely shorten my runs for a bit, so I am totally in." He took Dottie's leash. "Now that you and Brisa have gotten us some funding, we're headed to the shelter to meet with them about the dogs. Are you ready to kick this plan into gear?"

"I am. I understand the stakes so much better now. Thank you for that."

Sean tried not to show his pleasure. "You're welcome?"

She shook her head. "My modest hero."

That made it impossible to look at her. He would have kissed her. He would have. The urge was there.

Instead he made the "watch me" sign for Dottie and turned to go. "I'll bring her into the office when we get back." He didn't wait to see what she would say. She was too close; they were too close. He needed to leave.

A SLOW RUN with a clumsy dog would do a lot to set a man's mind straight. By the time Sean got back to Concord Court, he'd managed to shake off the sense of impending doom and the ache that came along with talking to Reyna one-on-one. That morning, it had been like staring something big and forever in the face. He'd blinked. He'd run.

Now? He was going to act as if nothing had changed. It hadn't. She was still his boss. She was still a Montero. And he was still happy exactly where he was.

Reyna bent to pet Dottie. "My girl. I did miss you, although I do not miss cleaning up bits of chewed toilet paper off the carpet." As she smiled at Sean, the balance shifted again. Just like that. He still needed space.

"Are you ready to go?" he asked Brisa.

She looked up from the laptop she'd commandeered since her arrival. He'd only used it while he was out on the grounds, so it was fine, but he wondered how often Brisa did that, saw something and claimed it.

"Almost. I wanted to do a graph with an estimate of four training sessions a year and how long our current funding would last. It might be enough to convince the shelter to give us a lower adoption fee."

Reyna's eyebrows rose. "You understand that's a charitable organization, don't you? They run on donations and adoption fees."

Brisa batted her eyelashes at her sister. "You understand we're a charitable organization, too, don't you? The better I negotiate, the less time you have to spend begging for money." Then she dismissed them to return to the screen.

Sean and Reyna exchanged a look. "It's hard to argue with her sometimes," he said.

"Cutthroat business acumen can be that way." Reyna shrugged a shoulder. "I used to think neither one of us was much like our father but…" She pointed with her chin at her sister.

"I heard that." Brisa stood and took the

papers off the printer. "I'd take it as a compliment, but I'm not sure you meant it that way." She frowned. "On second thought, I'm pretty sure you didn't."

Reyna cleared her throat. "I totally did."

Brisa wasn't buying it, but she also didn't seem to care, because now she was focused on Sean. "I'll coach you in the car, Sean. You let Mira, Peter and Marcus know their dogs are coming, didn't you? Four dogs. Don't tell the shelter we haven't built our waiting list. The money came in earlier than I expected, but we still have a good window to make up that time." She headed for the door.

He shared another look with Reyna and trotted to open the door for Brisa. "Yes, ma'am. How high, ma'am?"

Brisa's eyes narrowed. "Is that military humor? You know I don't get that."

Sean and Reyna shared grins and then he was sliding behind the wheel of the truck. "Mira, Peter and Marcus are meeting me at the shelter tonight before it closes, as long as they have enough dogs to meet the requirements."

Brisa frowned, a small wrinkle between her brows. "You didn't check on that?"

"I like to do my own evaluations." Jane, the woman who ran the shelter, knew what he wanted, but there was nothing like a one-on-one session.

"Let me handle the money conversation." Brisa flipped through her papers. "You have a relationship already with Jane Little, but she won't know me. I should be able to get some help with the fees." Brisa held up a hand before he could argue. "We're going to get so much publicity for this, I promise you. The only way to get your program off the ground is to draw plenty of attention to what we're doing. When we mention the shelter, we will plant the suggestion in other minds to go and find dogs there. That's an exchange. They can help us with the fees up front," she said, then buried her head back in the paperwork.

It wasn't long before Sean braked to a stop in front of the old gas station that had been turned into a dog shelter. The large glass windows that had made up the convenience store area now housed the lobby, and he could see three women waiting on him.

The garage area had been converted to air-conditioned dog runs, and a fenced area behind was the exercise yard. There were no cars parked in front. Brisa had a point. Publicity might increase traffic to the shelter.

And if she had her way, there would be plenty of publicity.

Brisa's phone dinged before she could slide out of the truck. She huffed and waved her phone. "The timing is too much. On top of my sister telling me that she could see my father in me, which she did *not* intend as a compliment, here he is on my phone to remind us both about the cocktail party he's hosting. We'll show off our perfect family, charm his clients and friends. Our presence is required but we can keep our opinions to ourselves." She scowled back at her phone.

Sean was tempted to ask questions, but he knew it would not go well.

"I warned Reyna she needed to find a date, but she doesn't take my advice seriously, either. These things pop up and he will pair her with some junior bond trader who has more hair than good ideas and she will be miserable, but did she listen to me? No. She thinks she can say, 'I don't need a date,' and Luis Montero will take the loss and give up." Brisa shot Sean a look. "He will not give up."

Sean was pretty sure she was right about that. "It's not too late to find her a date," he said. It was easy to picture himself in a suit and tie, even if he was always ready to ditch a suitcoat about five minutes after he put it on. He'd be happy to stand between Reyna and the rich guy with all the hair.

Brisa shook her head. "I can't think of anyone I can set her up with. My guy? He's rich, a pro football player who needs a little cover to keep his fans under control. We each have dates when we need to breathe at whatever events we're required to attend, and he can't be bullied by Luis Montero. That's who we need, someone above Luis Montero's reach."

Okay. Strike him from the list.

Brisa pulled out a mirror to check her lipstick. "I've been looking through the dating apps, but she refuses to play along with me, so what am I supposed to do, choose someone for her?" Brisa snapped and shook her head as she shoved open the door. "How well would that go over? She'd definitely tell me I was acting like Dad then. And what man am I going to find on a dating site who is good enough for the decorated Air Force vet whose one desire is to become a fire-fighter, of all things. It's like finding a date for Mother Teresa or something. Nobody is good enough."

Yeah, she'd named what he'd been experiencing all along.

Why didn't it feel better to have someone confirm his opinion? Reyna Montero had served her country with distinction. She was intelligent, tough, compassionate and brave.

He trained dogs. That was his heroic effort. Reyna might need his help now, but Brisa was right. She'd be happier with someone else, someone who didn't depend on Luis Montero for a paycheck.

Fatigue settled hard on Sean's shoulders, making each step an effort.

Sean followed Brisa slowly to the door and watched her inhale and exhale. Her eyes were doing that snapping thing. He'd seen Reyna's dark eyes do the same. When they were irritated, you could almost see the fire burning there.

"You okay to do this?" he asked.

"Of course. I do the money part. You can do the rest." Brisa pasted on a smile and gave a curt nod to him when he opened the door for her. "Let's do this," she said.

Sean needed a minute. Separately the Montero women were awesome, the kind of women who inspired people to follow them. Together they were too much, especially when they were arguing. But back-to-back like this? He didn't have the conditioning to stand up to the stress.

Right now, his mission was simple enough. Find four dogs who could be trained to serve as support to veterans. Brisa would handle everything else.

If imagining some other guy—a more suitable guy who could stand up to Montero scrutiny—with Reyna Montero had knocked some of his wind out, then that was too bad.

This program was his. He'd figure out some way to put a stop to this odd addiction to Reyna later.

CHAPTER FOURTEEN

REYNA WAS DETERMINED not to let the distance she was feeling between her and Sean bring a cloud to the day. They'd made it to their first stop in complete silence. This field trip to visit Charlie and introduce Dottie to children was going to be painful if the awkward silence lasted.

"I'm sorry the shelter didn't have enough dogs for the first class of training," Reyna said as they walked up the sidewalk at the Punto Verde facility. "Have you heard anything from Jane?"

He shot her a look before shaking his head. Had he forgotten she was following him or...? Why did he seem surprised to find her there?

"No, but this is going to work out fine. I can concentrate on helping Marcus, Mira and Peter with their training." He cleared his throat. "We have three vets lined up for the dogs once the training is complete, and Brisa says this is a large enough group to prove the merit of the program while we iron out the process."

Brisa says. Reyna wasn't used to her little sister giving the final approval on anything, but it was working. The whole experiment was succeeding beyond every fear she'd had. Whatever low bar Reyna had set for her sister, Brisa had soared over it.

That said so much about her expectations. Reyna realized she'd taken too much of her father's opinion to heart. Instead of trusting the judgment of someone she'd never been able to please, she should have known better.

"How was your first week at Sawgrass Station?" Sean asked. Sean's expression was one of interest. He wanted to know.

She didn't have to wonder why the gap between them had gnawed at her. This was it, the thing that she'd learned to love in a heartbeat: his attention. Sean gave his attention easily.

Being the focus of that was too sweet.

"Oh, you know how it is, lots of chores, so that we can 'learn the ropes,'" Reyna said, "but I got to drive a fire engine." She wrinkled her nose. "That was almost as fun as flying."

"With the siren and everything?" Sean's eyes danced. He was teasing but she knew he'd jump at the chance to go for a ride anytime.

"And everything." Reyna loved the way his eyes warmed when they joked like this.

"Nervous?" Sean asked and pointed at Reyna's grip on the leash.

She was. Charlie hadn't argued much when she'd explained why he had to go, but anger sometimes grew once you'd had a chance to think things through.

"Dottie will do great." Sean opened the door and led the way to the front desk. "This is Monique. She runs the place."

Reyna shook the nurse's hand as Monique playfully swatted at Sean. They had a thing, a routine. Did he have one with every woman except her? Brisa had a nickname. Monique had a routine. Was Sean's help for Reyna their particular thing?

That was depressing. She didn't like needing help. She wouldn't mind a cute nickname, as long as Sean was the one using it.

"Sign in and then introduce me to this

speckled beauty," Monique said as she came around the desk. "Mama was a Dalmatian but Daddy was something else, am I right?"

"This is Dottie. She's going to be a fire-house dog." Sean touched Dottie and gave her a thumbs-up. That was their new signal to tell her it was okay to be a dog. Dottie immediately stood and pressed her nose into Monique's hand. The nurse nodded and then stared expectantly at Reyna.

Eventually Sean noticed. "Oh. Reyna Montero. She's my..." He paused. Was he trying to figure out an alternative to boss?

"Nice to meet you, Monique. I was hoping to see Charlie Fox, too, while I'm here. Is he around?" Reyna did her best to ignore the heat in her cheeks. His boss. How hard was that to say?

Monique pursed her lips as if she was going to agree to let Sean's open statement ride, but she was not going to let that happen without telling them both she'd caught the awkward pause. "Charlie Fox," she repeated. "You are not going to believe the change to your friend, Sean." She pointed toward what looked like a common area. "When he got here, the man would not leave his room. I expected to have to call in reinforcements for the first fire drill because he was so committed to keeping to himself." She motioned with her head. "Then you introduced him to Dan and *things changed*." Her emphasis on the last two words was cute.

"How?" Sean drawled.

"I don't have much faith in soul mates or love at first sight or whatever you want to call this, but those fellas…" She whistled. "They spend every day together now. I kid you not. And the stories never stop flowing. It's like when you meet your best friend in kindergarten and you're certain you can't live without 'em. You go everywhere hand in hand."

Sean propped his hands on his hips and considered Monique before he turned to meet Reyna's eyes. "Good? I mean, we want him to be happy here."

"He honestly tells the best stories," Reyna said. "I don't think most of them are true, but he's so charming it doesn't matter in the end." She was relieved when Monique nodded.

"Yes, ma'am. He's one of those people that you go out of your way to help because he's pure joy to be around, and I will tell you that in his early days here, I did not feel that. At. All." Monique bent closer to murmur, "Fella was cranky, let me tell you."

Reyna tangled her fingers in Dottie's leash. Here was another spot where Sean had saved the day.

He'd never see it that way, but if she'd been the one forcing Charlie out, it would have been hard and yet Sean had come in and changed Charlie's world effortlessly. How did he always know the right thing or the right person or the right word?

"The gents are holding court out in the gazebo. Charlie prefers the shaded seats there to the noisy common room. He can't stand to listen to the news." Monique gestured at the French doors. "Step outside and then follow the noise. You can hear them all over the grounds on a good day." She tapped her desk. "Don't forget to get Miss Dottie a treat on the way out."

Reyna followed Sean to the doors but stopped when he paused. "All three of the guys Charlie's hanging with have dementia of some sort, but it doesn't matter. They're fun."

Reyna could see he was concerned that she might upset their fun. "Don't worry. I can follow your lead." When he hesitated again, she wondered if he doubted that.

Why would he doubt that? He was the expert here. She could let him lead.

Reyna made the "watch me" signal to Dottie and was relieved at how easily the dog stepped into her rhythm. They were side by side as they walked the shaded path through palms and the twisted branches of banyan trees to a large gazebo. As soon as the gents saw Sean, one of them shouted, "I knew it was going to be a good day. Sean is here and he's brought us a new dog." The dapper gentleman straightened. "And a lady friend."

Reyna licked dry lips as she met Charlie Fox's stare. She pointed down. "This is Dottie. She's deaf, but she's learning to talk to people. Would you like to meet her?"

The gents all clapped their hands. The noise was startling to Reyna, but Dottie's eyes were locked on her face. Reyna gave her the thumbs-up and watched Dottie transform back into a puppy. She cleared the three steps up to the gazebo in a single bound and headed directly for the man in the seersucker suit.

"This is Dan." Sean made all the necessary introductions, then said, "And you know Charlie."

"Did not expect to see you, Queenie." Charlie pointed at Reyna. "This is the one who kicked me out of my town house."

Dan clasped her hand. "Oh, honey, thank you." His face was completely serious. "If you'd waited even one more week, I would have missed him because I'm going home, and I cannot bear to think on it."

She met Sean's stare. The minute shake of his head was enough.

"Well, I hated to do it, Mr. Dan, so I'm relieved to find it's working out." She turned to Charlie. "How have you been?"

Charlie raised his hand to show her that Dan had tangled their fingers together. "Doing pretty good, Queenie. I do appreciate the company, though. I've told all the stories I can think of about running into royals in London. You want to sit down and tell that one about line dancing in the bar in South Korea?"

Everyone immediately turned her direction. "I could, or…" She grinned over at Sean. "I could tell you the one about how

I learned how to do the hustle in Coconut Grove."

Dan clapped. "Both. I want both and I want them now."

Reyna sat down on the floor of the gazebo and did her best to embellish both stories with as many flourishes as she thought she could reasonably get away with. Some of the worry that had sat on her shoulders since her father had told her she'd have to send Charlie away evaporated. Dottie worked the crowd and made sure every person in the gazebo had a chance to admire her beauty.

And Sean sat next to Reyna, his back against one of the posts, and he listened. He didn't interrupt or protest any of her embellishments. Since he was the funny one, he could have told Mimi's birthday party story better, but he let her continue.

Eventually she realized she'd been talking for almost an hour. "And that's how I learned that you can't play 'Achy Breaky Heart' too many times for a South Korean country-western bar. They say 'one more time' every time."

"Listen to me, young lady. You have to come back. I will not take any answer but yes." Dan shook his finger. "And if I'm not here, I'll have my daughter leave her address with the desk. I want to see you and this beauty again." He gave Dottie one more ruffle and checked his beautiful gold watch. "Almost lunchtime. Today is turkey clubs."

As the gents made their way slowly toward the building, Charlie stopped his wheelchair and glanced over his shoulder. "Hey, thanks for stopping by. I appreciate it. I appreciate everything." Then he dipped his chin at Reyna and rolled away to join his friends in the dining room.

"Thank you." Reyna wasn't sure how to put it all in words, but she owed Sean a lot for this visit. "For bringing me."

"We could have done that whole thing without you talking about my dancing abilities, but no." Sean shook his head, one corner of his mouth turned up in the crooked smile that she'd started to associate with him at his sweetest. Other times, he might be wicked or teasing or happy. This smile was the softer side, the one he didn't show to everyone. She'd seen it at Mimi's birthday party and every time she'd pointed out his help.

He didn't see it—that strong, solid core that made him irresistible.

A hundred different types of men could have landed at Concord Court and she'd have been fine. They'd have been great guys and good at their jobs.

Why was he exactly the wrong kind of man for her comfort?

"You could have talked over me or cut me off. Why didn't you?" Reyna grabbed his hand as he moved to leave the gazebo. "They were your friends. You could have changed the subject pretty easily."

"Why would I do that?" Sean squeezed her hand with his. "You were having such a great time." He shrugged. "My ego can take a pinch now and then." A breeze stirred the trees shading the gazebo, the quiet rustle around them covering any other noise. Here, they were alone. When he shifted away from her, Reyna moved closer.

"Are we okay?" Reyna asked. The distance she'd felt at the beginning of the day was gone, but there was still something there.

Sean brushed a hand across her cheek. Their eyes locked.

Kiss me. Reyna couldn't say it. Would he answer?

"You…" Sean tipped his head back. "We need to…" Then he shook his head.

Reyna glanced at Dottie, who was sprawled in the shade of the cool gazebo, patiently waiting for them to work out their problems.

"I like you, Reyna." Sean rumpled his hair. "I shouldn't. You can give me a list of reasons why this doesn't make any sense, this…whatever it is I feel. Anyone could. It's inconvenient. If you were smart, you'd put some space between us until it went away." He held out both arms. "When you look up at me like that, like I'm the one who is special, I can't…"

He turned on his heel and headed for the front door. Had he muttered something about a kiss as he went?

Reyna focused on the word *smart* until they were stopped in the shade at Heartfield Park. It was safer than *kiss*. No one had ever suggested she was unintelligent. It was the single thing she could always count on people to agree on.

Since Sean hadn't said another word since

the gazebo, she'd had plenty of time to think on the way. Heartfield Park was a recently updated development with a nice kids' playground on one end, the dog beach in the smallest cove and a wide public beach that spread for a couple of miles, most of it covered with people on that beautiful Saturday.

Sean's face was grim, determined when he stepped up next to her in front of the playground. She'd wanted to test Dottie around kids. This place had kids everywhere.

This should be fun.

The cold space between her and Sean was ruining the day. He didn't want to kiss her. Fine. He had always been ready to help her, though.

"Do you think this is too much for her for one day?" As the question left Reyna's mouth, Dottie spotted the kids and her tail started to rotate fast enough for liftoff. "Okay. She answered my question and she couldn't even hear it."

Sean laughed. It was a reluctant laugh, but he pointed at a water fountain. "I've got a travel bowl. We'll get her a drink and she'll be good for round two."

Reyna followed his lead. She liked following his lead. It was the *smart* decision here.

"Here you go, girl." He filled the dish and then shook his head. "Talking to them is second nature." Dottie took rude gulps of water and splashed it on Sean's jeans, but he wasn't bothered by it. Why was that patience so hot? If anything about them was nonsense, being hopelessly attracted to him because of his patience and kindness and...

Reyna rubbed her forehead. All of those things made perfect sense, even if he didn't agree.

"Don't look now, but we have an audience," Sean murmured.

Reyna turned to see a long line of kids pressed up against the fence. A tall, thin boy in the front elected himself spokesperson. "Can we pet your dog?" he shouted loudly enough to be heard in Miami Beach.

Sean pivoted. "Get permission from your parents and then make a line."

He might as well have said they'd get free ice cream. Every kid along the fence turned to run, the scatter immediate and fast.

"Wow. You get results," Reyna said, gratified when he chuckled. Whatever it was between them, this "inconvenient" thing, he still liked her. That was good.

"When you're working around kids, to protect your dog, you usually have to teach them how to approach correctly." He stared up at her before standing and clearing his throat. "Even the calmest dog can get rattled by a group of kids running up on him with their high-pitched voices. Their parents haven't always warned them not to reach out for the dog, and when the dog snaps to protect himself, you'll be the one having to settle everyone down. Best to take charge from the beginning."

Reyna could understand that. "Sort of like dealing with new recruits. Tell them how to be successful before they can mess up."

Sean frowned. "Are you trying to make a joke?"

Reyna wrinkled her nose. "I was. Someone has to because I can't stand your cold shoulder. The joke was bad, huh?"

His lips twitched. "It's nearly impossible not to kiss you. You get that, right?"

Impossible? Kissing her in the gazebo would have been easy, so very easy, but he'd had no trouble turning away. The flash of heat in her cheeks caught her off guard, but she didn't have any time to set Sean straight.

"We made a line!" The self-appointed spokeskid was front and center, one leg wiggling as if the strain of standing still for so long was getting to him.

Sean waved a hand. "All right. Come meet Dottie." He squatted down and placed his hand on the dog's back in their normal spot to signal she was working and gave her the "watch me" signal. Dottie sat strong and tall and so pretty as the kid approached.

"What's your name?" Sean asked as he squatted next to Dottie.

"Kevin," the little boy said as he held a hand under Dottie's nose. Someone had told Kevin how to meet new dogs.

"Good job. Everyone see what Kevin's doing? He's holding his hand out. He's moving slowly. His voice is low, and now Dottie can decide to say hello." Sean gave Dottie the thumbs-up and she immediately licked Kevin's hand to his elbow, sending the kid into a breakdown of giggles. It was adorable. Sean's happy grin, as he watched, was one of those things that shot all the way through her.

He was enjoying himself, and he was…

too much in that instant. She felt the sting of tears and wanted to kick herself.

The thump of Dottie's tail against Sean's shoulder didn't faze him, even though Reyna could testify to the power of the dog's joy-powered tail. She was either a large Dalmatian or a small Great Dane, so her tail was strong.

They stayed right where they were until every kid had a chance to meet Dottie. The dog was a pro through it all, and Sean? His grin never slipped.

She tried to imagine her father in such a situation and it strained her brain. The picture wouldn't form. She couldn't think of any other man who would squat next to a dog to introduce her to an endless line of kids on a Saturday afternoon.

He was the only one.

He was also the one who thought kissing was inconvenient, not smart.

Why didn't that surprise her more? Oh, yeah, a lifetime of dealing with others who assumed they knew how she felt.

If she didn't figure out how to handle this attraction, she was going to make a fool out of herself. He thought this thing between them was inconvenient, and she was starting to accept that it was like wishing on a star, never believing it would come true.

"Okay, kids, thank you for helping Miss Dottie today," Reyna said. "She's going to be at a photo booth for the Back to School Blowout next weekend. Tell your parents to come by and have your picture taken."

She decided to get her head back in the game. Sean was right. Again. At this point, he didn't need to be getting mixed up with her. There was still too much to settle, and his job would hang in the balance. Eventually she'd have to accept that Sean was always at least half a step ahead of her.

Reyna paused as she watched the kids slowly drift away, and she realized that she trusted Sean.

Whether it was all the things he did every day at Concord Court or teaching her to dance or helping her get the job she wanted by working with Dottie, she trusted him.

If he believed they were wrong as a couple, she trusted him. It was easy enough.

And if it hurt to think she might have found something better than a good friend, she'd adjust. Eventually.

CHAPTER FIFTEEN

AFTER ANOTHER SLOPPY drink of water for Dottie, Sean and Reyna had walked across to the gated area blocked off for large dogs. He was going to be perfectly professional here because this was the last thing he'd agreed to help her with. Then they could go back to work, where he would be distantly polite until Reyna told her father about her new job and the change of plans for Concord Court.

After the fallout, after he found a new job, after Reyna was settled in her new career…maybe he'd ignore everything Brisa said about the man Reyna needed and he'd open himself up to whatever happened when you put it all out on the line.

Maybe.

Until then, he'd watch Dottie.

He'd be perfectly friendly, because he

wanted the time with Reyna, but he would keep his hands and lips to himself. Easy.

"It looks like there's a snack shack over there. Want something to drink?" Reyna asked. Until she mentioned it, he'd been fine. "They have frozen lemonade."

Suddenly, he was certain he might die without frozen lemonade.

Reyna nodded. "I'll be right back." Did she mutter something about "lots of space" as she went?

She headed for the gate before he could stop her. Why did it feel like a total fail that he was letting her buy him a drink? They were coworkers, not dating. Friends, not dating.

Dottie sat at his feet. Instead of bounding away as he'd expected, she'd sniffed once or twice and then snuggled in close to his side. Every now and then, she shot worried frowns at her feet, so Sean brushed away the sand. "You don't know what to do with this stuff, do you?" He shook out the small blanket he kept in his truck for her to sit on.

"Still can't hear us." Reyna held out a cup. "But I do think she might be learning to read lips." When he took the drink, she turned aside to study the waves. It was a good demonstration of the cold shoulder.

He hated it.

"Whether she can or not, I can't break the habit of talking to dogs. I'll be the sad dog man when I'm eighty. Kids will ride by my house and find me talking to my collection of mutts as if they followed current events." Sean realized what he was doing. It was that easy. He was talking like they were friends. It was a natural rhythm they slipped into. From awkward silence to this…comfortable pattern. How many times had he wished to find something like this before?

He sipped his lemonade and immediately puckered his lips while pinching his nose against the brain freeze. Her reluctant chuckle reminded him they weren't doing this, they were friends, not lovers, but the warmth that spread across his chest suggested only his brain had gotten the memo. The rest of him was still connected to her.

He couldn't help it. Making her laugh was like a drug.

"She's not a beach dog." Reyna unhooked the leash. "Should we try walking down by the water? Let's see if she likes that better."

"Can't hurt." Sean stood and brushed the sand off his jeans. Dottie immediately snorted. She'd made her feelings clear about the sand. "And then we'll find a different dog park, one with lots of grass."

Reyna nodded and they slowly walked down toward where the waves wet the sand. Dottie perked up at the retreat of the water and followed it tentatively until the waves crashed back in. She ran away, her tail wagging wildly. She might hate sand, but she loved the new game she'd found. Sean sipped his sour lemonade and watched the dog chase the wave and then skip away before it could splash over her, and he definitely did not look down at his boss, who was dressed in shorts and a white tank top. A normal outfit a million other women could wear, nothing cute about it. Could he see her knees? Yes, but nearly everyone was equipped with a pair of knees.

"So now you aren't even looking at me." Reyna's sigh could barely be heard over the crash of the waves, but Sean felt it. "Let's call it a day. You've already done me a huge favor. Let's wrap this up so you can get on with your afternoon." She bent to attract

Dottie's attention, but the dog was busy, biting at the waves that chased her up the shore.

"She's having fun. There's no rush." Sean stepped farther away from Reyna, but she followed. If he was reading the look in her eye correctly, they were headed for a "conversation." It wouldn't be light and easy, about the weather or current events.

"Not smart. Inconvenient. You said that." Reyna shook her head wildly. "I reject that. If you aren't experiencing this connection like I am, that's okay, but you don't get to tell me a relationship with me would be silly. There is nothing about me that is silly." She pointed at him. "And you might deserve something better than what you could get with me. I can't argue that, but there are couples all over this globe who have less between them than we do. So..." She held her arms out as if she was prepared for him to take his best shot.

It took longer than he would have liked to close his gaping mouth. She was arguing for a relationship between them? He'd been doing the right thing for her.

"What about our jobs?" Sean asked. He didn't care about that, but watching her shoulders slump confirmed to him that Reyna did.

Sean was ready to make the sacrifice to help her—the least she could do was join in.

He didn't need to go any further, but he wanted to go all the way. If he could convince himself they were truly only ever going to be friends, the rest of their time working together would be easier.

"You know the charity dinner your father is hosting?" Sean asked.

Reyna stumbled to a stop. She'd been stomping along behind Dottie, or doing the best she could while being barefoot in the sand. "Yeah. What about it?"

"Who is your date for that?" If Sean could make her see what he meant, she would understand that he'd been right and could help cool this thing down. Honestly, the only way it would happen was if she pitched in. He'd been about to kiss her earlier today.

How romantic. Their first kiss could have been at a nursing home. What a story that would make for family and friends at their golden anniversary.

He was doing them favors left and right today. The least she could do was let him.

"I don't have a date." Reyna raised her eyebrows. "I don't need one. Are you afraid I'd force you to attend something like that if we…" She motioned between them. "Not that we ever could because I'm still your boss." She squeezed her eyes shut and he understood that they were on the same mixed-up ride, even if her focus was different. She worried about being his boss and his job.

His concern was bigger, like she could demand the stars but he was earthbound.

If her problems were eliminated, would Reyna finally understand she should aim higher than him?

"You won't be the boss forever. What do you want after that? What kind of guy fits your life when the question of who runs Concord Court is settled?" Sean didn't know how to fill in the blank. For some reason, he didn't think she'd consider anything short-term or just for fun. Everything about her made him think of forever.

"Okay. Sure." Reyna nodded. "Someday. What does that have to do with my father's command performance? That's one night. And that will never stop. I've been his daughter for decades. The only way we put an end to that is by moving halfway around the world."

For once in his life, he was facing off on the long-term side of this dating issue. How frustrating was it that his opponent was only concerned with next week?

"Brisa thinks you need a date or your father will set you up with someone suitable. In fact, she went on and on about what kind of guy he'll pick for you and who she thought would be better. Neither one of those types was me. I didn't even make the list of options. Wouldn't it be nice to feel this—" Sean motioned between them "—for someone your father actually approved of?"

Reyna tilted her head to the side. "In what world would that happen, Sean?" Her snort of disbelief almost made him smile.

"Fearing that I'll find what I've been looking for in my father's crowd? It's like you don't know me at all. I joined the Air Force to get away from that life of privilege and sometimes what can go with it, like being superficial or obsessed with material stuff." She touched his arm. "People like that aren't like us. That's why, although I will be forced to attend and I will make pleasant conversation in order to keep the peace with my father, I will never be one of them."

Sean studied her face. She meant every word that she said.

"When I first met you, I was pretty sure you would have said I wasn't one of your kind, either." He crossed his arms over his chest but she didn't let go. Her hand was still wrapped around his forearm and she'd moved closer. "Military washout. Collecting my paycheck by following your father's orders when you'd thumbed your nose at him. Playing at making a difference one dog at a time. That's where we are. You aren't one of them, but you aren't on my level, either."

This time, the wind gushed out of her.

"Okay, that's the biggest load of trash I've heard in a while." She yanked her hand away and propped it on her hip. "And if that's what you think, if that's what other people think about me, I…" She shook her head and took a few steps away. "I'm lost."

Sean closed his eyes. He was messing this up. "I don't mean it as an insult."

"Telling me I think I'm above everyone, even people who served their country like I did…" She jabbed a finger in his direction.

"That's not an insult? It is. You know how I know? I've been hearing something like it since I was a kid. Yes, my father has money, but I worked hard, too. And when I got the highest grade on every test, my classmates acted like I got lucky or didn't deserve it. All I ever wanted was to fit in, but they treated me the same way, like I thought I was better than they were. That doesn't come from me, Sean. If you feel that way, you look at yourself, because it's coming from you."

Dottie came to sit carefully between them, and Sean realized that they'd squared off and were honestly having a fight in public about whether they should date or not. As soon as he forced himself to relax, Reyna scanned the beach around them.

"It's almost like we're in junior high, isn't it?" She brushed the hair off her forehead. "I didn't fight with boys like this when I was fourteen, though."

His laugh was a short exhale of more tension.

"I'm sorry I got loud," Reyna added with a sheepish step forward. "I was strongly committed to what I was saying." She reached down to slide her hand over Dottie's head.

"When your shouting scares the dog, one who can't even hear the noise, you know it's time for a breather."

Sean followed as she led Dottie back up the sand. The dog paused now and then to shake her feet. She might have loved the water but sand was never going to be her favorite. Before Reyna snapped the dog's leash on, Sean held out a hand. "I might not have needed the volume, but I did need to hear what you said." He closed his eyes. "Everything you said was true. I wanted to be the military hero, but I didn't make it. That's stuck to me, like gum on the bottom of my shoe, for too long. You didn't have anything to do with making me feel inferior. All you've done since day one is come in and work as hard as you can to do the best job you could. That's who you are."

She drew a line in the sand with her foot. He wanted to hear what she had to say, so he waited.

"That's why I got loud. Some people have told me they won't like me unless I change." She held out both arms. "I can't. I'm almost forty years old, Sean. This is who I am. I get that it's not always easy to be around Reyna

Montero, but I also can't change my father or my baby sister or the money or the jobs I've had or what I'm going to do next. But that doesn't mean you have to put up with it, either. It's simple. You have to make your own choices."

Trust her to cut right through all the trash to get to the heart of the matter.

"Well, truth is…" Sean stepped closer. "I've been dying to kiss you ever since I met Dottie with part of your shoelace hanging out of her mouth."

Reyna's lips twitched. "That long, huh?"

Sean nodded. "That doesn't change any of our problems, though." He wasn't going to take anything for granted, not with Reyna. They communicated seamlessly on some things, but whatever was between them had them both rattled. "It could be so bad we'll know we're meant to be friends." But he knew there was no way their kiss would be bad.

Her lips curved as she stared up at him. "We're still on a public beach. It's the same beach we were yelling at each other on. Remember that?"

Sean teased, "I prefer 'loudly sharing our

opinions.' It wasn't yelling." He checked the crowd around them. "They've forgotten us anyway."

"For now." Reyna grinned. "This kiss should fix that." Then she took a step closer. Sean slowly wrapped his arms around her. Reyna rested on him, and he might as well have been a superhero. He lowered his head and she met him halfway, their lips soft as they found the way and then warmer as the kiss changed from the first kiss to the first kiss that mattered.

She stepped back before he was ready but tangled her fingers through his. "I... You know, I can't remember any other kiss. That one wiped every other kiss away."

He liked that. He liked it a lot.

"But..." Reyna pressed her fingers over her lips. "It doesn't change anything, does it? Have I magically resolved all your fears about being worthy? Because I've still got your job to worry about."

He groaned. How many ways could he say "forget the job"? She wouldn't let it go.

Then he reminded himself he'd been the fool who'd dug it up this time.

She snapped Dottie's leash on and opened

the gate to walk out into the parking lot. "I've got to tell my father. That's what needs to happen first. I'll tell my father I'm going to step down from leading Concord Court. Then we'll see what the fallout is. Your job will be...settled. I won't be signing your paycheck anymore. Some of the obstacles will be gone. We're having brunch the morning after the cocktail party. I'll tell him then." Reyna slid into her seat behind Dottie and closed the door.

As Sean walked back around to the driver's side, he tried to decide how he felt about the fact that, even after all the conversation and the kiss and the yelling and the *kiss*, Reyna hadn't asked him to be her date and her shield against her father at the cocktail party.

When they were in the truck, she turned to him. "What do you think about that?"

Now that he knew how wonderful it was to be her hero, he didn't want to miss an opportunity.

But he wasn't going to force her decision, not like her father tried to.

"It makes perfect sense. I hate it." He

shook his head at her offended frown. "For now, space."

Sean had his doubts that Reyna would ever resolve where he fit into her life, but she'd asked for time. He had to give it to her.

It might not happen immediately, but her father or her sister would set her up with men who fit the picture better than Sean did. Eventually the guy who deserved her would come along.

CHAPTER SIXTEEN

As the van the city was providing to transport all the workers for the Back to School Blowout in Bayfront Park slowed to a stop on Biscayne Boulevard, Reyna clutched Dottie's leash and tried to remember the first time she'd attended one of Miami's big celebrations here. Fourth of July fireworks, concerts—even Santa Claus partied in this park. It made sense.

If the rest of the world thought of Miami as South Beach, art deco and sandy beaches, Reyna could point them here to add to the picture. This park was the real heart of Miami. Greenery, palm trees and lots of space surrounded by tall glass buildings on one side and the bay on the other.

"Looks like you guys are right in the middle. Hop out here and head for the fountain." Nico, the driver, offered her a map. "Need this?" He'd been as good as a tour guide as they'd made the short trip from the parking lot where she'd left her car.

Reyna waved it off. She wanted her hands free for Dottie. "Easy enough."

He dropped it in the front seat. "You've got plenty of time to get to the booth if you get lost. Go north, toward the amphitheater, and hit a food truck before your shift. There's usually about a million choices, lotsa tacos, but my favorite is MaxCheese. Every sandwich has some sorta delicious cheese and you should try the tuna melt or…" The driver trailed off as if words failed him when he remembered the glories of MaxCheese. "Tell 'em Nico sent you."

The tiny rumble in her stomach made Reyna wonder if that was the best advice of the day or her life. A cheesy sandwich would hit the spot.

"Thanks for the ride, Nico." Reyna waved and then shoved open the van door, Dottie's leash wrapped firmly around her hand. She'd grown so attached to this dog that if anything happened to her…

Now words are failing me, Reyna thought, shaking her head. "You ready to work?" Dottie was watching her, even as Reyna realized she was doing the same thing Sean did: talking to a dog who couldn't hear her.

And the reminder that she'd kept her distance from Sean over the week hit almost as hard as the threat of losing Dottie.

She'd missed him. Dodging him in the office was easy enough because Brisa had nearly completed her takeover of the management of Concord Court. Reyna had gone to Sawgrass Station for three days and, for the remainder of the week, done her best to be in the Concord Court office when Sean wasn't. Brisa hadn't noticed.

Her little sister had gotten so wrapped up in identifying new veterans' groups who could benefit from Concord Court's programs that she'd barely come up for air.

"Food? Drink? Or work?" Reyna moved slowly down the path toward the large fountain that had always delighted her as a kid. Craft vendors had set up small tents to sell their items along the paved path, and there was a short line of families in front of one artist drawing caricatures.

Winding through the crowd took some time, so Reyna was happy she'd arrived early.

Before she made it to the fountain, off to the right, she could see a long line of people and several Miami Fire T-shirts. "Let's go this way first." She pulled out her phone to check the time. Nico had been right. She still had almost an hour before Dottie would start her two-hour shift in the working dog tent for her meet and greet.

When they made it up to the milling group of firefighters, she saw Alvarez and Jenkins, the two proctors for the city's physical aptitude test, talking with the Fields brothers. Before she could back carefully away in order to avoid being spotted, Mort Fields raised his hand. "Montero. Bring Dottie here."

Reyna pasted on her calm, definitely-not-nervous face and maneuvered through the crowd. If she'd been worried about Dottie's reaction, she was reassured, because the dog stayed close enough to brush against every step she took. They had become a team. What a great dog.

"Dropped anyone on their head lately, Montero?" Alvarez asked before Reyna had even come to a stop in front of them.

"No, ma'am," Reyna answered as she

met the other woman's stare. "And I only remove my gloves now for special occasions, so please pass that along to Marv."

Alvarez smiled and bent down on one knee to hold out her hand. "I like your new partner here."

Reyna gave Dottie the "okay" sign and watched the dog charm crusty Alvarez and Jenkins by batting her eyelashes and wagging her tail.

"Dottie ready for her first appearance?" the chief asked.

"Yes, sir." Reyna couldn't see over all the heads in the crowd. "Is this our tent?"

Mort Fields grunted. "No, but you're close. This is the dunking booth. That's why the line is so long. Firefighters line up to dunk the cops. Cops line up to dunk us. And your friend Pulaski has managed to draw an impressive crowd of both determined to send him into the water over and over and over." His crocodile grin was an expression Reyna had never seen. "We're gonna be able to issue so many scholarships to the academy this year, thanks to his exceptional personality."

A big Pulaski splash? That she had to see.

"Watch Dottie?" Reyna asked as she held out the leash. When the chief took it, she maneuvered carefully through the visitors so she could see, and there he was, Ryan Pulaski, dripping wet in the dunking booth. His eyes met hers and he raised his hand in a wave as another hit smashed the target and he landed with a splash.

If she were the kind of person to enjoy someone else's misfortune, she would have. It was so tempting, but Pulaski stood up, wiped his face and yelled, "Good one, Baptiste," before climbing back up on the seat. He met her stare again and mouthed, "Friendly fire, huh?"

Could she hit the target? Reyna slipped her hand into her pocket to see how much money she could donate to a good cause to take a shot. Then she remembered her pledge to herself to get along with her new team and Pulaski in particular. This was a good opportunity to take the high road.

Virtue and disappointment warred for victory as she turned away from the dunking crowd.

"Kid's taking it well," Mort said as she returned. "When it was his turn, Baptiste cussed like a sailor until I moved up to stand next to the tank." He frowned, his dark eyebrows a solid line. "There are kids here. Was it funny to hear Baptiste splutter and curse? Yes, but not appropriate for the day."

Reyna took Dottie's leash. "Pulaski's a tough competitor, but a good guy." She thought that was true. It seemed like a nice thing to say here. "I'm sorry I missed Baptiste's turn."

"How's training going?" Jenkins asked, his muscled arms crossed over his broad chest. Reyna was mesmerized by the muscles for a long second, so the chief answered.

"Montero here wants to be behind the wheel. Might have been born to drive a fire truck." Mort propped his hands on his hips. "That's what I heard, anyway?"

Sid Fields said, "Thinking about sending her back to the academy for defensive driving?"

Afraid she would betray her excitement, Reyna bent down to adjust the Sawgrass Station Firefighter vest that Dottie was wearing.

"Don't know. Finding someone who is good at community outreach is tough. If she's good. I guess we'll find out today or when school starts." Mort cleared his throat. "But finding someone ready to tackle driving the engines or trucks ain't always easy, either. She's a natural, so more training makes sense. Glad I found a spot for her on the team. You agree, Montero?"

Reyna cleared her throat as she stood. "Yes, sir. I wanted to join your station."

"That have much to do with being so close to Concord Court? Your daddy's grand gesture to the military men and women of America?" Alvarez drawled.

Reyna had to bite back her first response. This was close enough to the "your daddy bought your spot, didn't he?" stuff she'd dealt with that it hit an immediate button. The memory of how she'd yelled at Sean on a dog beach about the same thing flashed until she shook it off.

Eventually she was going to have to learn to let that roll off her shoulders. Changing people's minds was never guaranteed, and she knew herself, knew how hard she worked and what she believed. If Alvarez or Jenkins or Pulaski assumed something different, she'd prove them wrong. Reyna wouldn't even have to change her plans or her personality. There was no reason to cling to the chip on her shoulder.

Instead of icy anger, Reyna went for truth. It had never let her down. "Partially. I want to serve there, too. The place has lots of room for vets who'd like to volunteer to help the men and women returning home who might need a boost." She met Alvarez's eyes head-on. "And Sawgrass is obviously the best station in the city. Ask the mayor." She pointed at the woman standing to one side of the dunking booth, her politician-red suit and the large group of cameras and staff following her making her easy to spot.

Alvarez tipped her chin up to acknowledge the response while Mort grinned.

"Dottie and I are going to go find our tent." She touched the dog and gave her the "watch me" sign to make moving through the crowd of families easier. When she found the tent, she was happy to see that Hometown Rescue had set up an adoption event nearby.

And Marcus Bryant, Peter Kim and Mira Peters were there with their service dogs in training.

"I didn't know you were going to be here

today," Reyna said to the woman behind the Hometown Rescue table as she very obviously did not look at Sean.

The woman immediately knelt down to talk to Dottie. "Here's my girl. I'm so proud of you."

Had she met Dottie before? Reyna wanted to check with Sean. Except she was giving him "space."

"Hi, I'm Jane. Mort Fields is my dad. I twisted his arm to make Dottie his spokesdog. It had been too long since he'd had a dog running around the station."

This time, before she could remind herself of the space thing, Reyna traded raised eyebrows with Sean. Instead of his usual smile, he was serious as he listened. The warmth she wanted to see in his eyes was missing.

"And your sister set this up for us. She's what we call 'amazing' in the business," Jane said with a bright smile. "I've tried to get in here for years, but they limit it to Animal Control, which I get, but this could be huge for us." Jane pointed at Sean's dogs. "Fingers crossed for news coverage, too. Brisa thinks she might be able to make that happen. Sean's dogs. Dottie. The adoption event. It's all happening right here and makes for a great story."

Reyna couldn't keep it up. She turned to Sean. "That's awesome progress."

"Your sister is making a difference," Sean said. Jane turned her attention to a family that had stopped to see a beagle who was very interested in their corn dogs, and Sean added, "Which you would know if you'd stepped inside the office for any longer than fifteen minutes this week." He bent to scratch Dottie. "Oh, wait. Fifteen minutes while I was in the office. You were there other times, right? On my day off. When I went to lunch. After hours."

Irritated that he was confronting her this way in a public space, Reyna snapped back, "I have another job now, remember?" Then she held both arms out. "And you wanted *space*." She hated the word.

Sean snorted. "How could I forget your new job? It's everyone's focus, right?" Then he stood slowly. "And that's fine. Good. Let me know when we can move past it."

"After I talk to my dad next week, we'll be past my issue." She bent closer to stare up into his face. "When are you going to get over yours?"

He narrowed his eyes, but she wasn't going to back down. She'd given him what he'd asked for. He was acting like the one who'd been hurt because she'd been doing her best to avoid him.

As soon as she heard the statement in her head, things became clearer, but she didn't see a solution, not while the Back to School Blowout was happening at a loud volume all around them.

"We're about to replay the yelling-on-the-dog-beach scenario and I have to get Dottie to her spot. She's a featured entertainer, you know." Reyna fiddled with the leash wrapped around her fist. "You're getting lots of interest for the service dogs and the rescues. I'm glad." Her tone wasn't warm, but the words were true. She shifted toward the tent where Dottie would report for duty, but she was reluctant to leave. Even when she was mad at him, she wanted to be close to Sean.

"Brisa's been terrific. I'm not sure how much we've collected in donations, but she's also started a list of volunteers, people interested in learning to train the animals." Sean shook his head. "From being too small to growing faster than I even understand."

His words reminded her that she still had a part to play in his program. She'd spent years following behind Brisa and her flashes of inspiration. Slowing her down had never been easy. Sean didn't have the practice, either.

"If you need her to slow down, she will." Reyna studied his face. "Or I'll make her." She held up a fist in a weak attempt at a joke.

His lips curved in the sweet smile she'd missed. "I'm terrified of the vision of the two of you in a ring."

"It would only be a problem if we were fighting each other. Against anyone else? We could take 'em." Reyna pointed. "I've got to go."

"Be a star," Sean said to Dottie, then nodded to Reyna. "Both of you."

Reyna made it through the crowd as a beefy guy in a uniform stepped up to the small table where a beautiful German shepherd posed with two twin girls. The grins on all three models were huge. "Looks like you're a hit."

The big guy turned. "Daisy is a hit. Also a pure threat in a chase with a bad guy, but when she sees kids, that goofy grin pops up. She's about to retire, but I think she's got a career as a star." He glanced down at Dottie. "Big girl you got yourself."

Reyna touched Dottie's back. "Smart girl. Pretty girl, too, thank you very much. Watch a true talent." She hadn't been a firefighter long enough to pull her weight in the grudge match between the police and fire departments, but she needed to come out strong. When the cop moved to take Daisy's leash, Reyna stepped up and noted the long line of Sawgrass Station crew making the backbone of the crowd. Pulaski had been rescued from the dunking booth and had made his way to the food trucks, obviously. He was dangling a long string of cheese in front of his mouth as he waited for Dottie.

And Reyna realized it was time to step up. This was the job. In the distance, she could see Sean being interviewed by a reporter. Her sister had shown up and she was bustling around the tents and tables, making sure everything was picture-perfect.

Her new life on one side and her old one on the other.

Then she realized it had grown quiet.

And even Dottie had tilted her head to the side as if to ask, "What are we doing here, lady?"

"Good afternoon, everyone, my name is Reyna and I'm here to introduce you to my friend Dottie." She patted the chair that Daisy had vacated and Dottie jumped up as if they'd practiced the move a hundred times.

Since they had never practiced at all, Reyna decided Dottie must have been born with the modeling gene. "She's a young Dalmatian mix." She knelt down close to a young girl in the front of the audience. "Have you ever met a deaf dog?"

The girl stuck her finger in her mouth and shook her head slowly.

"Want to? Dottie's cute, right?" Reyna asked as she met Mom's stare. When Mom nodded, so did the little girl, who followed Reyna slowly over to Dottie.

"Can you do this?" Reyna showed the little girl Dottie's "okay" sign and waited.

As soon as Dottie saw it, she pressed her

nose forward into the little girl's hands with a sharp thump of her tail, and everyone in the crowd laughed.

That made Reyna feel ten feet tall. She'd commanded groups of all sizes—men and women who gave her the respect she'd earned through service and performance.

This was different. Being a performer was never her strong suit, but Dottie was the key.

And the men and women she'd be working alongside had seen her nail it.

"Working with deaf dogs isn't that different from working with other dogs. They love treats." Reyna held out her hand and Dottie carefully accepted her bite of cheese. "Dottie loves kids. Just remember to approach her slowly. Who wants to meet her? Parents, Dottie loves having her photo taken, so please have your phones out. We'd love to see posts, too, so please tag Sawgrass Station, the finest firehouse in the Miami area."

Reyna smiled at how Mort Fields tipped up his chin. The boss was pleased.

While Dottie worked, Reyna caught glimpses of Sean and hoped his program was attracting all the support he needed.

She'd taken all his help and his hints and his experience and turned it into this win.

That didn't mean she'd forgotten who she owed it to. Or that she didn't miss having him by her side.

Reyna told herself to make it through today, her first public appearance in community outreach. Then the next hurdle was her father and settling Concord Court.

Once she'd cleared them, all that was left was Sean.

CHAPTER SEVENTEEN

ON MONDAY, SEAN carefully attached the cover to the air-conditioning unit before wiping the sweat off his forehead. "High noon. Hottest time of the hottest day in a week and you're on the roof fooling around with a frozen AC unit. This is what you delegate," Sean muttered to himself before he stood slowly and stretched his leg, the ache in his knee a reminder that kneeling should be done on an emergency basis only.

He walked over to flip the breaker to return power to the unit. The immediate hum was so satisfying.

Could he have called in a company to deal with the frozen coils? Definitely. He still would during the week, but at this point, cool air had been restored to Concord Court's gym and all it had taken was time to thaw.

And if that problem had aligned with his need to get out of the office, even better.

AC in Miami was an emergency service, but he didn't have to be the one climbing up on the roof to check the unit or kneeling until his knee reminded him it was a terrible decision.

He would have been able to handle it all from his desk by making a few phone calls.

Except Reyna and Brisa were in the office, working on budgets together. Every now and then, he'd hear an excited jumble as they talked over each other, but no one was angry.

And he'd been happy to have a reason to step outside, away from roses and Reyna's voice and the reminder that hadn't been too far from his mind ever since that kiss at the dog beach. She was giving him the space he'd asked for.

But he hated it.

Since he was beginning to hate the sensation of being broiled on the roof of the office by the sun and his own stubbornness even more, Sean walked back over to the ladder. He'd climb down and take his time returning the ladder to the storage garage on the south side of the property. He could also take his lunch. Then he'd need to do a leisurely drive around to check for...something.

He'd raised his foot to step over onto the first rung when a car turning into the property caught his attention.

It was a dark sedan with tinted windows. At this height, it was impossible to see who was in the back seat, but the front seat was pretty clear.

Sean had never met anyone who had a driver to operate his vehicle for him in order to free up time for...important stuff.

No one except Luis Montero.

It had been a while since Reyna's father had dropped in to inspect his investment. Looked like today was the day, and unless Brisa and Reyna had decided to keep it from him for some reason, Mr. Montero hadn't called ahead to warn them.

He could stay up here on the roof. Reyna wanted to handle her father all by herself. By her estimation, she was the only one who could. Here was one more opportunity.

Then Sean remembered that Dottie had been stretched out on the tiles under the desk.

Dottie, who should not be there, because

there was only one person who had gotten the okay to have a dog and it was Sean.

The guy who didn't currently have a dog.

Reyna was about to have her whole plan blown up by one sleeping Dalmatian.

Not if he could get there quickly enough.

Sean hurried down the ladder and considered making a run for the office door, but he could see Reyna's angry face, midlecture about the safety requirements for a place like Concord Court, in his mind. Anyone could walk by. What if the ladder fell and injured someone? What if, what if, what if…

Sean lowered the ladder and collapsed it before moving it out of the way. Then he wiped his hands on his jeans and hurried around the building as Luis Montero hung up a phone call. They were frozen in front of the office door.

"Mr. Montero, I didn't know you were coming by today." Sean offered his hand and realized something had changed between them when Reyna's father stared at it coldly. They'd never been friendly enough to drink beer together, but Luis Montero had always given him a hearty handshake. Sean had never wondered where he stood. Montero gave him direction, and Sean carried it out. Both of them had been happy with that arrangement.

"Wakefield. Is my daughter inside?" Montero asked.

Sean would have asked for clarification, since the man had two daughters, but when Luis came to Concord Court, he was looking for Reyna.

"Yes, sir. Last I saw her, she was working on a budget for the final quarter of the year." Sean held the door open and relaxed when cool air floated out. The gym took up one corner of the building, while the lobby and offices, mostly empty at this point, filled out the rest. The building was big enough for three different units, and when one was down, things heated up fast.

He'd fixed that. Because he was good at his job. Whatever was going on, he wasn't going to forget that, even if Luis Montero had changed his mind about Sean.

Reyna and Brisa looked up, and Sean wondered where Dottie was.

As if he'd called her name and she'd heard him, the dog slid out from under the desk and approached Sean carefully. She didn't know Luis Montero and she was smart enough to pick up on the cold vibe rolling off him.

"Daddy, I didn't know you were coming," Brisa said as she stood and straightened her Concord Court polo. She'd taken to wearing them ever since Reyna had started filling three day shifts a week at Sawgrass Station. She'd paired it with a short skirt and high-heeled sandals that would be impossible to walk in for normal people, but she hurried across the office to hug her father's neck. "We've got some exciting things to show you. If you'd given us some warning, we would have put a presentation together."

Then she stepped back and clenched her fingers together.

Sean had watched Reyna face off with her father more than once, most memorably when she'd refused to tell Sean he couldn't train his dogs anymore. The temperature dropped and the silence was heavy.

He'd never been one of the participants, but somehow he and Brisa were included that afternoon.

"A presentation," Luis repeated and did a

slow survey of the room before stopping on the dog. "Who is this?"

Sean could read the intention on Reyna's face, but he hated that this conversation was coming before she was ready, so he said, "My service dog. This is Dottie. She's a big hit at the nursing home." Sean cleared his throat as Reyna tried to cover her confusion. "Punto Verde. We go there sometimes. To practice." Stop talking. The first rule of successful lying was to stop before he dug his hole too deep. Too many details and the lie would unravel.

"What sort of programs are you developing?" Luis asked as he moved closer to the desk.

Brisa looked to her sister, but Reyna had stopped where she was. She hadn't spoken. And it was her show to run. Wasn't it?

Everyone turned toward her when she shook her head. "Why don't you tell us what you already know and we'll go from there?" She turned to Brisa. "He's doing that thing where he asks us a question to see how deep we'll dig before springing the trap. You remember when he did that when I came in after curfew?" She rolled her eyes. "Both times it happened."

Sean would have laughed. If he'd had to bet money on which one of them had broken curfew, it wouldn't have been Reyna.

"Be careful how hard you push today, Reyna." Luis Montero pulled a folded newspaper out of his briefcase and then tossed it down on the desk. "Looks to me as if you have a couple of things you need to present to me, like a whole new career." He dropped into a chair and crossed his legs smoothly, prepared to wait like a benevolent dictator for his answer.

Brisa flipped the paper open and there on the front page was a spread on Hometown Rescue. "It's the service dog program. We've expanded it." She tapped the article. "We collected almost eight hundred dollars in donations, too. In one day. On top of that, we made a list of volunteers, people who'd like to foster more dogs, and we got some incredible publicity for Concord Court. Is this what has you so angry, Daddy?"

Sean crossed his arms over his chest and studied Brisa's delivery. She'd eased down next to her father, placed one hand on his arm, and her eyes were huge.

If Reyna had given him that look, with her dark brown eyes, he would have done whatever she asked.

Reyna wasn't playing the same game. She'd settled behind her desk, a calm mask on her face as she waited for the next line in the play.

How many times had they fallen back on their roles? Brisa went for charm. Reyna was building her argument.

"Unfold the paper." Luis's voice was sharp but patient.

If Brisa and Reyna had fallen back into their patterns, their father was comfortable in his, as well.

From his spot behind the group, Sean couldn't see the newspaper, but Reyna unfolded it and read, "Reyna Montero, the new community outreach person for Sawgrass Fire Station, works with her dog, Dottie, at Saturday's Back to School Blowout." Then she held it up and showed the full-color photo to him and Brisa. There was an adorable little girl giggling while Dottie sniffed her hair and Reyna pointed at them.

He'd battled the urge to go and watch them with the crowd because he was angry and disappointed about what was happening between him and Reyna, but he'd known the two of them would be a success.

"I got the reporter out by telling them about the way dogs from Hometown Rescue were finding new jobs that brought them homes. I included Dottie after Jane mentioned her part in finding the dog a home at the fire station. Mort Fields is the key to a lot of good publicity, I found out, and I want everything I do for Concord Court to succeed, so…" Brisa slumped back against her seat.

Reyna had trusted them with her secret.

They were so close to making it to the end with Reyna in control.

Except Brisa's plans had sunk the ship, excellent and ambitious and successful as they were.

If he had to guess, this had never been what Reyna expected, but she wasn't shocked that it was turning out this way. She was calm. Brisa was worried. And Sean could almost see the years roll back to when they were little girls.

The silence in the room was heavy. Luis Montero had crossed his arms over his chest.

"So you were all working on this deception. I had wondered if Brisa was a part of the group or a bystander." He sighed. "I'm not sure which would have been better."

If the stakes had been lower, Sean might have enjoyed the way Reyna and Brisa instantly stiffened and turned to face their father, as if they had learned special choreography that kicked in when someone pulled the alarm. They were both ready to battle, but for each other, not for themselves.

"I asked for her help," Reyna said.

"And I have been thrilled to have my sister again, to be a part of Concord Court, and I'm not a bystander in this family." Brisa stood up to pace. "I don't know what it will take for you to get that."

"Sir, if I may interrupt, I'd like to tell you about how much work your daughters have done to get this program off the ground. I could not have done any of this without them," Sean said, desperate to take some of the heat off.

Luis Montero's expression darkened. "Do you think that speaks in their favor?" He snapped up to stand tall and waved Brisa out of his way. "They ignored my wishes for Concord Court's policy regarding dogs and the programs we would pursue here." When Reyna started to speak, her father held up one finger to stop her. "Not only that, they lied about it. They worked to hide it from me. Right?" He slowly turned to Sean and waited for him to nod.

Then Luis Montero stepped up to face off against Reyna, as if Sean and Brisa were bystanders in the room. "But I could have straightened all that out, as I did with the wounded vet who had no place here. It's a terrible decision, one I never expected of you, but I could have straightened it out. If you had told me your plan, I could have explained to you how much better mine is." Montero shook his head. "But what do I do with my daughter, the one I have worried about for years as she fought battles she had no business entering, who thinks that instead of leading this worthwhile charity, she'll toss it aside and put herself in danger again."

Reyna opened her mouth, but he waved his hands angrily. "No, you don't speak yet.

You are putting yourself in danger. You made it home in one piece, so what do you decide to do? Risk your neck and this family to fight fires?" He pinched his nose. "I do not understand you at all, Reyna Ysabel Montero."

Sean had been on the receiving end of some serious speeches before. His mother had been able to shovel on the guilt and Mimi had been the one to teach her all she knew, but this? It was too much.

Before he could come up with something, anything to diffuse the attention, Reyna lifted her chin and drawled, "Am I allowed to speak, Father?" Each word spoken with a chill that crept up Sean's neck.

He hoped he never made her this angry. Ever. So far, her anger had ended in yelling and laughing and kissing and arguing and talking.

This Reyna was half a step from burning it all down.

The ridiculous poem he'd spouted around the pool to Mira and Peter popped into his head. Reyna was never cold.

Until now.

"Do you have an explanation?" her father asked. His tone approached Reyna's but lacked some of the cut. He might have been her pattern for icy delivery, but she'd perfected it.

"No." Reyna shook her head. "You don't want to hear it. Do you know how I know? Because I've already tried to tell you and you ignored me. I didn't want to leave the Air Force, so you laid the perfect beautiful trap. I wanted to join the Miami Fire Department on my own timetable, but you couldn't even pretend to listen. And the way you treat Brisa? She's the one who should be running this. It's been clear from the start, from day one, that she's the daughter who got all the best parts of your business brain, but you've been fixated on me, on putting me here and making me follow your rules. You're only interested in your daughter the hero."

Reyna covered her cheeks with her hands. "Well, I'm not. I ran away from you the first chance I got. The Air Force caught me when I needed a place to land, and it became a family. I would have stayed there until they kicked me out. In the Air Force, the orders are clear. You have that in common, but in the Air Force, I made my own plans, my own life, and I was free. Instead of fitting into the Montero box, the one everyone in Miami wanted to shove me in, I could become who I dreamed of. I flew, Dad. How could you not see how hard it would be to put me in a box after that?" She frowned. "Except you never tried to understand."

Luis Montero raised his head. If Sean had to guess, something Reyna had said had been unexpected, but it was impossible to guess what it might be. He'd thought his own family had issues. But this was hard to watch. He wanted to wrap his arm around Reyna's shoulders, but the glitter in her eyes wasn't begging for comfort. She was ready to fight.

"Then why are you here?" her father asked. "You don't need me. You don't want Concord Court. You've got your job. Go."

Had he had a change of heart? Sean traded a glance with Brisa, who shook her head slowly. Whatever was coming, she didn't expect it to be positive.

Reyna didn't, either. She propped her hands on her hips and inhaled slowly. "Dad, let's talk about this. You can have everything you want. Together we'll build Con-

THE DALMATIAN DILEMMA

cord Court up. It will be a Montero family legacy as you wished. We've been doing great things. The three of us—me, Brisa and Sean—we're a solid team, and that won't change. I want to be involved here, but I need more."

It seemed so reasonable. How could her father argue?

Luis Montero studied the floor and eventually focused on Reyna. "I have done everything I could for you." He looked at Brisa. "For both of you. Whatever you asked of me, I would have given you, but you've..." He laughed but it wasn't with humor. "I hate to admit this, but you've hurt me. Lying to me. Going behind my back. Ignoring my wishes." Then he nodded. "Have your career, but you won't have Concord Court. Pick one or the other. If you don't want my gift, give it back. I know what needs to be done here. I'll find someone to do it."

"Dad, I can do both, I will do both, but you're going to have to let go." Reyna moved to block his exit. "Your gift? It's about control. That's what you don't get and I can't forget. You want to control me, to direct how Brisa and I live, but we're not going to do that, not anymore. We're adults. Treat us like adults and let's make plans together."

Sean wished he was closer to Reyna. He would have stepped up behind her, a knight ready to follow her. She was right. Everything she'd said was true, but it was also true that they had everything they needed to make this work. All Luis Montero had to do was open his eyes.

"What did I tell you, Reyna? If you can't run this place, I'll bring in a team who can. They will follow my policies. There will be no need to evict people who don't meet the requirements because they will not be admitted in the first place. There will be no damage to the walls or grounds because we will have no animals here. I know what needs to be done," Luis Montero repeated firmly. "Don't question me and don't ever forget that you made your own choices."

He shot a look at Brisa and Sean. "I won't have dishonest employees here, so as I'm acting manager, they'll go, too."

Reyna shot her sister a look. "Don't do this. Don't punish Brisa because I'm not acting the way you'd like."

Her father pointed at Reyna. "You can

change this, Reyna. Quit the other job, the one you don't need, and commit to Concord Court. There are veterans here who need you. They depend on you. You understand them."

Reyna was shocked. It was clear on her face.

Brisa, who would wear a bright smile in the face of most challenges, was solemn.

"Nothing will change the way you see me, will it, Daddy?" she asked. "No matter how many events I run for you, how many programs succeed because of my hard work… nothing changes for you. Forever and ever, I'm… What? The girl who ran away from home fifteen years ago?" Brisa closed her eyes. "We've grown, Daddy."

"You're my beautiful daughter. There isn't anything you can't accomplish under my direction, but you thwart me at every turn. You refused my career advice and became a sometimes-model. You insult my friends and anyone I introduce you to, when an advantageous connection could mean huge returns. I see the things you can do with your charm, but you go behind my back and you fight me. You have for years." Luis Montero held out both hands. "How am I to see you? Do you know what my father told me when I left Cuba? 'Stand tall.' Because that's what the Monteros do. You? You have required so many bailouts, Brisa. When have you ever proven yourself capable of standing on your own two feet? I cannot entrust this investment to you."

Reyna reached for her sister's hand and met Sean's stare. Neither one of them deserved such harsh criticism.

Sean stepped forward. "Mr. Montero, you should look at them both again. I'm happier to serve at Concord Court because of your daughters. They are both impressive."

Luis frowned at him. "Why are you still here?" There was the ice again.

Sean straightened. "I care about Concord Court and your daughters, sir." Both of them. Reyna might pretend she didn't need any defense, but he had a hard time imagining how difficult it would be to fight your own father this way. And Brisa was a friend, had been since the first day she'd breezed in to pass on her father's directions on the building materials.

"You care about your job." Luis shook his

head. "But it's not yours anymore. My next complex manager will be hiring a new operations team. I'll have them here by the end of the week. I'll pay a severance if you'll remain in place for that long." He moved toward the door.

Before her father could leave, Reyna said, "Just to be clear, if I quit the fire department, nothing else changes here. Brisa stays on as the assistant manager. Sean keeps his job."

Her father paused. "Tell me you'll stay and we can discuss the rest. Come to the party. Step up into your role, the one I've made for you, and we can negotiate everything else."

Then he was gone.

Reyna and Brisa were both silent.

That was a concern.

Brisa got past the shock first. "Well, it's nothing less than Reyna has anticipated all along, so…why are we so stunned he has done exactly what we expected?" She looked at the knot of her hands clenched against her stomach and shook her hands out. "I've tried so hard to make this work, to show him I've grown up. Why am I always disappointed?"

"Because every time it happens, we hope something has changed. But it hasn't. It won't." Reyna bent to scratch Dottie's ears, then lowered herself to sit in the middle of the tiled floor.

Brisa watched her sister and then shook her head. "I hope you aren't considering martyring yourself for Concord Court, Reyna. For once, let's not do this thing where you're all noble and I'm the wretched little sister who makes demands of everyone around her. I can't stay here and do that, not anymore."

"I don't know what you're talking about, BB." Reyna gave a weak smile. "You're always so dramatic. It's simple. I can do what I want or do what helps others."

"Except what you want also helps others because Reyna can't be torn between a good choice and a bad choice. Either way she goes, it has to be perfect. You don't change. He won't." Brisa closed her eyes. "Fine. Let me make this simple for you. I've been ignoring calls all week from a friend who would love to have me in Mexico for a catalog shoot. I'm going to take that job. Then I'll find another that is not in Miami.

You stay here and learn what I've learned. I'm the one flying away this time." When Reyna started to argue, Brisa held up her hand. "This is our chance to make the break for good. You showed me how. What have I been waiting for?" She held out both arms. "Freedom. I'm going to go for it. Don't let him push you back inside that Montero box, Rey."

Sean waited for the smile, the one Brisa used to her advantage, and Brisa didn't disappoint. "You can cover the desk for the rest of the week, right? I need to pack." She didn't hesitate, but flashed her brilliant, completely unconvincing smile and made a grand exit.

Leaving him alone with Reyna.

"I don't suppose you have some dream job you've been holding off on accepting because of how badly Concord Court needs you, do you?" Reyna asked from her spot on the floor. "A fake construction job near the beach in the Bahamas, maybe?"

He couldn't laugh, even though that was her aim.

A sad Reyna cracking jokes to make the

people around her less sad made too much sense.

He'd used the same playbook more than once.

Sean sat down next to her. "You mean other than this Shelter to Service program that was a total dream come true?" He scratched his chin. "Nah, but I can find a way to pay the bills. That's the least of my worries."

"Least, huh? Lucky you." Reyna fiddled with Dottie's ears and very obviously didn't meet his stare.

"Tell me Brisa's not right. Tell me you aren't considering giving up on the firefighting." Sean wished Luis Montero was still in the room. He'd grab the guy and force him to see what he was doing to his daughters. They'd been best friends and happily discussing budget numbers before he'd walked in. Now Brisa was going to give up Concord Court again to save her sister's plan, and Reyna was as miserable as he'd ever seen her.

That included the night she'd been convinced Dottie was going to be sick because she'd eaten bills.

"How am I supposed to give her up?" Reyna asked, her voice breaking. "Working here is fine, but Dottie…" She met his stare then, tears welling up. "I wanted what I wanted and now everyone is going to pay for it. Losing my sister and my dog…" She wiped away a tear that streaked down her cheek. "It's a mess."

Sean scooted around Dottie, who had crawled to put her head in Reyna's lap. "There's a way to fix this. Keep the job you love and the dog. Brisa is an adult. She'll figure out her next steps."

"But you've seen her. She's been so on top of it here. She was meant to take on a leadership role for this mission. It could be everything. I came home because I missed my family. I missed my baby sister." Reyna wiped away another tear. "There's no easy choice. I'll stay here. Dottie will be fine." Her voice broke again. "But not without Brisa. I'll negotiate with my father and we'll go back to how we were." She blinked and wiped a tear off Dottie's ear.

When she tried to firm her shoulders and nod bravely, Sean realized this was it, the job that would prove his right to hold on to Reyna Montero. He'd find the solution. There had to be one.

Now that he'd seen Luis Montero in action, Sean knew it would be a battle. Their father had ignored everything but his own selfish wishes, even in the face of his daughters' successes and their requests for his support. It was impossible to imagine saying no to women as extraordinary as the Montero sisters.

Determined to take his shot against Luis Montero because the prize was so great, Sean wrapped his arm around Reyna. "I think, if we put our minds to this, we can come up with a new plan that works."

Reyna squeezed her eyes shut. "Some problems don't have answers, Sean. Don't you know that?"

He pressed his forehead to hers. "No matter what you bring me, I'm going to find the answer. Have I failed you yet?"

"There's a first time for everything." She laughed at his shocked face, the exact effect he'd been going for. "What do you suggest?"

He tipped his head down. Her question was fair. He needed time and assistance to find the answer.

"Meet me at the pool tonight." He brushed away her tears. "One thing I know for sure, if there's an answer to be found, we can come up with it out there. Greatest minds I know and some cold beer, the world's most efficient think tank."

She frowned. "Are you serious?"

He sighed. "Hardly ever, but this one time, it's all I've got. Let's pull the family together and brainstorm. Meet me at the pool?"

She blinked as she considered it. "It's against policy, you know." Then she shrugged. "But neither of us works here any longer, so let's go for it."

CHAPTER EIGHTEEN

WHEN REYNA LOCKED her door, she paused with one ear pressed against it to make sure Dottie settled back down. She'd considered bringing the dog, since she'd been tearing up all afternoon every time she remembered Dottie belonged to Sawgrass Station, not her. Facing the loss of her job was one thing. She would have recovered from that eventually, because Concord Court was a good place.

But losing Dottie would leave a hole she wouldn't be able to fill. Spending every second she could with her dog was important.

But keeping things quiet while they broke the complex's pool rules was important, too. Reyna wasn't sure whether Marcus Bryant would be there or if he'd have the Lab mix he was training. The Lab and Dottie were either best friends or mortal enemies, and no one could tell the difference. Both required frenzied barks, so Dottie was going to catch up on her beauty sleep while Reyna went out to see if a miracle had happened.

Now she was worn out, dehydrated from crying, mad at her sister and her father, and desperate for Sean's easy distraction. No matter what happened, she would feel better, stronger, after some time with Sean.

Halfway out to the pool, Reyna realized how unfair it was to rely so heavily on Sean for this. He'd never volunteered to be tangled up in this mess.

This should be something she did herself. Indecision slowed her progress. She'd walk a few steps and then slow down as she considered returning to her town house. Something kept pulling her forward.

When she made it to the pool, her sister was closing the gate. Reyna paused in the shadows. She hadn't known Brisa had joined the group. But as Sean introduced her around, Reyna realized she was a special guest.

Apparently she hadn't hopped a plane to Mexico yet.

"Are you going to tell me what this is about?" Brisa asked as she hugged Marcus, Peter and Mira. Of course her sister had made friends with all of Sean's friends. She collected new admirers like seashells at the beach.

"Let me grab you a chair," Sean said. Reyna could hear quiet steps as he moved to grab one of the chairs near her hiding spot. Then he stopped and said, "Are you going to join us or spy on us all night?"

His quiet tone told her the question was for her alone, so she stepped closer to the fence. "How did you know I was here?"

Sean tapped his nose. "Roses." Then he crooked his finger. "Come inside."

Reyna followed his directions and held up a hand as everyone in the shaded corner of the dark pool area turned to watch her. Everyone shuffled quietly to make room for the chairs Sean brought over. When they were seated, Reyna realized everyone was looking at her as if they were waiting.

She turned to her sister to ask if she knew what was going on, but Brisa was staring, too.

"What? I thought this was a group effort." Reyna had been trying to come up with a way to fix this all afternoon, because she wanted to drive the fire engine every day.

And she wanted to love Dottie and go to schools and talk about fire safety and whatever the chief wanted. That was what she wanted. Giving it up hurt.

But she also wanted to share inside jokes with her sister over boring brunches and fight with her over budgets and stand next to her against Luis Montero.

And she was so tired. Reyna said, "I need help. I don't want to quit. I don't want Brisa to leave. I want what we've built the past few weeks to last." She'd never meant to say it so plainly, but the ache in her chest convinced her that it was no time to be noble or stoic or reserved.

"I want Brisa to take over the control of Concord Court. Whatever new project it is that she's working on, I want her to make it a success. I want Sean's service dog training program to grow until there's not another dog in a shelter or a vet who worries all night long because the nightmares come and there's no dog on guard to chase them away and I want Charlie Fox to be happy and the vets who come here to have everything they need. I want my dog." Reyna covered her mouth and tried to still the words that would not stop. "I want it all. I don't know how to get it."

She gulped for air and took the cold beer Peter Kim held out. He said, "Drink this. Three big swallows, please."

Reyna realized everyone was going to watch and wait for her to follow his instructions and all she wanted them to do was not focus on her, so she sipped once, twice and a third time before waving the bottle. "Okay. I'm better."

"Sean's given us the rundown of the situation with your father," Peter said as he braced his elbows on the table. "Except for the whole 'building this awesome place for us to live out of his own pocket' thing, he sounds like the worst. What would it take to get him out of the picture?"

"Like permanently?" Brisa asked, her voice a squeak. "Nobody wants that. He's our dad. We love him, even if we wish he was on another planet sometimes."

Peter frowned. "Okay. Think smaller than hit man. What I meant was, is there a way to take control of this place? If we could do that, then whatever Luis Montero said would be... Who cares? No one cares, that's who."

"Money. It would take so much money," Marcus said. "Place runs on money, man. Unless you got a rich uncle who can float us a big loan, I'm guessing Luis Montero holds the keys."

"Well, he does own the place, no matter what we do, but what if we could raise enough money on our own to keep it open?" Brisa said, looking around the table. "I had to sit through countless meetings while he explained his plans to his terrified accountants. They were convinced this place would take the whole Montero fortune, and then who would keep them in memberships to the Cutler Bay Club?"

"Hey, I'm a member there. The marina is top notch. Did you know I have a boat?" Peter asked as he leaned closer to Brisa.

Brisa shook her head.

Was he flirting with her sister? Now?

Of course he was.

"Even if I could get the commitments quickly enough to keep him from firing us," Brisa said slowly, "it wouldn't change the fact that this is about control. It's not a money question. He has a plan for the money, and even if we were to bring him a different one, it wouldn't change that we'd lied to him or that Reyna is about to ignore his demands."

Everyone around the table was silent.

"What if you told him about your plan for the veterans' small-business lab to run out of Concord Court?" Marcus asked, his voice excited as if he was certain he'd found the answer. "I mean, ol' Luis ain't dreamed that big yet. A concentrated effort to find vets who want to build their own businesses, with mentors and funding and networks of support to nearly guarantee success? That's you. You did that. I'll be your witness to that, and I'd be shocked if he can find anyone else who will step in here at Concord Court who can dream like that and back it up."

Reyna watched Brisa squirm in her seat. Since Reyna had no clue what Marcus was talking about, it seemed Brisa had been doing more work on her own.

It was such a good project that Reyna was angry she hadn't thought of it. She'd wanted to help Marcus when he was planning to buy into his landscaping business, but she didn't have the tools or the connections. Brisa did. What a huge impact her sister could make here.

"I told you I had a couple of ideas," Brisa murmured as she rolled her eyes at Marcus.

Turning her attention to Reyna, she explained, "I met Marcus that morning I first came to talk to you about working as assistant manager." She crossed her legs. "He mentioned how glad he was to have this corporate account because he was getting ready to expand his business, and he gave me a business card. I don't know if it was the heat or if coincidence started simmering in my brain, but I needed more time to develop it. Marcus has been helping me understand some of the city and state requirements, the legal issues he's had to work through by himself. If we can build this, it will be a program that changes lives and communities." Brisa lifted her chin. "I want this. So much."

"More than a modeling job in Mexico," Sean drawled. "Does that even exist, Breezy?"

Brisa groaned. "Of course it doesn't. I said it because that's what Reyna expected and it would allow her to get what she wanted.

I mean, it should be true—I am a great model—but…it doesn't change the fact that I need to get out of Miami. I don't have a job lined up yet, but I've got to make a change. We can't go back to the way we were as kids." She faced Reyna.

"You're a good model, BB. You're an even better manager, an entrepreneur at heart, and a real chip off the old block." Reyna draped her arm over her sister's shoulders. "I admire you, sis. I don't know if that idea ever would have come to me, and now that you've mentioned it, there's no way we can walk away. We have to fight and we have to win."

Everyone was quiet, and Reyna started running through different scenarios in her mind.

"She does this. Goes silent when the wheels are turning," Brisa said to the rest of the group. "I don't know if explaining to her that we could help if we could take part in the conversation would work but—"

"Okay." Reyna stood up to pace in a tight, small line.

Everyone swiveled to stare at her again.

"Here's what we know. We need to cut the financial strings to gain independence." She waited for everyone to agree and ticked the point off on one finger. "Brisa and I have been summoned to an event and that would be the perfect opportunity to ramp up the donations." She ticked off the second point. "Everyone there will be Dad's circle, the Cutler Bay Club types who understand writing checks." She waved her hand at Peter. "And there might even be some people in the crowd who understand true service to the country, as well." She ticked off that point. "What if we seized the chance to publicize Brisa's big idea there with a full range of reporters to document it? Dad won't risk the public embarrassment of shutting us down. He'll have to support the project and the new manager of Concord Court or at least keep his mouth shut until it fails." Reyna stopped pacing and stared hard at the concrete while she thought. "We go loud, we go public and we go together."

Brisa clamped her hands together as if she was prepared to cheer or clap. "I'll follow you anywhere, but I'm going to need a few more directions."

"Do you remember my Sweet Sixteen party? It was on the club's yacht." Reyna braced her hands on the back of the chair she'd been seated in, the cool, heavy metal the perfect anchor to help her think.

"Yeah, I was there. It was terrible." Brisa winced. "For me, that yacht was high school graduation and it wasn't much better, but that was mostly because you weren't there." She wrinkled her nose. "And I was making plans to run away with my boyfriend, and a voice in my head was shouting it was a bad idea. I was too silly to understand that the urge to vomit with nerves while ignoring that voice was a terrible sign."

Reyna squeezed her sister's shoulder. "I'm sorry, BB. From now on, we're in this together. What I meant about my party was that it was all for show, for Dad's friends to see how awesome he was and how beautiful his daughters were—so what if, instead of letting this cocktail party be the same, where we smile at all the right spots and stick to the script he writes, we turn it upside down." She could picture it in her head. "I'll tell Dad I'd like to make an announcement at his party, make him think it'll be all about my role at Concord Court, which will continue. He'll hope his clients eat that up. And

I sort of do that, but I turn it into an intro-duction of the new head of Concord Court." She fought the urge to jump up and down. "I'll be right there beside you, but you will address the budget needs for the new year, talk about the past year's programs and an-nounce exciting plans for this small-business development. You'll allow a few questions from the reporters you invite—you'll have to get them there without letting Dad know somehow—and we'll take some photos, with Dad, of course." Reyna clamped her hands together. This would work. She knew it would. "What do you think? Can you get reporters to show up for this?"

Brisa made an obvious show of pretend-ing to consider the notion. "For a Montero event on the rooftop of one of Miami's most luxurious hotels? Uh, yes, but let me tell you I'm not the only one with a bit of Luis Mon-tero running through her veins. You want us to take the battle to him, head-on, with an audience, trusting that his own ego will be the fatal blow. It's brilliant. It's inspired. It's diabolical and I want us to always be on the same side because I do not have the guts to go there alone, but with you and your shield, I'm in."

Reyna clapped her hands and immediately made fists when Sean shushed her. He added, "Would you keep it down? It's against the rules to be out here and my boss is a real stickler for those rules."

She'd run them out before for making much less noise, so Sean was absolutely right.

But the urge to celebrate was too strong. Instead of a war cry, she bent and pressed a hard, quick kiss to his lips. "Thanks for the reminder."

When he didn't answer, she said, "I'm going for all of it. One way or another, I am not going to be your boss here at Concord Court. We are going to come to terms with the rest of this stuff between us. I want my dog and my sister and you and I can get it."

She waited for him to answer.

He tipped his head to the side and nodded.

Which was less than she'd hoped for but good enough for the minute.

The stunned silence around the table was awkward, so Reyna made the "gimme" motion with both hands. "What else? This is a chance to brainstorm."

Mira recovered first. "If you want a grand slam, something to open checkbooks, bring in people that Concord Court is helping. We can show up, work the crowd. We could bring the dogs, if that's helpful."

Brisa straightened. "I like it, but we need to make that a surprise, too, since Dad will absolutely know something is up if he finds out ahead of time."

"Can you get us in?" Peter asked seriously, as if they were planning a heist to steal the crown jewels instead of sneaking into a cocktail party.

"Of course." Brisa waved her hand. "Security will take my word even if you aren't on the list. I'll get you in."

"Sean needs to be there, too," Mira said, "because he deserves the credit for the service animal program."

"And so much more," Reyna added. It was true. He'd held this group together at that pool. He'd assisted Brisa in the earliest days of Concord Court, and he'd saved Reyna over and over. If they were going to celebrate Brisa, then Sean definitely deserved his own applause.

"And I have a plus-one in mind." Reyna tapped her lips. There was something there at the back of her mind, but it was only an itch. "Do I have to add him to the list?"

Brisa frowned but shook her head. "Nah, security will let him through on your say-so. Who is it?"

She wasn't sure it would work, so Reyna said, "Let me make sure I can get a commitment, because this is a big fish to convince Dad we've got the clout we need, but there is one more piece."

Brisa raised an eyebrow.

"Can you find a dress for me?" Reyna asked. "If I choose, it'll be understated."

"Drab. Dull. Boring. Serious? Is that what you mean?" Brisa asked.

"Exactly." Reyna blinked slowly. "And if there's ever been a time to draw attention to us, it's this party. This is it, turning the tide. It deserves a standout dress."

Brisa shook her hand. "Count on me, big sister."

Reyna high-fived everyone at the table

and ended up face-to-face with Sean. "Thank you. Again."

He would have waved it off, but she caught both his hands. "Listen, you may not see how important you are, but I would have walked away. Brisa would have, too, and we would have both been convinced we were doing the right thing, but if you don't see that Concord Court, Brisa, and I are going to be so much better now that you've glued us back together, I can't help you."

He tipped his head back. "I'm listening, but there's one thing you need to remember."

Reyna crossed her arms and waited.

"Your father knows. Your concerns have been addressed, and you still haven't asked me to step up beside you at his big party and that's fine. But we both still have things to work through, boss."

Reyna watched him stroll away with his group and turned to her sister. "One more item on your to-do list."

"Name it," Brisa said. "I'm not afraid of anything anymore. I can do it."

"Sean thinks you're going to find me the perfect guy and that you're sure he's not the one. He told me so at the dog park." Reyna had replayed that argument and the kiss over and over until something clicked. Sean had some help coming to the conclusion that they were a mismatch. "Whatever you said to Sean to make him think I'm too good for him or that *I* think I am anyway..." Reyna pointed at her sister. "Fix it."

Brisa huffed. "Wish you'd filled me in on this development sooner because now it means I have another problem to unravel, thanks to your secret *whatever* with Sean, but I will give it my best."

Reyna stared hard at her sister and waited for Brisa's nod. She'd done the same thing whenever they'd fought over the remote control as kids. Brisa's nod was the only agreement Reyna required. They had a lot to do before the cocktail party, but her sister understood how important this final item was.

CHAPTER NINETEEN

ON SATURDAY EVENING, the light sounds of a string quartet floated through the air on the rooftop deck of the South Beach Hotel. Pink lit up the clouds on the horizon as the sun set, and the ocean was gently rolling in. All in all, Luis Montero couldn't have picked a better time or place to make an impact on his collection of business associates. Even Sean understood that building this one-of-a-kind atmosphere was important to drawing these men and women back every time Luis wanted to ask for their business.

In a setting like this, it was easy to have faith in peace and prosperity.

Sean stared at the biggest shrimp he'd ever seen in his life and reminded himself not to pull on the tie that was slowly strangling him. It had taken three different tries to get the thing knotted in the first place. As he moved down the fancy buffet line, he carefully checked out the people around him. His tie and suitcoat were fine, not the best and not the worst in the crowd. That had been his worry. He didn't move in circles like this, and Mimi had told him to go with a Hawaiian shirt.

At least he had enough sense to know that was bad advice. Mimi had finally listened to the salesman in the men's shop she'd chosen in Coconut Grove. Bud had gotten his last suit there, which had made Sean nervous—his grandfather died in 2007. But the place had felt right when he walked in. If he ever needed to escort Reyna to one of her father's events, he'd be prepared.

"Anything good?" Brisa asked from behind him. "I can't remember what I told the caterers. They do all these events, so it's almost autopilot at this point." She frowned. "I should try to give contracts like these to a veteran." She rubbed her forehead. "If I'm ever asked to contribute to anything Montero ever again. I've always gone with the chef from the Cutler Bay Club because that's the Montero standard." She said the last with a sniff. "I wanted to be a rebel, but I hated to rock the boat and..." She held her hands out at both sides before miming turning the lock on her lips. Light glinted off the sequins of her deep pink cocktail dress as she moved. In a sea of dark suits and subdued matrons, Brisa had chosen to match the sunset.

The dress she'd chosen for Reyna was the perfect contrast, a pale pink with more sway than sparkle.

Not that he'd spent entirely too long watching Reyna out of the corner of his eye, but he'd taken a spot so that he could see her but not appear to be staring.

Like a creeper. Wonderful.

"Great dress. Nervous?" Sean asked as he picked up one of the crackers with some kind of spread on it. He would pretend everything was normal. After tonight, he'd know what normal could be. "Can I get you something to drink?"

Brisa reached out to snag a glass of champagne as a waiter walked by, then immediately gulped it.

"Quick reflexes. I'm impressed." Sean noticed all eyes were on Luis and Reyna as they moved through the crowd. Luis's grin was wide and satisfied. He was convinced things were working out as he'd planned.

Reyna was composed, her hair perfectly controlled in the light breeze. Sean saw the wink of a delicate gold chain around her neck and wondered if she was wearing the rose pendant.

As usual, she was giving nothing away. It was no wonder she'd made it to officer status.

And the guy trailing behind Reyna? The one who was smiling and nodding with every introduction? Sean didn't recognize him, but his salt-and-pepper hair and the complete lack of suitcoat suggested he was too rich to be bothered by any rules, written or otherwise.

Somehow, Reyna had managed to do exactly what her sister said she should: find a man who could not be intimidated by Luis Montero.

Sean's only consolation was that he wasn't getting any romantic vibe off the two of them. Their faces read business, polite business. The guy was only a part of the game plan.

"I can do this," Brisa said, then turned big brown eyes Sean's way. "I can do this, can't I? I don't give speeches. I can sing, dance a

little, but I don't deliver budget numbers."
She gripped his arm and Sean refused to
wince. He'd been caught off guard by how
delicate Reyna had been. The power of
Brisa's grip was shocking, too.

"You've already done the hard part. Now
you execute. Easy." Sean waited for her eyes
to meet his and calmly returned the stare
with as much certainty as he could. "Remember negotiating with the shelter? That
was money. You nailed it. You can do this."
Her grip eased.

"I need to run downstairs to let the dogs
in." Her forehead wrinkled. "As soon as Dad
steps up on the stage, I'll go."

"And then all you have to do is hold on.
Follow Reyna's lead and this is going to
work." Sean held out his plate. "You should
eat something, in case the champagne hits
hard."

Brisa immediately grabbed the shrimp
and took a bite. He had to admire a woman
who took him at his word, even if she was
also taking his food.

"Listen," Brisa said after she swallowed,
"you know that foolishness I mentioned at
the shelter that day? Of course you do—you

reminded me of how I negotiated the adoption fees away."

"From the nice charity, yes," Sean drawled, wondering where she was going. She'd obviously been correct. Reyna had the chance to ask him to be her plus-one, and here he was, hovering near the buffet. Alone.

"It was trash. Don't tell my sister this, but I do have a small streak of my father in me." She grabbed his arm again. Sean did not wince. He didn't want to distract her from her train of thought. "I think I know what's best for other people, even if I forget important pieces of information sometimes."

"Like what?" Sean asked, ready to follow where this was headed.

"You know how the rest of us see Reyna? Like she's some kind of perfect model of service and honor and being really smart?" Brisa asked, her nose wrinkling at the suggestion. "Or maybe that's only me, but I've run into enough Montero haters to know that Reyna has, too. People who think they know us because of what they can see on the outside. Montero money. In her case, we can see her success."

Sean nodded. Right. So far, she was repeating what she'd said at the shelter, not wiping it away.

"The part I forgot is that Reyna doesn't see things how I do or you do or all those haters do." Brisa sighed. "Reyna has always been so logical. Sometimes that seems like a lack of emotion. Now that she's home and we've gotten close again, I understand it better. For her, all of those successes, they're logical. To her, it's just a day. To me, this cocktail party, without a speech, would be just another party, even if I had to talk her into putting on the perfectly lovely dress I chose instead of a *pantsuit*." Her scandalized face would have made him smile, but she was serious.

Sean nodded. He thought he was following. "So what does that mean about who she deserves to be with?" That part he couldn't get. Brisa wouldn't be going this far out of her way to tell him Reyna was too good for him, would she? Not again.

"That means my sister—my smart, hotshot, beautiful sister—wants nothing more and nothing less than what all of us want." Brisa bent closer and met his stare. "Someone good and strong. She was never distracted by some of the things that dragged me off course, like money or power to stand up to Luis Montero. She's always been enough. All along, she's known there's only one kind of man to change her whole world for."

"And who is that guy?"

"The one who makes her confident and better and braver. She got a job she couldn't handle at Sawgrass Station. Who helped her learn what she needed to work with Dottie? She would have given everything up because she couldn't see her own way out. Who waded into the mess instead of walking away?" Brisa poked him in the chest. "On a whole planet full of people who can't be bothered to help the person next door, much less the men and women who come through on their way to somewhere else, there aren't many men like you, Wakefield. I say silly stuff. Don't let that keep you from what you know is right."

Sean wrapped his hand around her poking finger. "Have you been working out?"

Brisa laughed and balled her hand into a fist. "Tell me you understand."

He held up both hands in defense. "I get it. Stop the violence."

Brisa started to answer but Luis Montero stepped up on the stage. "Gotta go," she whispered and disappeared into the crowd.

Sean moved closer to the railing to lean against it. The show was about to start and he didn't want to miss a thing.

"Good evening, friends." Luis Montero nodded at the quartet and the music stopped. "I hope everyone has had a chance to fill a plate and grab a drink. We wanted this to be an easy gathering, filled with family, as we celebrate the first year of operation of Concord Court."

Polite applause filtered through the crowd.

String music might not be Sean's idea of a good time.

Disco balls and the collected hits of ABBA and the Bee Gees were fun. Watching dogs chase waves at the dog beach was fun.

String music might not be fun, but it was rich.

And perfect.

So when Brisa cut through the crowd with a small wave of veterans and three dogs following in her wake, there was no record scratch, but it was easy to imagine.

From where he stood, Sean could see Bo, his last rescue, with the vet who'd adopted him. New dogs, old friends, the reporters converging on the low stage. Brisa and Reyna had set the scene perfectly.

Luis Montero frowned at Brisa, but Reyna was still there, smiling at his side. That must have been enough to convince him that whatever this disruption was, he was still going to get his way. It was sad. Any guy who was committed to being that wrong was someone to pity.

As Sean looked at Reyna and found her watching him, he realized that he didn't want to be that guy. He was guilty of trying to make decisions for Reyna, as well. Brisa had changed her mind when she'd figured out she was wrong. He could, too.

"Let me introduce you all to my daughter Reyna. If you haven't met her yet, I haven't listed all of her Air Force accomplishments for you, but I will." Luis waited for the crowd to chuckle, but he lost the microphone as Reyna stepped up and gently shouldered him aside.

"Thanks, Dad. We'll have copies of my résumé available on the way out. Let's keep this party moving," Reyna said with a brilliant smile.

Sean raised his eyebrows when her gaze landed on him. Reyna had made a pretty good joke and that wasn't her forte—she needed support in that moment and she turned to him first. He clapped silently, showing her she'd done well. She dipped her chin and they might as well have been the only ones in the room. In that heartbeat, Sean understood.

Reyna was wonderful. She'd accomplished so much already.

She set goals and had high standards, but she needed him. That made him a hero, too.

"If we've never met, I'm the oldest Montero daughter and I've been running Concord Court since my retirement from the Air Force. I haven't been doing that alone. Since day one, Mr. Sean Wakefield has been the strong backbone of Concord Court." She pointed at the crowd. "There are a few veterans here who are lucky enough to call the Court home. Raise your hands."

Reyna waited and Sean spotted Mira,

Peter, Marcus, Jason Ward, and a pretty brunette who had to be his professor, in the crowd. He had never questioned whether they'd let Reyna and Brisa down. He knew his friends.

"And if you haven't met the dogs at their sides, please make sure to introduce yourself. I'm standing here to tell you about the programs we've instituted at Concord Court this first year. With your generous support, we'd like to expand them." Reyna cleared her throat and returned her gaze to Sean in the crowd. "In addition to the counseling services that have been a part of Concord Court's programs since day one, this summer we've added job counseling, including interview preparation and coaching to build a professional appearance, and a pilot program called Shelter to Service. Sean Wakefield has given his extra time, talents and connections to train dogs from a nearby shelter to provide emotional support service dogs to vets. With the help of two important people, this is a program that will expand next year."

Reyna held out a hand toward the man she'd been leading around all evening. "Julius Stewart. It's a name everyone knows, thanks to years of success at Stewart Foods. Julius has supported the Shelter to Service program since its inception and is poised to become an even more important donor to Concord Court. He has pledged significant funding for the next five years." She held up her hands to applaud and everyone followed.

The guy who'd been glued to Reyna's side dipped his chin in acknowledgment and Sean finally understood why she'd gone with the plus-one she had.

He also made a mental note to make a straight line for the guy to offer his heartfelt gratitude.

Her father's frown was growing.

"And the other person who has come into Concord Court and changed everything is my little sister, Brisa Montero." Reyna motioned her toward the stage. This was something they'd all agreed would happen, but Brisa seemed to be having second thoughts. She dragged her feet, but eventually, she stepped up between her sister and her father.

Reyna held up a picture. "I've traveled all over the world in the service to my country and everywhere I went, I carried this snapshot. Brisa was a baby. We'd attended the Back to School Blowout at Bayfront Park. In those days, it was called the Miami Safety Fair or something like that. They've improved the show." Reyna waved the picture. "Me, my father, my baby sister and a station dog for the Miami Fire Department, named Smokey. East Coast. West Coast. Hawaii. South Korea. This photo has been there. And now, because of my sister, I'm going to pursue my second dream. I'm going to be a firefighter for the Miami Fire Department, and Brisa is going to lead Concord Court. She has proven herself to be a creative thinker with well-placed strategic ideas and a person who does not quit until the job is done. Could you all give a round of applause to the newest manager of Concord Court, Brisa Montero?"

Sean clapped as hard and loud as he could and was gratified when the vets in the crowd followed suit. He wasn't sure this public showdown would accomplish what they hoped it would, but it didn't matter. Brisa deserved the applause.

Her nervous glance over her shoulder at her father drew Sean's attention to Luis.

Reyna had handed her father the snapshot she'd waved at the crowd and whispered something in his ear. He nodded once and then crossed his arms over his chest. Was he angry? It was hard to tell, and that was the best they could hope for.

Brisa's hand shook when she raised the microphone. "Thank you, thank you. Most of you, I already know. Expect me to make an appointment next week to ask for more generous donations, because I have great plans." She laughed. "I've had them all my life. I never had the backing to make them work. If you ever need a crew to make dreams come true, look for veterans." She flashed a brilliant smile around the crowd. Sean enjoyed watching the trees felled in the woods as a wave rippled through the crowd, a silent shuffle of reaching for checkbooks in their hearts, even if they hadn't carried them with them.

Sean was pretty sure Brisa would meet and exceed the budgetary goals she and her sister had set.

"Next year is going to be an important year." Brisa faced her sister. When Reyna nodded, Brisa straightened her shoulders.

All she needed was backup and she was prepared to step out in front to lead. "We're going to be launching a small-business lab for veterans. We'll start with vets at Concord Court, but my new volunteer liaison, Reyna Montero, will work with local veterans' groups to build a network of people with experience, mentors who can help, and eventually a portal to connect people searching for those businesses." She glanced at her sister again. Reyna raised her eyebrows before nodding. They hadn't discussed any of that. Brisa was either thinking on her feet or she'd had a few tricks up her nonexistent sleeves, too.

"Concord Court has been a family labor of love to honor the men and women who have given their time to protect us. Going forward, I plan to open the doors to anyone who wants to come alongside the Montero family because the mission is still growing. Veterans need us. They answered when their country called and now that they've come home, it's our turn to step up. Join us at Concord Court to be a part of that." Brisa held out the microphone and barely waited for her father to take it before stepping down off the stage.

Luis Montero shifted awkwardly back and forth for a minute and Sean was pretty sure everyone involved in this plan to perform a coup at Concord Court was on edge. Eventually he said, "Enjoy, everyone! There's plenty to eat and to drink!" Then he switched the microphone off and waved an impatient hand at the quartet. Music immediately flowed and the partygoers returned to pleasant conversation, completely unaware that an earthquake rumbled all around them.

Luis headed for his daughters, who had met in a corner of the rooftop. Sean followed suit. Whatever happened, he was going to be a part of it.

And again, he and Luis skidded to a halt at the same time.

Luis pulled the photo out of his jacket pocket. "Is this intended to convince me that I bear some of the blame for your new career choice?" He pushed the photo at them.

"Blame? If we're talking about blame, you bear a large piece of it for both of my career choices. I wanted to be free, so I chose the

Air Force, but firefighting… Do or don't take any blame for that. But I showed you the photo to help you understand that it didn't matter where I was or what I was doing, my family was always there. I was always thinking of what it meant to be a Montero, and I knew I had a little sister who looked up to me and a father who expected the best." Reyna snatched the photo out of his hand. "Understand, we are always Monteros, even when we don't follow your orders. And what we make of ourselves is something you should be proud of. We couldn't have done this without you, but we will do it in spite of you if we have to."

Sean sighed. "I came over here to defend your honor. You never need my help with that, do you?"

Reyna laughed and wrapped her arm around his waist. "Not with that, no."

Luis's clenched jaw twitched before he asked, "And you're dating Wakefield now?" He motioned over his shoulder. "Better than Julius Stewart."

Reyna blinked up at her father. "What? Why? It doesn't matter, does it? How many battles are we going to fight today, Dad?"

Luis looked Sean up and down. "This one knows how to dress for an event such as this. That's all I meant. None of this has been settled. Next week, we will discuss all at Concord Court." Then he held out his hand for the photo. "Text me your schedule at the fire station. You, your sister and I will meet. I want to show this photo to some friends."

Reyna put it in his palm but didn't let go. "Don't lose this. I need it."

Sean watched them exchange a glance. When her father nodded, Reyna let go. Luis faded back into the crowd, an extra bounce in his step.

Brisa covered her cheeks with both hands. "I think we pulled it off."

"Yep, although giving me a title was unexpected. We should definitely talk about these things before you volunteer me." Reyna shook her finger. "Except this fits me perfectly, so, of course you can count on me."

Brisa hugged her sister and then hugged Sean. She poked his lapel again and Sean winced. "I fixed this problem. I have one more mess to clean up and then we're set."

"Do you need help?" Reyna asked.

Brisa shook her head and faded into the crowd.

"What was that about?" Sean asked. "What problem?"

"I'm not sure what the second mess is, but the first one was you and whatever Brisa said to convince you I believed my father's hype about me." Reyna frowned. "You do know she was wrong, don't you?"

Sean slipped his hand in hers and pulled her toward a balcony that led to the other side of the hotel rooftop. From here, he could see the beach and the water, but the party might as well have disappeared. "Let's talk about that. Want to?"

She tangled their fingers together and pulled him farther away from the crowd. Sean laughed. Eventually he'd get used to how strong and determined these Montero women were. He hoped he had a lifetime.

CHAPTER TWENTY

As soon as they reached the deserted side of the rooftop, Reyna pushed Sean down onto one of the lounge chairs clustered near the railing. They had a beautiful view of Miami lights glowing in the growing shadows. She wished she'd rehearsed what she planned to say here, but she'd been so focused on getting Concord Court handed over that she…

"You remember how we had a couple of issues with being together? As I recall, number one on the list was that you were my boss," Sean said as he leaned forward and braced his elbows on his knees. "You were worried about what would happen if I lost my job."

"Because of me. If you lost your job because of me, that would have caused a problem. One way or the other, that had to change." Reyna paced one direction and then stopped in front of him. "I was doing it again, wasn't I? What Brisa accused me of? Deciding to make the sacrifice and taking your choice out of your hands."

"Taking the whole weight of the world and making decisions based on what you thought was right instead of whatever anyone else thought? The same way Luis does?" Sean nodded. "Yeah." And she was going to do it again and again. This was the first time they'd work through this, but he understood he had to be okay with talking things out with Reyna.

If the other choice was living without her, he'd happily talk things out for the rest of his life.

She eased down next to him, the swirl of her dress settling over her knees. "I should stop doing that. I know."

Sean tapped the rose pendant dangling on the gold chain. "I remember this. Sometimes it flashes through my mind from that day you wore it to brunch." He ran his finger over the chain, her warm skin tickling his fingers, and watched her shiver again. "This is an address that requires diamonds. I'm shocked there's no Montero vault with family heirlooms tucked away."

Reyna snorted. "There might be, but this rose means everything to me. I wore it because I thought Brisa might need to see it. She gave it to me a long time ago and it's been around the world, too. I never went anywhere without it. Whatever my father thinks, my family was always with me. Miami is a part of me. I'll always be a Montero. I hope you're ready for that. We don't change easily. You're going to have to remind me that we make decisions together."

Relieved, Sean ran his hand over her nape. When she shivered, he celebrated his stupid suitcoat for the first time that evening. He draped it over her shoulders. "Training. You and I are both going to need some work." There would be more yelling.

"Instead of cheese, let's use kisses. Food doesn't work as well on me as it does for Dottie." Reyna wagged her eyebrows at him.

The cute, in this moment where the two of them were locked together, was too much. Sean experienced that breathless, overwhelmed sensation of diving too deep, as if he'd been paddling along in love and a wave had washed over him.

"You do know that I've trusted you, don't

you?" Reyna wrapped her hand around his. "More than anyone ever, I've trusted you. I *trust* you. It's important you understand what I'm saying."

"I do. It's been the most jaw-dropping thing I can remember, stepping up beside this completely capable hero when she needed me. Honestly, tonight I realized something. All my life, I wanted to be a hero. I thought that meant a career like my dad's, but..." Sean brushed the hair away from her eyes. "My mom and grandmother made him into that hero. If he'd been a mechanic or a policeman or a doctor, they'd have done the same thing because they loved him. He was a regular guy, but that love made him more. Your father does the same thing for you because he's proud of you."

Reyna wrinkled her nose. "You get how it's different for me, though? Your father is gone. He can't fall off the pedestal that other people built for him, but I'm still here and teetering on the edge of falling. That was the pressure I felt growing up Montero and coming home, too. Other people have called me a hero, lifted me up here, but I'm human. I'm going to make mistakes. It's so shaky up on the pedestal when you have a whole life to live. I don't want to disappoint anyone, so I've got to get down before I fall, you know?"

That was the part he'd missed all along. "Absolutely. Now I do. I couldn't see it before."

"I should have chosen better words when I was yelling at you on that beautiful beach." Reyna's lips were curved when he met her stare. Together, they smiled slowly. "We're going to have to get used to emphatic conversations, aren't we?"

Sean grinned. "Maybe. But when you look at me like this, I can't imagine disagreeing with you. That look in your eyes… It's what I've been missing, seeing myself through your eyes. We aren't that different after all. We love our families. Our work is important. And when we're together, we're unstoppable."

Her sweet smile was the boost he needed. Words weren't his talent, but he was speaking from the heart. It was working, too.

"Is love really like this?" she whispered as she moved closer. "From one heartbeat to the next, you're in so deep you can't imagine living without someone?"

"I've only been in love once." Sean stared at her lips. "And yes, it is."

Reyna's lips held the warmth of a smile as she met his, a sweet promise of a lifetime of dogs, some yelling and more kisses.

* * * * *

For more romances in the Veterans' Road miniseries by acclaimed author Cheryl Harper, visit www.Harlequin.com today!

Get 4 FREE REWARDS!

We'll send you 2 FREE Books plus 2 FREE Mystery Gifts.

Love Inspired books feature uplifting stories where faith helps guide you through life's challenges and discover the promise of a new beginning.

FREE Value Over $20

Get 4 FREE REWARDS!

We'll send you 2 FREE Books plus 2 FREE Mystery Gifts.

Love Inspired Suspense books showcase how courage and optimism unite in stories of faith and love in the face of danger.

FREE Value Over $20

THE WESTERN HEARTS COLLECTION!

19 FREE BOOKS in all!

COWBOYS. RANCHERS. RODEO REBELS.
Here are their charming love stories in one prized Collection: 51 emotional and heart-filled romances that capture the majesty and rugged beauty of the American West!

YES! Please send me **The Western Hearts Collection** in Larger Print. This collection begins with 3 FREE books and 2 FREE gifts in the first shipment. Along with my 3 free books, I'll also get the next 4 books from The Western Hearts Collection, in LARGER PRINT, which I may either return and owe nothing, or keep for the low price of $5.45 U.S./$6.23 CDN each plus $2.99 U.S./$7.49 CDN for shipping and handling per shipment*. If I decide to continue, about once a month for 8 months I will get 6 or 7 more books but will only need to pay for 4. That means 2 or 3 books in every shipment will be FREE! If I decide to keep the entire collection, I'll have paid for only 32 books because 19 books are FREE! I understand that accepting the 3 free books and gifts places me under no obligation to buy anything. I can always return a shipment and cancel at any time. My free books and gifts are mine to keep no matter what I decide.

☐ 270 HCN 5354   ☐ 470 HCN 5354

Name (please print)

Address   Apt. #

City   State/Province   Zip/Postal Code

Mail to the **Reader Service:**
IN U.S.A.: P.O. Box 1341, Buffalo, N.Y. 14240-8531
IN CANADA: P.O. Box 603, Fort Erie, Ontario L2A 5X3

#343 MONTANA WISHES

The Blackwell Sisters • by Amy Vastine

A life-changing family secret, two impulsive proposals and best friends navigating feelings they're both afraid to share. Will Amanda Harrison and Blake Collins's new relationship survive when truths are revealed on the Blackwell Ranch?

#344 RESCUING THE RANCHER

Heroes of Shelter Creek • by Claire McEwen

Firefighter Jade Carson had no problem handling the Northern California wildfire evacuations until Aidan Bell. The stubborn rancher refuses to leave his sheep and appears to care little for his own survival. Will they survive the night—and each other?

#345 HILL COUNTRY SECRET
by Kit Hawthorne

Lauren Longwood lived a carefree existence, but pregnancy from a failed marriage leads her to a friend in Texas. There she instantly connects with Alex Reyes, a man who can't afford the distraction from saving his family's ranch.

#346 ALL THEY WANT FOR CHRISTMAS

The Montgomerys of Spirit Lake
by M. K. Stelmack

After her aunt passes away, Bridget Montgomery is surprised when her ex-fiancé, Jack Holdstrom, returns with two adopted daughters in tow. But she's downright shocked to discover Jack's been willed the other half of Bridget's home and business!
